Love, Lies & Lust

BY MZ. ROBINSON

Published by:

G Street Chronicles
P.O. Box 1822
Jonesboro, GA 30237-1822

www.gstreetchronicles.com
fans@gstreetchronicles.com

Cover design:
Hot Book Covers
www.hotbookcovers.com

ISBN: 978-1-9384420-2-5
LCCN: 2012942901

Join us on our social networks

Facebook: G Street Chronicles
Follow us on Twitter: @gstrtchroni

Dedication

This book is dedicated to my uncle Kenneth Leslie. Thank you for listening, the laughs, and always having a useful word to say. Thank you for giving selflessly and staying real. You are a wonderful man and I thank God for you. I love you "Uncle Bay".

Acknowledgements

I would like to take this moment and say that I have been blessed throughout this series, to have been shown so much love and support. I have tears in my eyes as I think about how much my list of supporters has grown and how thankful I am for each and every one of you. Please, please, forgive me if I forget to list your name. You can blame all the characters and voices running around in my head but please know it was not my heart.

~ Kisses~

To my Lord and Savior, I say with a humble spirit and a heart that overflows with gratefulness: "Thank you". You are the center of my joy and my provider and I know that without you, I am nothing.

To my parents Ray and Shirley, the two of you offered your love and support from book 1 and you continue to do so today. I love you so very much and I am so very proud to be your daughter. Thank you for your continuous prayers and encouraging words. I love you Daddy. I love you Mommy. P.S. Thank you for watching after Dolce during my travels. (Lol)

To my Bestie, Banita Brooks, thank you for your continued support, riding with me, and listening to me vent. I love you sis.

To my cousin Tammy, You've supported each and every book. Thank you and I love you!!

To my cousins Quiana, Kenyetta, and LaNisha, thank you for showing your love and support on my page. I Love You All!!

To my family: The Caudles, Leslies, Walkers, Masseys, Warners, and Rice.. I love each and every one of you!

To my girls Valerie Ann Williams, Cassandra Allen, and Doris McDonald, you ladies ROCK! I love ya!

To Robyn Traylor, I know before the release of this book you had personal things that took place that were difficult to handle but you still managed to go hard for me. You showed up at G Street Books and Café and showed out! I am so very thankful to have you on the team! You are a Diamond.

To JeaNida Luckie Weatherall, your strength and courage is amazing. I am so thankful we connected. Keep going strong, Gorgeous!

To Naomi B. Johnson, Thank you for the uplifting - inspiring words and your continued support!

To Denia Turner, Danielle Churcher -Straub, Andrea Anderson, Sonjia Baker- Lee, Marissa Palmer, Erica Kinder, Qiana Drennen, Leslie Gray, LaBrina Jolley, Shae Hobbs, Samantha Pettiway, Morgan Robertson, Timiska Martin Webb, Natasha Potts, LaShawone Powell, and Althea Justbeingme. You ladies are wonderful! Thank you!!

To each and every one of my followers on Face book, Good reads, and Twitter. Thank you!

To The Literary Joint, Black and Nobel, and Horizon Books, Thank you for your support and introducing my work to your customers.

To all of the other bookstores, street vendors, and online stores who carry my titles, Thank you!

To the talented Authors: Red Snapper, Aleta Williams, and Thomas Long, thank you!!

To Ms. Detra Young, thank you for your support and just being you! Love ya!

To all of the book clubs reading and reviewing my series right now or who plan to in the future: Thank you!

To Shantelle, Malika, Anjela and all of the members of Fun(4)daMental: Thank you! To the members of Sistah Reading Sistah Clubhouse: Thank you! To Mary Green and the members of My Urban Books: Thank you!

To my editor Autumn, Thank you! To Hotbook Covers, thank you for another hot book cover!

To George Sherman Hudson, the same thing applies today as it did from day 1, I'm thankful and grateful for the chance you took with me. And you know.. Love & Loyalty ALWAYS.

To Shawna A. Grundy, thank you again for everything!!

To my label brother Joe Awsum, thank you for the laughs. Beastmode, get it!

To all the authors that make up Team G Street, we have the honor of being where many only hope to be, let's show the world why we were chosen. We're destined for greatness. Let's get it!

To all of my fabulous readers who continue to buy each and every book that I write. Thank you!!

To all those out there with a hope, a wish, a dream, and a prayer: keep PUSHING. Let nothing stop you from pursuing your dreams. No Fear. No Excuses.

Remember: In life you can choose to stand tall against the Big Dogs or you can stay on the porch with your tail tucked in between your legs and get mauled in your own yard. Either way you're going to fight, it's just up to you how you enter the ring! ~ Mz. R

Prologue

I'd never been one to dwell on how or when I'll die. Why would I? I was too busy living, trying to claim what was mine. I won't lie, though. My current situation has me rethinking a lot of things.

Days ago, when I awakened, I found myself tied to a chair in the middle of an abandoned warehouse. Inside the warehouse were several chains hanging from the ceiling, and four dust-covered fluorescent lights, along with an equally dusty mattress. For the first two days, I sat thinking about ways to escape, until I finally concluded there wasn't one. The metal doors opened from the outside, and the windows were so high that it would literally take a lift to reach them. When I first came to, my head was still throbbing from the blow I'd received, but now the spot was numb. I knew without even touching it that there had to be a knot, undoubtedly a large, disgusting one. It was unbearably hot and humid in the warehouse, and there was sweat dripping from my body like rain falling from an umbrella. I hadn't heard nor seen anyone since I'd been dumped in this hellhole, and I was beginning to wonder if they had forgotten about me. My lips were chafed and cracked to the point that when I licked them, I only tasted blood and raw meat. I swallowed, attempting to cool the burning sensation in my dry throat, to no avail; in fact, it seemed my saliva only made things worse. My dress and panties felt like they were singed to my skin, saturated by my own sweat and urine. I was so miserable with all the pain in other parts of my body that I had no time to focus on the hunger pangs that coursed through my stomach in waves. All I could do was wait for my captor to return so he could do whatever it was he had planned.

But then it hit me: *Maybe this IS the plan. Maybe he WANTS me to suffer and rot slowly away.* Either way, I was already tired of waiting to find out. I was ready for whatever he had prepared.

Chapter 1

Octavia

I stood frozen in place, watching Kelly and my mother-in-law, Ilene. Kelly stood smiling lovingly at her, while Ilene stood with one hand pressed against her chest, just above her heart, and the other pressed against Kelly's. *What the hell?* I thought to myself. The two of them were close, toe to toe, and with one slight movement, it seemed they'd end up right in each other's arms. It was apparent that Kelly and Ilene were having a private moment, but my curiosity had me wondering just how private—no, better yet, just how *intimate*—that moment had been before I entered my home. I watched as Kelly took Ilene's hand in his, then pressed his lips to her palm. *Oh, hell no!* I thought.

"There you are!"

The sound of Contessa's voice startled me, and I turned on my heels quickly, almost knocking her down. "You scared me," I said, trying to catch my breath.

Contessa smiled. "Oh, I'm sorry, sweetie," she said gently. "I just wanted to let you know your mother is looking for you."

"Oh...okay," I stuttered, my thoughts running rampant about what I'd just seen.

A few seconds later, Kelly came strolling past the two of us in the hallway. "Excuse me," he said as he walked by.

I turned around and saw Ilene looking in my direction, looking like she'd been convicted by a jury of her peers; she looked guilty. I wanted to run up and ask her what was going on with her and Kelly. To my knowledge, it had been the first time they'd met, but they sure as hell didn't look like it. Ilene didn't strike me as the loose type, but on the same note, you never know. After all, Kelly was good-looking: tall, with an athletic physique, smooth skin the color of milk chocolate, and a round, smooth baby face. As for Ilene, even though she was old enough to be his mother, she could still turn heads with her mocha complexion and penetrating gray eyes. *But would she risk creeping, especially with her husband—and worse, her son—right outside?* I was lost in my thoughts.

"Octavia?" Contessa said, interrupting my questioning mind. "Hello?"

I pulled myself from my mental blackout and looked at my nanny. "I'm sorry," I said, shaking my head. "Tell Mama I'll be right out."

Contessa hesitated, then nodded her head and went on her way, leaving me alone.

I wanted to confront Ilene about what I thought I had seen, but as my luck (or hers) would have it, she had disappeared. The bathroom door was closed, so I knew she'd taken refuge in there, and I decided it best to leave well enough alone at the moment.

I rejoined my family and extended family outside just as my parents, Charles and Charlene, were saying their goodbyes.

"I had a wonderful time," Mama said. She walked up to me with my father following close behind her. She gave me a kiss on the cheek, then smiled. "Where's Ilene?" she questioned.

"Here I am, darling," Ilene purred, coming up from behind me.

Hmm. It's like everyone has perfect timing today—almost scary how perfect.

"Damon Sr. and I are also about to make our departure," she said, hugging my mother and then my father. "However, we must all do this again soon. Maybe next time, Damon and I can host our family gathering in Atlanta," Ilene suggested.

"Sounds good!" Mama replied excitedly.

I stood listening to the two women go back and forth about holidays and events they should organize to bring our families together. It was all fine and good, but I had some questions I needed answered; at that moment, that was my main concern. "Mama Ilene, I'd like to speak with you before you go," I said, gently interrupting her conversation.

She looked at me with raised eyebrows and a look that clearly stated she knew why I wanted to talk. "Yes, darling, we'll talk," she said, giving me a smile that looked as if it had been plastered on.

"Is everything okay?" Mama asked, looking from me to Ilene.

I would never put my husband's mother on blast, no matter how desperate or nosy I might have been. I also didn't want to worry my mother. She looked good and said she felt good, despite her recent cancer diagnosis. The last thing I wanted to do was send her radar up. "Everything is fine," I finally answered. "I…well, I just wanted to surprise you with a shopping spree in Paris, and I know Ilene is familiar with the hottest boutiques there." I cut my eyes in Ilene's direction.

She smiled her picture-perfect smile, then nodded her head. "Of course I am," she answered. "The two of us will get together soon to discuss the hottest spots for shopping and *anything* else you would like to know."

I took the emphasis she placed on the word "anything" as my hint that she would later explain what had taken place between her and Kelly, if anything. Then again, I wasn't even 100 percent sure she knew I'd even seen them. All things considered, I decided to dismiss my questions for the moment.

"Octavia, I do not need a shopping spree," Mama told me, taking my hand. "The trip is more than enough—too much, if you ask me. In fact, I think we should decline."

After Mama had advised me of her illness, Damon and I had agreed to treat her and my father to an all expense-paid vacation to Paris, France. I had originally wanted to give my parents the package Damon had gifted me with, but Damon—being the loving and kind-hearted person he was—decided to purchase a separate package for my parents.

"Speak for yourself, woman!" Daddy spoke up. "I love you, Charlene, but I'm going to Paris with or without you." Of course my father was teasing, as we all knew he'd never leave the country or even the state, for that matter, without my mother, especially at a time like that.

Laughing lightly, Mama slipped her arm around Daddy's waist. "Baby, I said, we *should* decline," she clarified, "not that we *are*."

"Just making sure," Daddy said before kissing her sweetly on the lips.

"Well, let me grab my husband," Ilene said, exhaling lightly. "We need to get back on the road before it gets too late."

Five minutes later, my parents were gone, and Ilene and Damon Sr. were on their way out the door. I noticed that before Ilene and Damon Sr. departed, Ilene nonchalantly shot a glance at Kelly, then nodded her head. I looked at Kelly and caught a glimpse of him blowing Ilene a kiss. There was definitely something not right. Seeing Kelly and Ilene together was not the only strange occurrence that had taken place at my family get-together. There was also the case of Kelly introducing us to his two-year-old son.

Donovan was a beautiful little boy with light brown skin, jet-black curly hair, and big brown eyes. I was surprised when I met the child for two reasons. First, I didn't even know he existed. When I'd first met Kelly, during a job interview at my restaurant, he had advised me that he had a daughter, Ciara, who had passed from complications due to leukemia. He had never mentioned that he had another child. Second, Donovan, who had no known relationship to my daughter, really favored Jasmine.

I sat with Jasmine sitting on one knee and Donovan on the other, watching Kelly and Contessa as they sat closely, talking to each other. My husband stood a few feet away from where I was sitting, cleaning off the grill of our outdoor kitchen. The conversation between Kelly and Contessa seemed intense and less than pleasant. Kelly's face held an expression I had never seen before, one of stress and trouble. Earlier, when Contessa had told me Kelly was coming to visit, she'd informed me that he was bringing her some additional insulin. I began to wonder if Contessa was feeling well. I watched as Kelly placed his hand on her forearm, and I continued to stare at them until Kelly finally looked up and our eyes locked. I watched as his hand slid down Contessa's forearm to her hand. The two of them held hands briefly.

Contessa turned in her chair and gave me a bright smile. I returned her smile, then redirected my attention to my husband, who stood by the outdoor kitchen looking like a king. The baby-blue button-down and dark jeans he wore were just the right size, unable to conceal his toned, muscular body. I loved looking at my husband. From his smooth bald head to his caramel-colored skin and dark brown eyes, everything about Damon turned me on. I noticed he had been somewhat quiet throughout the day. I assumed he was just consumed with preparing such a delicious meal for everyone. I decided I would show him some extra special attention later to let him know how much I not only loved him but appreciated him.

I set Jasmine down on her feet, then did the same for Donovan. "Go to Daddy," I told Donovan, pointing in Kelly's direction.

He looked up at me, slightly hesitating.

"It's okay," I gently coaxed the beautiful little boy. "Go to Daddy."

Donovan immediately ran to Damon and wrapped his arms around Damon's legs.

Damon looked down at the little boy, then back at me, then lifted Donovan up into his strong arms.

I could only assume Donovan had heard Jasmine calling Damon "Daddy" and had gotten slightly confused. I smiled and walked over to the two of them, holding Jasmine's hand.

"Hey, love," Damon said, kissing my cheek.

Stroking the soft curls on Donovan's head, I smiled. "Jazz is gonna get jealous," I teased.

"No need for that," Damon said. He gave Donovan a hug before easing him down. He then lifted our daughter up into his arms and gave her a big hug all her own.

Jasmine squealed loudly; she was undoubtedly a daddy's girl.

"It's so cute," I said. "I told Donovan to go to his daddy, and he paused, then marched right over to you."

"Really?" Damon asked, staring at me.

"Yes."

"Should I be concerned?" Kelly asked loudly, walking up to us.

"What do you mean?" I questioned, turning to face him.

Kelly's face was stone, completely serious, to the point where I wondered if he was slightly jealous of how Donovan had latched onto Damon. "The four of you are over here looking like the perfect family portrait," he answered. "You, Damon, Jazz, and *my* son." Kelly rubbed the well-groomed hair on his chin, then loosened up a bit and laughed lightly. "Damon, you're not trying to steal my kid, are you?"

"You should know better than that," Damon said seriously. "*My* family is perfect just the way it is."

Kelly's expression softened. "That it is," Kelly replied, looking at me. The silence between us was uncomfortable until Kelly finally turned to Damon.

"I'm just playing with you, brah." He smiled. "After all you and your wife have done for me and my aunt, my son is your son." His voice dropped an octave, and his gray eyes grew even softer. "Besides, Donovan is going to need a strong female figure in his life," Kelly continued. "Unfortunately, Donovan's mother passed away recently. She died during a home fire."

"I'm so sorry to hear that," I said empathetically. "Did Ciara have the same mother?"

Kelly looked surprised at my mention of his daughter.

I remembered Contessa telling me Ciara's mother was a little on the trifling side, and I assumed my mention of her must have opened up an old wound. I instantly regretted asking the question, but I patiently awaited his answer.

"Thanks…and no she did not," he said flatly. "Donovan's mother and I…well, we hadn't seen each other in a long while" Kelly finally continued. "I thought she was living halfway across the country, but as it turned out, she was living here in Huntsville the entire time."

I didn't want to jump to any conclusions, but in my mind I wondered how and why Kelly could have avoided being an active part of his child's life. *How could he not know where his son was living? What does that say about him as a parent?* I looked at Damon, who was just staring into space. I knew he was listening, though, and I wondered if he was asking himself some of the same questions.

"I didn't know I was Donovan's father," Kelly answered, like he was reading my mind. "When she told me about her pregnancy, she also told me someone else was Donovan's father."

I shook my head. *What is it with women lying about their child's paternity? Is it that they really don't know, or are they just hoping the other man—the better man—is the father?* "Do you think she really believed the other guy was Donovan's dad?" I questioned. "Do you know who he is?" Yes, I was being nosy, but I needed some details, and I was gonna get them.

"I think she always knew I was his father, but she was just so hooked on this dude that she couldn't accept the fact that he isn't her baby's daddy," Kelly replied, shaking his head. "I don't even know who the guy is. She never talked about him, and now…well, she's gone."

"That's just crazy," I said.

"Yeah, it is," Kelly agreed. "Her mother contacted me and told me she was dead. It was also her mother who told me Donovan is my son. She thought I already knew and that I was just being an absent, deadbeat father. I went to go visit the two of them, and I took a DNA test just for my confirmation. And I guess the rest is—"

"History," I finished. I was in awe at hearing Kelly's tale. I had been curious about the child's mother, and my questions had been answered, but I never would have expected it to be such a tragic story. It sounded like something off the big screen, tragic and triumphant at the same time. I imagined that memories of Ciara still flooded Kelly's mind, but at least he had Donovan and the opportunity to make new memories and be a father again. Suddenly, as if the heavens were trying to jolt me out of my thoughts, I felt a droplet of rain on my arm. Looking up at the sky, I noticed a bundle of semi-gray clouds gathering.

"Babe, why don't you take the kids in?" Damon suggested, finally breaking his silence.

"Yeah, Damon and I will wrap up here," Kelly added. "You don't mind if I give you a hand, do you, Damon?" he asked, looking Damon in the eyes.

"Not at all," Damon answered.

"All right," I said, pressing my lips to Damon's quickly. "Let's go, babies!" I said to Jasmine and Donovan. I held their hands as we quickly walked toward the patio doors.

* * *

I sat inside our family room watching Jasmine and Donovan play on the carpeted floor. The two of them were commercial perfect, as cute as could be. The short time I'd spent with Donovan that day had me thinking about having another child. *Would it really be that bad?* I asked myself. Damon hadn't brought it up in months, but I knew in my heart that the hope and thought was still in his mind. I was slowly beginning to feel selfish for not wanting to honor his request; my excuse was that I was running two very successful restaurants, and I didn't want my career to fall on the back burner again for another pregnancy. However, I'd learned a lot from my mother and her cancer diagnosis, one of the most important being that we should always love and live to the fullest. I loved being a career-oriented woman, but I loved being a wife and mother more. I decided to let the thought rest for the moment, for another thought began reeling through my head: the memory of Ilene and Kelly in the hall of my home. I was eager to have a discussion with my mother-in-law and vowed that I would call her the next day to try and get some answers.

Contessa entered the room quietly and eased down on the sofa next to me. She looked completely lost in her thoughts, and the worry etched in her mocha complexion revealed that those thoughts were troubling.

"How are you feeling?" I questioned, sincerely concerned.

"I'm feeling fine, baby," she said, giving me a weak smile. "Why do you ask?"

"You look like something is bothering you," I said. "You looked that way earlier too."

Contessa removed her small-framed glasses from her face and looked at me. "Damon is a good man," she said. "He reminds me of my husband Johnny—strong, hardworking, and willing to do whatever he can to take care of his family."

I smiled, knowing she was right. My Damon was all of those things.

"I know my nephew can be very charming," she continued, "but all the charm in the world isn't worth risking what you already have." Contessa looked at me with raised eyebrows.

Visions of Kelly's head in between my legs replayed in my head. The night the two of us had almost had sex was one I was sorely ashamed of. Although, I had been way past my tolerable alcohol limit, I couldn't use my drunkenness as an excuse. The fact remained that I should have never been there in the first place. I wondered if I had been unknowingly giving off some sort of silent signal—to Contessa or others—that something had taken place between Kelly and me. *Stop trippin'!* I thought to myself. *Of course you haven't. Maybe the signal came from Kelly.* "I…uh, I don't understand," I said, feigning innocence.

"I may be old," she whispered, "but I ain't blind. Be careful when it comes to my nephew. Don't get yourself involved in anything *else* you may regret." Contessa winked her eye at me, patted me on the leg, then exited the room.

She had placed great emphasis on "else," and while I doubted that Kelly had openly admitted to her about the night we'd crossed the line, it was obvious that Contessa knew more than what she was letting on. That scared me most of all.

Chapter 2

Damon

My heart pounded loudly in my ears as Kelly provided Octavia his explanation of how he'd discovered that Donovan was his son. I remained quiet, but I was hanging on Kelly's every word, waiting for him to reveal that my ex-lover, Nadia, was Donovan's mother and that I was the man she had originally said had fathered her child. Although Kelly didn't spill that deep, dark secret, I still felt no relief. Octavia was satisfied with his explanation of how everything had unfolded, but I was not convinced. In fact, I was confident that Kelly knew every detail of what had unfolded between Nadia and me the months before she passed. If, by chance, his story was true, that could only mean that Nadia had spun a web of lies—alone. Nadia was good at manipulation, but I was sure she wasn't that good. *Even if Nadia had done it alone, I pondered, how is it that Kelly just so happened to walk into my wife's restaurant the day she and Kelly met?* It didn't make sense.

Kelly waited until Octavia and the children were inside our home and out of earshot before he directed his attention toward me. "Man to man, I just want to thank you," he said, smiling at me.

I waited for him to elaborate. When he didn't, I decided to probe. "And exactly what are you thanking me for?" I questioned.

"Well, first, you gave me a job until I could find full-time employment," he said. "Then, you put me up in a nice crib. Not as nice as what you have here," he said, looking around, "but nice nonetheless."

My gut feeling was whispering to me that Kelly was not just expressing his gratitude. I was still waiting for him to admit to knowing that the other man was me. "Like I told you before," I said, "you should thank my wife."

It wasn't the first time he'd thanked me and given me credit, even though Octavia was the one who'd hired him to do the landscape at our home. I was man enough to admit that the brother had done a good job. Not only had he brought life back to the hedges and flowers surrounding the front of our home, but he'd also built a Japanese garden in the back, complete with a sitting area, Japanese cherry trees, various climbing plants, and even a pond filled with koi fish. However, he would have never been given the opportunity if it hadn't been for Octavia. My wife was also the one who'd gone out on a limb and had an associate of hers pull some strings to get Kelly approved for his own apartment. Due to previous credit issues and debts that Kelly had incurred during the treatment of his daughter, he'd fallen into hard times. According to Octavia, Kelly had sunk so low that he was living with Contessa in her one-bedroom apartment, sleeping on her couch.

"I know Octavia had a lot to do with it," he said, "but you could have easily waved your magic wand and made things go a completely different direction."

"I don't own a wand," I said lightly, "and I don't believe in magic."

"But you do have a way of making things happen," Kelly concluded. There was a certain undercurrent in his tone that I didn't like, but I chose to let it go for the moment.

The rain began to trickle down in a light but steady stream. I took my eyes off Kelly and focused my attention on cleaning up before the downpour came. I wiped the inside of the grill down with a clean hand towel, then eased the hood down to close it.

"Well, let me at least thank you for the delicious meal," he said.

"Not a problem," I answered. I continued to straighten until I was satisfied that everything in the outdoor kitchen was back in its proper place.

"Well, I'd better get Donovan so the two of us can ride out," Kelly said, extending his hand to me.

I greeted his hand with a firm handshake. "Take care," I said, releasing his hand.

"No doubt," he said and he started to walk off. "Oh, Damon…" he called, stopping to look back at me.

"Yes?"

"Don't worry," he said. "Yours and Nadia's secret is safe with me."

I watched as the corners of his lips turned up into an arrogant smirk. I remained quiet as Kelly walked back up to me.

"I know you're the man Nadia claimed was my son's father."

I didn't respond.

"I guess it's true what they say, huh? It's a small world."

"Is it?" I questioned. There was a hint of sarcasm in my voice that Kelly obviously missed.

"Most definitely," he said, unfazed by my tone. "I mean, can you imagine how surprised I was when I went to see Nadia's mother Bernice and saw all those pictures lined up on the coffee table, photos of Nadia and this dude. They were throwback, of course, but that dude was you for sure. When I asked her about the guy posed up with Nadia, she explained that you were an old boyfriend."

"Really?"

"Yeah," he continued. "She went into this spiel about how Nadia was madly in love with you and how they thought the two of you were going to get married someday and so on and so forth. Then, Bernice started explaining how crazy Nadia was about you. I put two and two together and figured you had to be the other man."

"How can you be sure?" I questioned. I was calling his bluff, waiting for him to trip on his own words.

"Because I knew Nadia," he said, shaking his head. "I don't mean to speak ill of the dead, but the bitch was money hungry. Hell, I'm a good man, and I know the only reason she'd try to pin my son on another man was if that man had money."

"When I spoke to Bernice a few days ago, she advised me that Donovan was returning to Huntsville with his godmother," I said, gauging Kelly's reaction. "Do you know whom she was referring to?" I wanted to know if Kelly knew of anyone else Nadia may have pulled into her circle, anyone else who might be aware of our dirty little secret.

Kelly frowned then shook his head. "I have no clue," he said. "As soon as Bernice called me, I hopped the first available flight out to New York. Bernice talked a lot while I was there, but she never mentioned Donovan having a godmother."

I decided I would leave the rest of my questions concerning Bernice's involvement for her to answer. "So, how did the two of you meet?" I interrogated. "When did the two of you become...an item?"

"A little over two years ago," he continued. "I was working at the airport, doing some janitorial work. I was mopping up a spill when I saw this beautiful woman sitting alone in tears, and I offered my assistance."

"And *Nadia* fell for that?" I inquired. I knew if Kelly had been pushing a mop bucket, it would have been a clear indication that he was a blue-collar worker; Nadia was money hungry, like he'd said—the kind of woman that even if she didn't have a pot to piss in her-damn-self, she would have still considered a man who made less than $80,000 a year far beneath her standards.

"C'mon! Nadia with a janitor? We both know better than that," he chuckled. "She cursed me out, and I cursed her out. We exchanged words back and forth until she finally apologized—told me she'd just been dumped and was having, as she put it, the worst day of her life." He smiled, as if reminiscing, and then went on, "But after talking for a minute, she invited me to dinner. After dinner, she caught a late flight out to LA. Then, a couple days later, she hit me up and invited me out to visit her. I went, and the two of us began kicking it on a regular. That went on for about six months, until she finally gave me the boot. I didn't hear from her again until she told me she was pregnant by another man."

"So, if this is the truth," I began, "why did you tell Octavia otherwise?"

He paused, looking at me in deep thought and concentration. "Because," he finally answered, "Octavia is a woman, and women don't always understand simple things. They take the basics and make them extravagant. Small disagreements turn into all-out blow-ups. The things that took place between you and Nadia were before Octavia's time. I don't feel it's necessary to taint a beautiful present with toxic waste from the past."

What an eloquent sermon written with an underlying load of bullshit. "Okay. Well, that explains why you did it for Octavia," I said, "but why would you do it for me?"

"Because despite what you think," he began, "you and I have a lot in common."

I grew angry at the thought of what Kelly felt we had in common. He had to be talking about Octavia. It was obvious at times, when Kelly spoke of my wife, that he had some sort of feelings about her. The way he looked at her further confirmed his underlying attraction. I couldn't blame Kelly for being attracted to my wife, for she was naturally beautiful. She had a brown sugar complexion and honey-brown bedroom eyes, as well as a body that could harden even the strongest man's dick with one look at her. I'd never been a jealous man, and I also noticed and admired attractive women, but the truth is, if I could ever confirm that Kelly had violated my look-but-don't-touch policy about my wife, he'd discover he'd have more in common with Nadia than just their child. Like her, he'd meet an untimely death.

* * *

After Kelly and Donovan left, I showered and told Octavia I had some work to do. I excused myself to the home office and sat behind the mahogany desk, staring at my laptop, thinking about the events that had taken place that day. From Donovan to Octavia, I had more than one issue with Kelly and more than one reason to question his intentions. I reached into my pants pocket and pulled out the diamond stud, I found earlier. I knew the earring belonged to Octavia, but I wanted to know why it was lying, of all places, by the bed inside our guesthouse—the guesthouse Kelly had occupied before Octavia found him an apartment.

Flashbacks of the day Octavia had mentioned the missing diamond replayed in my mind. It had been following the night she'd gone on a drinking binge, after her mother had informed her that she was battling cancer. I was sure that day had been hell for Octavia. Before having what I imagined must have been a heart-wrenching conversation with her mother, Octavia had learned that I had been withholding information in regard to Lena, my former high school sweetheart and mother to Octavia's best friend's deceased husband's child. I wasn't having an affair with Lena, but I had chosen not to disclose the fact that I had given her a substantial amount of money, amongst other things, to help her and her daughter Janai start a new life. After the murder of Janai's father Kenny, I felt it was best that Lena and Janai leave town. I was sure a fresh city was the perfect answer to a fresh start. Octavia thought my assistance had started and stopped with getting Lena a job in Los Angeles; however, due to a few slip-ups, her suspicions had increased. Later, she found out that I had not only helped Lena get a job, but I'd also funded and supported her in starting her own business, and the two of us had remained in contact, even after her relocation. I hadn't told Octavia because I knew the shit didn't look good, and honestly, I didn't want to explain why I felt compelled to offer my assistance.

My decision to assist Lena was purely innocent, whether my wife would believe that or not. I knew Lena could do so much more with her life if the opportunity presented itself, so I presented her the opportunity. I had faith that *my* daughter would never fall off or allow her self-esteem to drop so low that she would settle for being the side chick and baby-mama to a man who was not only married, but also a sorry piece of shit (Kenny was all of those things), but we never know what life is going to throw at us. When it comes to our children, we can pray and wish and pray again that they turn out to be upstanding, confident, successful individuals, but we cannot live their lives for them. Sometimes those children choose to take a left turn, despite the fact that we've given them a road map, plenty of fuel, and practically carried them in the right direction. Lena had taken my helping hand and made a good life for her and her daughter. Although I wished I had been honest with Octavia from the beginning, I didn't regret the things I had done for Lena.

Nevertheless, to make matters worse, when Octavia had tried to contact me for emotional support on that dreaded day, I was MIA, and the person who just so happened to be available to offer support and comfort when she needed it most had been Kelly. Looking at the earring again, I wondered if the comfort and support he'd provided included taking advantage of Octavia in her state of inebriation and depression. I decided to push those thoughts from my mind, at least for the moment. I was positive I would have my answers soon enough. In the meantime, I needed to focus on regaining control of my home and my life. I had been so caught up in trying to cover my own tracks that I hadn't realized that Kelly was quite possibly making and gaining headway with my wife, right under my own nose.

I signed onto my PC and logged into my e-mail account to check my mail. The first e-mail in my inbox was from Lena, and it was a short one, informing me that she'd received the deed for the home I'd sold her for $1 and thanking me for all of my help. She ended the letter with, "I love you… and I hope to see you soon." I had explained to her that while I valued our friendship, I felt it was best that we put some distance between us. Although I didn't say it to her, what I meant was that it was better that we end our friendship altogether. After confronting Lena, Octavia had advised me that she felt Lena had romantic feelings for me. I never got any vibes from Lena that indicated that, but I wasn't willing to take any chances. I had enough on my plate without having to deal with any unwanted feelings. I deleted her e-mail and emptied my recycle bin so it was gone for good.

After reviewing my other e-mails, I got to the reason that I had logged on in the first place: my business associate, Lawrence. He was my go-to guy whenever I needed a problem researched or resolved. Kelly was the problem this time, and I needed a resolution.

I had just finished e-mailing Lawrence when Octavia appeared in the doorway wearing a silk red robe. The robe stopped inches above her knees, revealing her toned legs. "Baby, are you coming to bed?" she asked sweetly. She entered the room and pulled the door shut behind her.

"Yes, I am," I answered, quickly minimizing the screen I was looking at. "I was just wrapping up down here."

Octavia stepped barefoot across the wooden floor and slid in between me and the desk.

I eased the chair back slightly to give her enough room to sit on top the desk.

Her robe fell open slightly, revealing her full breasts. The scent of Shea butter and vanilla floated in the air, teasing my nose, while the sight of Octavia's flawless skin awakened the man in between my legs. She flashed me a smile, then frowned. "Ouch," she mumbled, turning slightly to the side.

"What's wrong?" I questioned, concerned. I watched as Octavia slightly elevated her hips.

"I sat on this," she said, facing me again, "and it stuck me in my ass!" She held up the earring that I had completely forgotten about. She studied the jewelry carefully and concluded, "Hey, this is the one I lost. Where did you find it?"

I contemplated before I answered. Part of me wanted to lie and tell her

I found it stuck in the carpet or outside. I wanted to forget about at least one of many thoughts that were troubling me, but I couldn't. I had to see her reaction, and I craved her response. The only way I was going to get that was to tell her the truth. "On the floor of the guesthouse," I finally said. "I stepped inside earlier to make a phone call, and I found it lying on the floor by the bed." I watched every detail of Octavia's expression, gauged every inch of her features.

She looked slightly surprised but not shocked. "Oh," she said coolly before clearing her throat. "I—"

A light knock on the office door interrupted my wife's response, and I looked from her to the door. I knew it was Contessa at the door, and I thought about asking her to wait until Octavia and I finished our conversation; however, when there came another knock, I assumed whatever she wanted was important.

Octavia stood up and adjusted the robe she was wearing so it once again covered her breasts.

"Come in," I said.

Contessa opened the door. She was smiling and holding Jasmine's hand.

Before the two of them could step across the threshold, Jasmine let go of Contessa's hand and ran over to me. I lifted her up onto my lap and gave her a big squeeze. She was dressed all cozy in a pink gown with the word "Princess" embroidered on the front and a pair of plush pink bunny rabbit slippers. Her curly hair was pulled on top of her head in a big afro puff. She looked more and more like Octavia with each passing second: absolutely beautiful.

Contessa looked like she was also ready for bed as well, in her very modest and comfortable cotton pajamas, slippers, and a floral print scarf around her head. "Sorry to disturb you two," she said, looking at me apologetically, "but the li'l princess wanted to give you goodnight kisses."

"It's no trouble, Ms. Contessa," I said sincerely. "Daddy will still be up to tuck you in," I said to Jasmine.

"Goodnight, munchkin," Octavia said, leaning down to kiss the top of Jasmine's head.

"And I want to thank the two of you for a wonderful day." Contessa sighed, extending her arms to Octavia. "Give an old lady some love."

Octavia laughed lightly, then stepped up to her so the two of them could share a brief, friendly hug.

"Oh!" Contessa said nonchalantly as she pulled away from their embrace, "Something poked me!" Contessa rubbed the back of her arm lightly.

"I'm sorry," Octavia apologized. There was a look of bewilderment on her face. "I must have stuck you with this" She held her hand open, revealing the earring.

Contessa smiled and shook her head. "You just walk around with diamonds in your hand? Such a diva," she teased.

"Actually, this was a lost one," Octavia replied. "Damon found it for me."

Contessa pushed her glasses back on her nose. "Wait a minute," the nanny said, rubbing her finger across her eyebrow. "When did you lose this?" she asked, looking like she was deep in thought.

"I woke up the morning after Mama told us," Octavia said, "and I was missing an earring."

Contessa sighed. "I thought so," she said. "I found an earring tangled up with the laundry the next morning. I knew it was yours and planned to return it, but I just got caught up in my housework. I remember dropping it in the pocket of my apron, but I completely forgot about it." She shook her head. "It must've fallen out somewhere during my cleaning rounds."

"Ms. Contessa, I found it in the guesthouse," I informed her. I looked at Octavia, who looked like she was hanging on Contessa's every word, clueless to where the conversation was headed.

"I was in the guesthouse," she said. "Remember? Kelly had spent the night that night and…well, I wanted to make sure he left everything in place." She shook her head. "I love my nephew, of course, but sometimes that boy can sure leave things a mess." She looked at Octavia, then back at me. "I must have dropped the earring in there when I went to check on things and tidy up." Contessa took a deep breath, then exhaled. "I'm sorry, sugar. I shoulda given it back right then and—"

"It's okay." Octavia smiled, patting Contessa's arm. "I'm glad you remember now, though, because to be honest, I didn't have a clue."

I looked from one woman to the other: Octavia looked relieved, and Contessa looked satisfied. I was content with the answer I had been provided.

"Well, I better get the little one up to bed," Contessa announced, yawning slightly. "It's past her bedtime...and mine."

We said our goodnights, and Contessa exited with Jasmine walking at her side. I pondered her explanation for a second, then decided to put the subject to rest.

Octavia assumed her previous position, again sitting down on the desk in front of me. "Mystery solved?" she asked, staring at me lovingly.

"Mystery solved," I smiled, sliding my chair forward. I reached out and stroked her thighs with my fingertips; her skin was smooth and soft, like silk. "Show me where you stuck yourself," I whispered, staring into her eyes.

Her lips spread, giving me a seductive smile. I watched closely as Octavia slowly untied the belt of the robe, then stood, allowing the material to fall to the floor. She turned around so her back was facing me, then ran her hand down her wide hip to the curve at the top of her ass. "Right here," she said, pointing with her finger.

My nature was slowly beginning to rise just from looking at her naked body, and I knew it wouldn't be long before I needed sexual relief, but I wanted to take my time and admire the majestic piece of art before me. Octavia's brown skin appeared to glow underneath the lighting inside the room. I leaned forward and pressed my lips to the spot she was pointing at. "Feel better?" I asked.

"Almost," she said, looking over her shoulder at me.

"Almost doesn't count," I said, shaking my head. I grabbed her waist and pulled her toward me. I rolled my tongue along her lower back, licking from one side to the other, then back again.

"Mmmm..." Octavia moaned.

"Closer?" I asked. I moved my hands lower, until I was cupping her firm, round ass.

"Yes."

I pulled her down so she was sitting on my lap. I could feel the warmth from her kitten through my pants, and I couldn't wait to feel the direct heat on my dick. I turned the chair so the desk was on our right side, allowing us more room to move. "Stand up, baby," I whispered.

Octavia did as I requested.

"Bend over and grab your ankles."

She looked over her shoulder, lowered her eyes seductively, then did as I requested.

I wasted no time in getting to what I wanted. I kissed her left cheek, sucking softly, then her right cheek, before sliding my tongue in between the two. I started at her crack, then moved down and around the rim of her tightest hole. I gave Octavia's back door extra attention, alternating between licking and blowing warm kisses. I then massaged the outer perimeter gently with my thumb before licking her hole again. Octavia moaned deeply as I saturated her most delicate area over and over again with the wetness from my tongue. Once I was content with the job I had performed, I moved further south, gliding my tongue down to her hairless, phat lips. I nibbled, then sucked on each before latching onto her clit. I was thirsty, and her clit was the handle leading to the faucet that I knew would quench my thirst. Octavia's legs began to tremble as I tugged and pulled continuously on her chocolate knob. I held her lips open with my hands while dipping in and out of her warm wetness. I rolled my tongue inside her pussy, then traced my name against the inside of her lips. I used her juice box as my tablet as I spelled D-A-M-O-N, giving new meaning to "put your name on it." I sucked, then licked, licked, then sucked on her pussy until my mouth was covered in her juices and I had to come up for air. I inhaled her aroma while replacing my tongue with my index finger.

"Damon..." Octavia moaned.

The sound of her voice calling my name made my soldier jump. He was standing at attention, completely hard. I pushed my finger as deep inside her as nature would allow it to go. The heat from inside her playground, combined with the swishing of her wetness was almost too much for me to bear. Between my own legs there was a throbbing that was quickly beginning to match the slowly increasing pounding of my heart. I reached down with my free hand and carefully unbuttoned and unzipped my pants, setting my man free. He was ready. I told him to be patient, letting him know his time would not be much longer.

I heard Octavia moan and moan again before screaming, "Oh shit!"

I could no longer resist. I removed my hand from her body and quickly stood, allowing my shorts to fall down around my ankles.

Octavia stood up straight and turned around and looked at me. The hunger in her eyes both satisfied me and made me want her even more, so I grabbed her by the back of her head, pulling her to me. We kissed each other quickly but with passion. I sat back down, holding my dick in my hand. "Sit on it," I commanded.

I watched her, anticipating and anxious for her to honor my request, but she didn't. Instead, she dropped straight to her knees and wrapped her lips around my stick. Octavia plunged completely down on my man, deep-throating him and causing my knees to shake. She took her time licking, then sucking my dick, going up, then down, then up again. Her soft lips, warm mouth, and wet tongue were a triple threat, and I was quickly falling victim. I could feel my body growing stiff, my muscles tightening involuntarily.

"Sit on it," I groaned.

This time she obliged. Octavia rose from the position she'd been occupying on her knees and turned around and eased down on my lap. I kissed her shoulder blade, then the back of her neck, all the while grabbing and squeezing her breasts. Octavia rotated her hips, grinding on my dick. Her movements were strong and swift, and I matched every, one stroke for stroke. She leaned back against my chest, looking up at me, almost hypnotizing me with her eyes. I pressed my mouth to hers and kissed her hard on the lips. Our tongues mated while our hips continued to move in unison. I could feel her getting wetter and wetter with every movement. Reaching between her legs, I placed two fingers on the hood of Octavia's clit. Rotating my fingers quickly, I applied just the right amount of pleasure and pressure to her button. The sensation of her muscles grasping my hard-on elevated me toward the mountain of climax. When she arched her back, grabbed her breast, and screamed, "Damon!" so passionately, it almost pushed me completely over the edge. I stood and pulled out of her creamy filling long enough to turn her around, then lifted her up on the edge of the desk. Octavia wrapped her legs around my waist in a grip the jaws of life would have envied. I rolled my torso back and forth; my dick had sat sail in her chocolate waters, and I was enjoying every moment of the ride. I kissed each of her moist lips before moving to her breasts. I licked, then sucked each of her nipples slowly. I was savoring the moment, indulging on the taste of her skin. I felt the walls of her pussy closing in as her muscles began to tighten gradually around my dick. I pushed further, diving deeper with every rotation of my hips. I could feel the sweat on my forehead, the sensation in my stomach, the tightening in my thighs as the load I was trying my hardest to hold a little longer broke free, and I erupted inside of her.

Chapter 3

Kelly

Kicking my feet up on the coffee table in front of me, I sank down into the cool leather sofa while bobbing my head to Bootsy Collins. The sound of Bootsy crooning, "I'd rather be with you," beat loudly through the speakers mounted on the wall just above my head. Taking a long pull from the blunt I pinched between my fingers, I hummed along with Bootsy.

I inhaled deeply, allowing smoke to fill my lungs, held it there for a few seconds. then exhaled slowly through my parted lips. I was in my zone, a place of complete relaxation—relaxation that was long overdue for me. The past few weeks had been filled with chaos and stress, and this day was no exception. First, I had chosen to confess my true identity to Ilene. I'll admit it hadn't been part of my plan; however, when I saw her looking like something out of the movies, I had to. I wasn't a bad-looking man, and it was obvious I'd come from a good gene pool, but damn, no one had told me my mother was so beautiful. When I hit her with the news that I was the baby she'd given up at birth, her reaction was one of shock and I'm sure disbelief, until I revealed my birthmark. I had never dreamt of that moment before, but I'm sure if I had, I wouldn't have anticipated her reaction. I could have been wrong, but I'd seen something in her eyes that looked like joy and another something that resembled love. The two of us barely had time to talk before Contessa and Octavia interrupted us. I don't know how much Octavia saw, but Contessa advised me as the two of us were later sitting on the patio that Octavia had been watching Ilene and me when she walked up. I figured whatever questions Octavia had about what she may or may not have seen or heard would eventually come up. When Contessa disrupted Octavia's spying, I thought for sure she was still on the same team as me—that was, until she also informed me she was no longer feeling our plan.

"I can't do this anymore," she said, looking at me. "These are good people, and they don't deserve to be hurt."

I was baffled at how quickly some people could suddenly grow a damn conscious and want to live with integrity. "Did you say that when Lena pulled your ass off the streets?" I whispered. "If I remember correctly, you were digging through trash and collecting cans."

"I was," she said, pushing her glasses up on her nose, "but I ain't no more. Besides, that was before I got to know Damon and Octavia."

I looked across the patio at Octavia. She sat with my son on one leg and her daughter on the other. She was dressed in a sexy, off-the-shoulder dress that accentuated her every curve. In that dress, which flowed down to her ankles, and with her hair pulled up like that, she looked like a goddess. Beyond Octavia's beauty, she had a giving, sincere heart and an outstanding personality. At that moment, I couldn't admit it to Contessa, but I understood her loyalty to Octavia.

"You are the hired help," I said firmly, staring at Contessa. "You will do as you're told, when you're told." Yes, I could understand Contessa's loyalty, but the fact still remained that she was getting paid to do a job.

"No. I'm done with this," she said strongly.

To be honest, I was proud of the old broad. She had heart, and she was attempting to stand for what she now thought was right. If her standing for what she believed to be right wouldn't have screwed up my plans, I would have had her back; however, she was overplaying her stroke, and I had to let her know it. I reached over and grabbed her arm. Her eyes looked like they might pop out of her head when I began to apply enough pressure to leave a mark. "Say one fucking word and the next time you feel my hands, they'll be wrapped around your bony neck!" I threatened through clenched teeth. "Do you understand?" I could see the tears swelling in the woman's eyes, but that moment was not the time for compassion. I was too close to getting what I wanted to let her fuck things up. I couldn't allow that, and I needed to make sure she understood.

"Yes," she whispered.

"You will do as *I* say," I continued. "Do you understand?" I pulled my eyes from hers and noticed Octavia watching us. I nonchalantly slid my hand down to Contessa's. I held her hand, hoping the picture I was creating for Octavia was one of peace and harmony. "Smile," I said, "and turn around."

Contessa did as I said, and it seemed from Octavia's reaction that I had saved the moment, but I knew if Contessa was feeling guilty, there was a great possibility she'd jump ship and sell me out. *What ever happened to the ride-or-die hoes who'll hold up their end of the bargain when they make a vow?* As I thought about it, it seemed every female I'd dealt with had been on some more shit.

I hit the blunt again as images of Nadia filled my head. The first time we'd met was as fresh in my mind as if it had taken place that very morning. The story I'd told Damon about it had been slightly altered. The truth was, I was not working at the airport, but at the University of Alabama in Huntsville, as a member of the maintenance team, doing odd jobs. I had been working that particular gig for about three months. Of course ninety days doesn't seem like much, but I spent more time unemployed than employed, so ninety days of continuous employment made me feel extremely good. It wasn't that I didn't want to work or that I was some trifling-ass bum. People simply didn't want to hire an ex-con.

At the university I barely made minimum wage, but my money was tax free since the school director paid me cash under the table. She told me it was because she wanted to help a brother in the struggle. She believed in the whole rehabilitation movement, and she felt it was her duty to help her fellow man. Of course, she told me all that five minutes before I had her face down and ass up behind the closed doors of her office. I kept giving her the dick, and she kept coming up with bullshit tasks for me to perform. However, my job and our little love affair would soon come to an end, not long after I met the mother of my son.

At the time, Nadia was living in Los Angeles, but she was at the university teaching a dance workshop. The day we met, I was in the Student Center, down on my hands and knees, removing gum from the carpet. She entered the room wearing a short dress that revealed a pair of legs that would have put the chicks on the Nair commercials to shame. She had dangerous curves to complement her legs; clearly, she kept her fine body in shape through the art of dance. Nadia was light-skinned, with flawless, beautiful features and long, sandy hair. She had the body and the beauty, and I couldn't help noticing her when she entered the room. She noticed me as well, despite the fact that she was completely out of my league, she made the first move. After watching me for a minute or two, she said, "Hello." I returned her greeting, and the two of us engaged in a little visual flirtation. Finally, she passed me her phone number.

We started talking on the phone on a daily basis. I learned that not only did Nadia teach dance from time to time, but she was also a professional ballerina. She told me her mother had died during childbirth, so she'd been raised by Bernice, her grandmother. Nadia had never met her father, and Bernice had advised her that his identity was unknown. I was intrigued by her story and even shared my own. Not only did I tell Nadia about my criminal past, but I also shared with her the details of my childhood and that I had been adopted by my parents, Delia and Eric. I opened my heart, going into great detail about when I was ten years old and my mother passed from injuries she sustained during a car accident. I also told her that four years later, my father drank himself into an early grave.

"I was fourteen when I was dropped into the foster care system and started bouncing from home to home," I explained one night on the phone with Nadia. "The so-called families I was placed with were nothing more than a bunch of fake muthafuckas who wanted a check. By the time I was sixteen, I was a high school dropout and a D-boy. By seventeen, I'd caught my first case, and—"

"Say no more," Nadia said. The tone in her voice sounded so empathetic and filled with compassion. "None of that matters to me. All that matters is who you are now. I want to know *that* man." Nadia never asked me for any further details about my past. The only portion of my history she seemed slightly interested in was my family tree.

She occasionally asked if I had ever considered finding my biological parents, but I told her I hadn't. Truth was, I felt if the people who'd conceived me wanted to know me, they never would have given me up in the first place. I didn't dwell on the subject because at that time, I didn't give a damn. I couldn't miss someone I'd never known.

After two weeks of talking on the phone, Nadia asked me to come visit her. She flew me out to LA, and from the moment she greeted me at the airport, she began treating me like I was the best man who'd ever pissed on Earth. She clothed, fed, and fucked me like I was the man of her dreams. She spent a lot of time on the road, so we didn't have time to get on each other's nerves. She never even complained that I hadn't found work.

Thing was, I'd never been a stupid man. I have always completely understood that if something seems too good to be true, it probably is. It seemed too good to be true for me to have met such a beautiful, professional woman by chance, one who just so happened to want to establish a relationship with me. In the end, it was neither good nor true.

Nadia was on tour with the Alvin Ailey American Dance Company when she suddenly got sick. She came home early from the tour, and the two of us found out she was pregnant. At that point, I thought my life couldn't get any better, and I began to think I'd really been given a second chance in life.

Nadia, on the other hand, seemed mad with the world. "How did I let this happen?!" she screamed, pacing back and forth across the hardwood floor of our kitchen. She was holding the positive home pregnancy test in her hands, and there was a look of utter disgust etched across her face. "I can't believe I've gone and fucked up like this."

"Baby, calm down," I said gently, watching her. "Everything is going to be fine."

"Fine!?" she snapped. "Fine?!" Nadia stopped pacing and looked at me like I was the world's biggest idiot. "Bringing a kid into this world is going to crap on all my plans! I'm not doing this shit for nothing, and—"

"Boo, you can still stick with your plans," I said, certain she was referring to her career. "You'll just have to change it up a little and—"

"Change it up a little? You are so clueless," Nadia snapped, cutting me off. She shook her head, staring at me. "I'm not keeping it."

"Huh? Wait a minute," I said, walking up to her. "Let's talk about this."

"We already did," she said coldly, "and the conversation is over. I won't discuss or justify *my* decision to bring or not bring a life into this world. It's my body, and it's my choice and mine alone."

"Yours alone? But I'm your man, the father of your—"

"The fact that you have a dick has nothing to do with being a man." Nadia laughed. "No matter how good that dick may be, I pay the bills in this bitch. And as such, I make the decisions." She pointed at herself. "Me. You got that? It's up to me."

I looked at Nadia and was speechless. What could I say? She was right. I had been lying around, leeching off her, thinking I was some big man with a strong woman carrying me. The truth was, I was *her* bitch. I was too caught up in enjoying the finer things in life—all the things Nadia was providing—to realize that I was slipping on my job as a man.

"I need some air." Nadia sighed, looked at me, and rolled her eyes. "I'm going to see my grandmother. I'll see you in a few days." And with that, she marched off and left me standing there with my mouth open and my manhood in her back pocket.

I blew Nadia's cell phone up for three days straight, wanting to get her to change her mind about the baby—*our* baby—but every time, I got her voicemail. Finally, a week later, she contacted me and told me she was fine. I told her we could make everything work, but she explained to me in no uncertain terms that she'd already made *her* decision, and she'd see me soon.

Nadia's little trip out for air eventually turned into a two-month hiatus. During her trip, she occasionally called to let me know she was okay and ask me about my day, but every time I even mentioned the baby, she hastily ended our conversation. I finally came to the assumption that Nadia had already terminated it without bothering to tell me.

Despite the fact that I had my own bank account with a few hundred dollars (money she'd given my broke ass, of course), I knew I needed to reestablish myself as the man. I decided to make some changes and spent our separation putting in work; I went back to hustling. Although, I'd been trying to stay on the straight and narrow, I needed a quick come-up, so I called my old connect. He made the trip out to LA, and just like that, I was back on with my hustle. I wasn't moving half as much or as fast I had in the South, but it felt good to make my own money again. It also kept my mind off Nadia.

When she finally decided to return from visiting Bernice, she advised me that she had changed her mind and was, in fact, going to keep the baby. She apologized for the things she'd said before she left and explained to me that she was just terrified of ruining the career she'd worked so hard to build up. She gave me one of the sweetest kisses I'd ever had in my life, and then the two of us made love for hours. We were happy again.

After Donovan was born, though, I noticed that Nadia seemed detached. I thought she was dealing with post-partum depression, but as time went by, I discovered that she just wasn't interested in being a mother since it required her to take focus off herself and make someone else her priority. She was too shallow and far too damn selfish to allow that; anything or anyone that took attention away from Nadia was an issue.

She decided to put off her dancing career in favor of doing some acting, and her pursuit for landing a role had her on the go even more than when she was working as a professional ballerina. Thinking back now, I'm not sure what she was really doing with her time. The only thing I *was* aware of was that she was more of a part-time visitor than a full-time mother. She did manage to land a few roles in stage plays, and she even got casted in one of Tyler Perry's productions.

For the most part, I was happy with the family we'd created, though I was getting more and more fed up with Nadia's selfishness. As if things at home weren't bad enough, I took a hard hit in the game when an associate of mine ran off with more than half my supply. I blamed myself for the mishap, for I should have known better than to trust any man, especially one I hadn't created myself.

Donovan had just turned two when Nadia and I decided to relocate. When Nadia suggested Huntsville, Alabama, I was puzzled. Since she had begun performing in stage plays, she'd been spending a lot of her time in Atlanta—so much time that she'd even rented a home there. Therefore, I naturally assumed Atlanta would have been her city of choice. I didn't trip about Huntsville though. I'd been raised in the South, and I had always enjoyed the Southern comforts, but I did question her intentions.

"The cost of living is cheaper down there," Nadia explained, "and it's a great city to raise children in."

My radar should have gone up at that moment. I should have known there was more to her decision. Nadia had never bothered checking a price tag in her life, and she knew nothing about caring for and nurturing our son. A woman who spent so frivolously and couldn't care less about good parenting wouldn't have bothered to check cost of living or child safety in any neighborhood, but I failed to realize it at the time.

The sound of my cell phone vibrating on the coffee table pulled my attention from my reminiscent state. I took one last hit from the roach between my fingers, then dropped it in the ashtray sitting next to my phone. I picked up my phone and glanced at the caller ID. "Shit!" I exhaled loudly, looking at Lena's name. It was the fifth time she'd called me in the last two hours, and just like the times before, I sent her to voicemail. I was avoiding her for one reason and one reason only: I was not in the mood for her interrogation. I knew she was calling to ask for a play-by-play on what had happened at the barbeque, but I wasn't in any kind of mood for a recap—not to mention I hadn't done what I'd promised her I would. Then, of course, there was the fact that I was simply growing tired of her.

Lena had walked into my life shortly after Nadia, Donovan, and I moved to Huntsville. I'd received a phone call from her, asking me to meet her for lunch to discuss a business opportunity. At the time, I had a few flyers posted up around town, advertising handyman and odd jobs services. I had a position waiting for me with an old connect, but I knew that acceptance would come with several conditions, one of them being possible fed time. I wasn't trying to get caught up again, especially now that I had a son. Returning to the university was an option I considered, but since they still had the same director, and her coochie was probably all hot and dry, I decided that was not my best option. When Lena called, I figured, *Why the hell not? I got nothing to lose meeting with the woman.* I didn't lose a thing, but everything I thought I knew about my life and the woman I was sharing it with changed.

As it turned out, Lena and Nadia had met before, back when Nadia and I were still living in LA. Lena advised me that Nadia had been running game—that Nadia had only taken an interest in me because she knew the one thing I never cared to know: She knew who my birth mother was. The only reason she'd shown any interest in me was because she saw me as a meal ticket. Nadia was a manipulator but not a smart one. She had invested more time and money in me than she gained in the end. That's what happens when a slow bitch thinks she's a boss and doesn't plan properly; it results in an epic fail.

During our first meeting, Lena presented me with a copy of my birth certificate, as well as other supporting documentation that named Ilene Lawson as my birth mother. Ilene Lawson was a twenty-one-year-old single woman when she had me, but just a year later, she would marry a man who would end up being one of the wealthiest brothers in the Southeast, Damon Whitmore. I was impressed by the information Lena provided about my past, but I was even more impressed when she looked me directly in my eyes and let me know her sole purpose in filling me in was to enlist my help. What Lena had planned was scandalous, yeah, but I respected her for keeping it real. She wanted me to help her make Ilene and Damon's son, Damon Whitmore Jr., her man by helping her get Octavia out of the picture. Lena was so stone-cold serious about putting me on her team that she dropped me a $10,000 advance and promised to drop another $50,000 once the task was complete—as long as she and Damon were rubbing elbows, making the bed wet.

Lena had everything figured out, and she'd put together a flawless plan, complete with a new background and history for me. Part of that contrived history was a daughter, Ciara, who passed from leukemia; of course that was only a lie, meant to evoke emotion and pity from Octavia, since my first time being a father was when Donovan was born.

Her brilliant plan also included Nadia's participation. Lena explained that Damon and I shared a common interest, Nadia. Nadia failed to tell me that she knew the identity of my birth mother and that the man she'd once told me about, the one she was so "in love" with, was really my half-brother. According to Lena, Nadia was still in love with Damon, but if she couldn't have him *and* his money, she'd just settle for money. It then occurred to me that she chose to have Donovan because she thought that one way or another, she'd have access to the Whitmore fortune. Once I realized I was nothing more than a pawn in Nadia's great scheme, I decided to take control and make her a pawn in mine. I agreed to help Lena.

Lena's elaborate plan included Nadia, but of course Nadia wasn't going to be part of it for long—just long enough to cause a little havoc in the Whitmore household. Granted, Lena sold Nadia out, but Nadia had burned her own bridge. She could have kept it 100 percent real with me from the beginning, and things might have turned out differently. She might have been there with me and our son. I would never have trusted her again, and I probably would have dropped her ass and only maintained a relationship for the sake of our son, but I know without a shadow of doubt that I would have *never* killed her.

My phone began vibrating again.

"Damn it!" I grumbled. "This bitch is relentless!" I snatched my phone off the table. "What?!" I snapped into the phone, without looking at the caller ID.

"Now is that any way to greet an old friend?" the voice on the other end of the phone didn't belong to Lena, but much like hers, it belonged to someone I didn't want to hear from.

"Gator?" I said, sitting up straight.

"I've been waiting to hear from you, Kelly," Gator said.

There was complete silence in the background, and I wondered if he was sitting in his home or—worse—parked somewhere in front of mine. "I've, uh...I been a little busy," I said calmly, easing up from my spot on the sofa and carefully making my way to the living room window.

"Busy getting my money, I hope."

"I told you I got you," I said lightly. "Give me another month, and I'll be straight." I stood by my living room window, peering through the blinds. It was dark out, and the moon rays radiated down, bouncing lightly against the paint of the parked cars. I didn't see anything or anyone that looked out of place, but I was paranoid as hell—and that paranoia had nothing to do with my little smoke session I'd engaged in moments earlier. The sick feeling in my gut and the perspiration on my forehead were coming from the voice on the other end of the phone. I knew all too well that when Gator called about his money, there were only one of two possible outcomes: Either I'd have to break him off what he was looking for, or he'd break me, simple as that. There was no in between, no compromise. Hell, I learned that personally when he'd sent a couple of his street soldiers to beat my ass. The reason I'd ended up living in Damon and Octavia's guesthouse was because I'd been robbed at a fleabag motel where I'd been planning to crash for a few nights. The plan was for me to stay at the motel just long enough to play on Octavia's sympathy, but I didn't have to stay there long. As my bad luck would have it, the motel was one of many low-budget locations members of Gator's team frequented. One of his goons recognized me, and they jumped me.

"You've got two weeks," Gator said firmly. "I like you, Kelly. Don't make me come looking for you."

Click.

He hung up before I could respond.

"Fuck!" I cursed, slamming my hand against the wall. "Son of a bitch!"

Donovan was only a few feet away in the other room, sleeping, and I knew my rant might awaken him, but at that moment, I didn't care. I paced back and forth across the living room floor, and it felt like my thoughts were bouncing off the walls. *How did I allow this to happen?* Things had been going so well for me, but in an instant, they'd disintegrated. I had to make some major moves and make them quickly. If I didn't satisfy my debt with Gator, I knew things were only going to get worse.

Chapter 4

Lena

"Why aren't you answering your phone, Kelly? I've been blowing your ass up!" I screamed into my cordless handset. "What's going on? You need to call me back…immediately!" I hit the end button, then slammed the phone down into its charging cradle. My nerves were wearing thin. I hadn't spoken with Kelly since the two of us had parted ways at JFK International after picking Donovan up from his grandmother's, and I was a nervous wreck, wondering what in the hell could be going on.

I blamed Nadia's simple-minded ass for my current situation and my panic. *Why'd she have to be such a gold-digging whore? All she had to do was follow the script and keep Damon occupied with Donovan while Kelly cozied up to Octavia and got her in the sack. Damon would find out about her infidelity, and Octavia would find out about Damon's so-called illegitimate son. I would comfort Damon, Kelly would comfort Octavia, and Nadia would…well, die. I mean, really, how fucking hard would that have been?* Granted, Nadia didn't know she would be axed out of the plan, but she still didn't stick to it. If there was one thing I couldn't stand, it was a disloyal woman.

After I'd approached Kelly with my offer, the two of us had gone to Nadia and offered her an in. I personally thought she would have told me to kiss her ass and go to hell, seeing as though I had ruined whatever intentions she had to use Kelly, but Nadia wasn't that type. If money was involved, she'd overlook anything. Even *after* we had a deal, though, she threw me under the bus by sending Octavia a gift from my spa. That gift, along with the fact that Octavia was too nosy for her own good, led right to me. I was in good with Damon, and I would have been even better—meaning lying in his arms—but Nadia's school-girl move had caused my future husband to receive pressure from his current wifey; thus causing a major setback in my future nuptials. When Octavia found out that Damon and I were friends, she'd pulled rank, and Damon was forced to tell me we had to cool our friendship for the moment. *What kind of bullshit is that?!* Of course I refused to accept Octavia's demands and conditions, but I was still pissed about her making such an inappropriate request in the first place. *What kind of woman comes between friends?* I know, I know. I didn't have any intention of remaining just friends with Damon, but Octavia couldn't prove that. The way I felt about Damon may have seemed a bit crazy, but I didn't care. He was the only man I'd ever come in contact with who deserved me.

Yes, I was quite aware that I'd played the fool for Kenny, and I'd often said the same thing about him, but my feelings for Kenny and what I felt for Damon were on two totally different levels. I loved Kenny, but I was hopelessly in love with Damon, and I knew Damon loved me too. Besides, Kenny wasn't shit, and Damon was *the* shit. I was so close, but Nadia ruined it.

As if Nadia's antics weren't enough, Gia, the dumb blonde we recruited to tamper with Damon's and Donovan's paternity test results, had the audacity to off herself, but not before she committed the gallant act of leaving a note of confession, stating that she'd switched the results. I would have never known that if Contessa—perhaps my best investment—hadn't intercepted Damon's mail and informed me that a letter had come for him from DNA Diagnostics. I informed her to hold the letter to give me enough time to contact the center. When I called, I pretended to be Nadia and was advised that it had been discovered that there was an error with the test they'd performed.

I told Contessa to destroy the mail, of course, but Kelly insisted on letting the truth about his son's paternity get out. "I should have never agreed to that," he said, staring at me. "Donovan is my son. The thought of him calling another man Daddy disgusts me."

It didn't disgust you when you were cashing my check! I thought to myself. But

I decided to let it go. After all, Kelly still had an inside connection. He had bonded with Octavia, and he was Ilene Whitmore's son. Plus, he assured me that the shit would hit the fan when he crashed the Ellis-Whitmore family gathering. "I'm gonna tell Octavia everything," he promised. "When she hears that Damon's been lying to her about his whereabouts because he thought he had a son with Nadia and that he was breaking her off bread to keep her quiet, she'll walk out on his ass. She'll crumble right into my arms, and she'll leave Damon behind for you to console."

I decided I had nothing to lose by trusting Kelly, but I still wanted to know what happened when it all went down. *Did Damon flip to the crazy when he saw Donovan? Did Octavia throw the massive diamond that hung on her finger (which, by the way, should be mine) in Damon's face and declare their marriage was over?* The suspense was killing me. I was anxious to hear what had taken place, but believe I was not investing all my stock in Kelly with the hope that all would go according to plan. I had learned that lesson the hard way. Therefore, I had chosen to secure myself a back-up contact.

Knock-knock-knock.

I took a deep breath through my nostrils, then exhaled slowly through my mouth. I was not in the mood to deal with anyone at the moment, but I still had a business to run—a very successful one at that. "Come in," I said, forcing a smile.

The door opened and Joni, my hostess, stepped into the room. "Your 10 o'clock is here," she said happily.

My visitor was early, and it was just like her to be that considerate. To make matters more irritating, on days when I was not the most cheerful person, I wished I'd hired someone who knew when and where to turn their perky on. Joni only showed two emotions around me: happy and happier. I'd always believed in fake it till you make it, but she played that role a little too well for my taste. However, my clients loved her, and she was efficient, so I kept her around.

"Thanks, Jo." I smiled and stood. "Tell her I'll be right out."

Joni flashed her pretty blue eyes at me and then nodded her head. "I certainly will," Joni said before exiting my office.

I reached down into the top drawer of my desk and pulled out my Mac compact. After dabbing at the shine in my T-zone with my powder puff, I dropped the compact back in the drawer and exited my office. I smoothed my hands over the front of the silk blouse I was wearing as I walked toward the VIP room of my salon. If someone had told me five years earlier that I'd own one of the hottest salons on the West Coast, I would have laughed in their face and asked them to let me hit whatever it was they were smoking. But, there I was, accepting the fact that sometimes, dreams do come true. That was why I knew that my dream of standing by Damon's side would also become a reality. I smiled brightly as I stood in the hallway outside the VIP section as I imagined that fantasy all over again.

My client sat at my styling station with the latest edition of *Essence* magazine spread open on her lap. She appeared to be in her own world. I allowed my eyes to travel from her open-toe wedge heels up to her long, chocolate legs. From where I was standing, her legs appeared smooth and hairless. She had well-defined calves that were tight and big, revealed by the short dress she was wearing. I touched my hand to my chest in an effort to calm my pounding heart as I scanned her up and down, admiring the daring peek that the low-cut V in her dress gave her big breasts. I had paid good money for the D cups I proudly carried, but hers were all natural, and I found myself silently wondering what they looked like beyond the restraints of her clothes. I was completely turned on as I took in the beauty of her full cheeks and plump lips, neither hidden behind makeup. Her jet-black hair was blown out into a massive afro that very few women, myself included, could pull off.

I hadn't been with another woman since Donna, and until that moment, I was sure I would never want to be again. But the quiet throbbing in between my legs was a heated reminder to never say never. *Calm down,* I silently told my kitty. I didn't know why I was suddenly attracted to the woman, as we'd been around each other before without me ever feeling a spark. Then again, maybe I was looking at her in a new light. Maybe it was because I hadn't been laid in God knew how long. I was pulling for the latter, but I couldn't be sure.

I ran my fingers through my hair and cleared my throat as I stepped into the room, closing the door behind me. She instantly looked up at me and smiled. Her eyes grew wide as she stared at me, and I was so happy at that moment that I'd chosen the blouse and fitted pencil skirt that day. It had been a while since I'd seen her, and I wanted to make a good impression.

"You look gorgeous!" she said sweetly. I watched as she stood, giving me a full view of her curvaceous body. "Come here!" she ordered. "Give me some love."

You have no ideal how much I'd love to do just that, I thought. I knew her request was innocent, but I was willing to give her the extended dirty version. I stepped across the floor, swaying on my stilettos until the two of us were standing toe to toe. I couldn't name the scent she was wearing, but I loved it; it smelled like jasmine and honey. She pulled me into her arms in what I'm sure was a friendly embrace for her, but it tempted me something terrible. I allowed my hands to rest on her back while inhaling her sweet scent. The feel of her breasts pressed against mine made my nipples hard. She stepped back and took both my hands in hers. She stared at me as we stood there hand in hand. There was a familiarity in her eyes that I had not seen from another woman in years. The two of us had history, and although our stories were very different, in many ways, they were the same.

"It's been...too long," I said softly.

"I know," she said. "I'm so happy you reached out to me."

Hearing her say those words made my heart happy. I had been hesitant to contact her at first, afraid that she would reject my invitation to spend time together. Looking into her beautiful dark brown eyes now, though, I realized I should have known better. *How could a woman so kind, so tender-hearted reject anyone?* "Janai is going to be thrilled that you're here," I said, thinking of my daughter.

"I didn't know if you would want me to see her...um, well, I mean... after everything, and..." Her eyes filled with tears as she halted her words.

"It's okay," I said, stroking her cheek with my fingertips. "You don't have to say another word. Of course I want you to see her. You were an important part of her life, and she loves you. Despite everything that happened, we are forever bonded, and I'm glad we finally have time to reconnect." I brushed away the single tear that had escaped her pretty eye. "It's really good to see you," I said, pulling her into another hug. "Thank you for coming, Shontay."

* * *

"The country is absolutely beautiful!" Shontay exclaimed.

I nodded my head and smiled as she gave me details of her trip to Africa. After I showed her around my salon and basically claiming my bragging rights, the two us of picked Janai up from school and went on a tour of the city, followed by a late lunch. I loved the way Janai clung to Shontay and the way Shontay treated Janai. Shontay was the perfect stepmother, and although I couldn't see it when Kenny was living, I could now see why he'd chosen her as a wife.

The sun had gone down, and the two of us now sat side by side on my living room sofa, talking. After dinner, I sent Janai up to her bedroom so Shontay and I could be alone. I listened as Shontay continued with her story, but then she abruptly stopped.

"I've been babbling all day," she said. "Let's talk about you."

"There's not much to tell," I said lowly. "I work and take care of *our* daughter." I put extra emphasis on "our" just to see her reaction. I was pleased when the corners of her mouth stretched upward into a huge smile. "Tell me more about you," I insisted. "Are you seeing anyone?"

Her smiled lowered slightly. "I'm in what you might consider an, uh, open relationship." She sighed.

That piqued my curiosity. "Open?" I asked. "Really?"

"Yes," she said, looking away. "We've agreed to see other people."

"How do you feel about it?" I questioned gently. "You don't sound too thrilled."

"Believe it or not, it was my suggestion," she said. She looked at me and shrugged her shoulders. "I love Savoy—I promise I do—but…well, I'm just not ready to make the commitment he wants and deserves."

I had to respect that about her. She wasn't ready to fully commit to Savoy, and she wasn't about to pretend she was by stringing him along. "So you're keeping all your options open?" I asked suggestively.

"Most definitely." Shontay smiled. "What about you? Are you seeing anyone?"

I ran my fingers through the layers of my hair while contemplating whether or not I should tell her the truth. Granted, Octavia was Shontay's best friend, which was one of the reasons I was hesitant about inviting Shontay to visit in the first place. I didn't know if Octavia had talked badly about me to her or what. When I heard how happy Shontay was to hear from me, though, I pushed that thought out of my mind. Besides, Shontay and I shared a separate bond—a bond held by blood. She was my daughter's stepmother, and despite the fact that Kenny was now planted six feet under (thanks to me), the connection Shontay shared with Janai was unbreakable. The connection I shared with Shontay was equally unbreakable. We'd shared the same man for years, and we had both loved him deeply in our own way. Call me crazy, but I'd always thought that what's wrong with the women of the world today is that instead of celebrating what connects them, they bicker and argue and go to war with one another over men, of all things. I hoped that someday, when Damon and I were together, Octavia and I would remain cordial for the sake of the children, but considering that Octavia took me for the bitter, man-stealing type, I sincerely doubted it could ever be like that with us. Finally, I answered Shontay's question. "I'm in an open and long-distance relationship." I giggled, thinking about Damon.

"I guess that's yet another thing we have in common," she said, laughing lightly.

I casually dropped my eyes down to her breasts, wondering what else we may have in common. I felt comfortable with Shontay, but I wasn't confident enough to make a move. I decided to take my time and see if getting a taste was an option. Besides, playtime with Shontay was not on my original agenda.

She reminded me of why I had asked her to come in the first place. "I was a little relived when you contacted me," Shontay confessed.

"Relieved? Were you?"

"Yes. I've been avoiding returning to Huntsville for weeks and weeks now."

"Why?"

"Everything has changed for me," she said. "I've changed. I'm not the same woman I was, and I really don't know how or where I'd fit in there. I don't know what I want to do with my life."

"I understand," I said honestly. "I wonder the same thing. I mean, my mother is there, but...well, I just don't know."

"You'd fit in anywhere," Shontay said. "You have a new name, a fabulous new look, and you're handling your business very well. You've got your path laid out, and you know the direction you want to go. I'm sure if you wanted to return, you'd be just fine."

I loved the encouragement Shontay gave me, and it felt good to hear her confirm aloud what I already knew. "Thanks for that," I said softly, "but I don't think others feel the same about me...or that they are as willing to forgive." I lowered my eyes to add dramatic effect.

"What do you mean?"

"Octavia hates me because of what happened between me and Damon, and—"

"What are you talking about?" Shontay asked, cutting me off.

Octavia didn't tell her, I said to myself. "She…she didn't tell you?" I asked innocently.

"We haven't had the opportunity to talk lately," Shontay said quietly.

I wondered exactly how long it had been for the two of them. "Oh… well, I just assumed she would have told you…" I took a deep breath and then slowly exhaled. I wanted to give Shontay the impression that I was struggling to open up, that I had been torn with the secret I was preparing to reveal. The look of concern and anxiety on her face told me my act was working. After a few seconds of wasting time and silence, I said, "Here's what happened…"

Twenty minutes and a few tears later, I'd completely filled Shontay in on my history with Damon. I told her how the two of us met in high school and he helped me get established in Los Angeles. I also educated her on my run-in with Octavia, telling her that she'd accused me of trying to break up her home, thus driving a rift into my friendship with Damon. I may have exaggerated a tad, but I needed Shontay to feel my pain.

"Wow." She sighed. "The world gets smaller by the minute. So Damon found out you were his friend from—"

"*Girl*friend," I corrected.

"Girlfriend," she said slowly, "from high school? After he hired an investigator?"

"Yes," I answered.

"And he funded your business?"

"Yes, because he wanted to help me establish a better life for Janai," I stated, "but when Octavia found out, she refused to understand."

Shontay shook her head, and I could only assume she was just as disgusted as I had been. "Unbelievable," she whispered.

"I know it is," I said, dabbing at my eyes with my fingertips. "I would have never imagined in a million years that Octavia would have reacted the way she did. She basically belittled me and made me feel like I am the most disgusting, pathetic woman on the planet. Then, to make matters worse, she had the audacity to presume that I was sleeping with her husband! After every thing I went through to change my image and turn my—"

"I understand she may have hurt your feelings," Shontay said, interrupting me again. "Octavia sometimes has a way with words, and some people can't handle it. She's a little too real like that sometimes. However, you have to look at things from her side as well."

What the fuck? I asked myself. "What do you mean?" I asked, trying hard not to give away my developing anger.

"Lena, the two of you first met when she and I ran up on you in a motel...with *my* husband," Shontay said firmly. "You had a child with my husband, and Octavia was there through the entire thing. She was the one I cried to when your affair with Kenny began to unfold. I've forgiven you for those things, but it's only natural that Octavia would be defensive or harbor ill feelings, and I'm sure she had justifiable suspicions when she discovered that you were connected to her husband too."

I was completely caught off guard by Shontay's reaction. "So you agree with her? You share her ill feelings?" I concluded.

"No. I know you better than that. I'm just saying that I understand why she was concerned," she said.

"Oh..." I had no ideal where to take our conversation from that point, and the unsettling silence in the room made it clear to me that Shontay didn't know what to say either. "Would you like something to drink?" I asked, standing. I decided it was time for me to go into recovery mode and attempt to salvage the rest of our evening. I was disappointed that Shontay hadn't instantly empathized with me, but I wasn't completely defeated. There was still plenty of time for me to use my power of persuasion to win her over.

Shontay looked at her watch, then glanced back up at me. "I don't think so," she said politely. "I better get to the hotel and get some rest. I'm a little tired."

"You're leaving already? But it's so early," I stuttered. "You should stay. We have an extra room where you can take a nap or even stay the night. Janai would love to wake up to find you here in the morning." Despite the fact that she had taken Octavia's side, I was willing to forgive her, and of course I was still interested in getting between the sheets with her. I was beginning to think I should have tried that first.

"It's nice of you to offer," she said, standing and smiling, "but I'm already checked in. Maybe Janai can come stay with me tomorrow night. It'll be like a sleepover."

A sleepover? But I'm the one who wants the fucking sleepover! I wanted to blurt out, pun completely intended. I thought about pleading my case and presenting what could possibly be a winning argument, but the tension between the two of us was still thick, and I knew it was because of my remarks about Octavia. It was as if everyone else thought the bitch walked around in a halo, fluttering little angel wings behind that presumably perfect ass of hers. Everyone and everything loved her ass. I knew I had to move fast. I grabbed Shontay by the face and pressed my lips to hers. I kissed her hard, right on the mouth, releasing all the passion inside of me. I was lost, completely caught up on the Island of ecstasy, but when I opened my eyes and saw Shontay giving me a blank stare, I realized I was on that damn island alone. I released my grip on her and stepped back.

She frowned, touching her lips. "I…I'm sorry," she said. "Did I somehow…Lena, did I give you the wrong impression? I'm not a…what would make you think I'm gay?"

"I…uh, I don't know what came over me," I stuttered. "I just…I guess I sort of got caught up in the moment."

"Well, on that note, I'm going to leave," she said slowly. "I'll call you about Janai coming over."

I decided I needed some time to process my thoughts, though it was obvious by Shontay's reaction to my kiss that I should have done the processing sooner rather than later. Also, I still wanted to try and track Kelly down. Shontay had told Janai that she'd be in LA for at least a week, so that would give me plenty of time to work my magic. "Sure," I said, forcing a smile. "Janai will love that."

"Great. Well, uh, I guess I'll talk to you tomorrow," Shontay said, hurrying toward the door.

"Sounds good." I followed her to the front door and attempted to give her a hug.

She stuck her hand out for a casual handshake and bolted out the door.

I watched her as she did what I could only describe as a walk-run to the curb in front of my townhome, getting into her rental car as quickly as she could and speeding off.

Chapter 5

Octavia

I knew Contessa's warning to me came with justification. Although she had not said it directly, she knew something had taken place between Kelly and me. I was further convinced when she lied to Damon about the earring he'd found in the guesthouse. First of all, there was no possible way I could have poked her with the earring, as I had it in a death grip in my palm. Second, I remembered feeling something drop when I was hauling ass to get out of the guesthouse and away from Kelly, the night his tongue made acquaintance with my kitty. I wasn't about to question Contessa's loyalty though. I was thankful and extremely grateful for it, so much so that I left her a note stating my appreciation, along with a cash bonus, on the kitchen counter before I left for work. Of course the note said nothing more than that she was doing a wonderful job. I wasn't about to write anything so telling as *"Thanks for covering my ass,"* but I knew she knew the deal.

It was Monday, and I was busy as usual. My morning had started off perfectly, and my husband and I had shared a nice, invigorating shower before we sat down for breakfast with our daughter. On my way to the Ambiance, I placed a courtesy call to Ilene, only to be informed by her housekeeper, Isabella, that she and Damon Sr. were spending the day together on the lake. I decided to put my desire to speak with my mother-in-law on hold for the moment and focus on the other tasks I had before me, such as taking care of payroll for both of my establishments and going over inventory.

I had given Amel a few days off so she could visit her mother in Selma. The two of us had finally worked out the last minor details for her big day, and we were just counting down the days to the event. After it was all over, she and Tarik were going to take a short honeymoon while Damon and I, along with my parents, jetted off to Paris. I was excited for Amel and for myself.

I was calculating the hours for the last employee on my list when Tabitha knocked on the door and announced that I had a visitor. Damon and I had plans to go to lunch together, so I assumed he was my visitor. "Is he tall and handsome?" I asked, smiling.

"Um, well, one of them is," Tabitha advised me . "The other is short and adorable."

Aw! He must have brought Jasmine along, I thought to myself. "Send them in," I told Tabitha. Prepared to greet my husband and daughter with hugs and kisses, I was caught off guard when Kelly and Donovan strolled through my office door. The two of them were dressed alike in jeans, pink polo shirts, and classic white Nikes. I was slightly disappointed that it wasn't Damon and Jasmine, but when I saw the small bouquet of flowers in Donovan's hands, I couldn't suppress my smile.

"I see you're still screening your visitors based on their looks," Kelly teased, staring at me. I observed his eyes as they traveled from mine down over my physique. Although my two-piece, champagne-colored suit was relatively conservative, he managed to make me feel naked with one glance.

"Actually," I said, clearing my throat, "I was expecting Damon. We have a lunch date." I bent down so I was eye level with Donovan. "Hey, handsome." I smiled.

He gave me a shy smile, then extended the flowers to me.

"For me?" I asked sweetly.

He nodded his head.

"Aw. Well thank you, sweetheart." I took the bouquet from his hands, then kissed his cheek softly.

Kelly frowned. "I swear I'm always just a little too late when it comes to you," he said, shaking his head.

"What do you mean?" I questioned, walking back around the desk to my chair.

"First, I missed the opportunity to marry you," he said, smiling slyly. "I'll never forgive myself for that one." He shook his head dramatically.

I rolled my eyes then laughed.

"Second, I let the kid here…" he said, looking down at Donovan, "I let him carry the goods and steal my thanks."

"I can't help you with the first one." I laughed. "But as for the second… well, thanks to you too."

"I was hoping for the kiss," Kelly said, looking at me. His tone was friendly and upbeat, but I knew he meant every word he was saying.

I eased back down in my leather chair, ignoring his comment. "What are the two of you up to today?" I questioned, changing the subject. "And shouldn't you be at work?" It was a little after 12:30, and it wasn't a holiday, which meant the school where Kelly taught was in session.

I waited for his response, watching him carefully as he sat down in one of the two armchairs on the opposite side of my desk. Donovan followed his lead and climbed up onto the other one.

"I should be," Kelly responded lowly, "but considering I just met my son and he just lost his mother, I figured dumping him in daycare with a bunch of strangers would not be the best move for the time being."

I looked across the desk at Donovan. The boy sat there with his arms on the armrests of the chair, kicking his feet back and forth. He looked like he didn't have a care in the world. I wondered if Kelly was just being overprotective for fear that something would happen to Donovan and he would have to deal with the loss of another child or if he was trying to make up for lost time. I couldn't knock him either way. Dealing with the death of my child is something I hoped and prayed I'd never have to do, and I couldn't even imagine the pain and fear that Kelly had to be dealing with now that he had another child to think about. I'd also never had to spend more than a few days away from Jasmine, and even those were by choice. I hadn't missed any major milestones, and as far as I was concerned, I never would. I imagined it must have been hell for Kelly, knowing he'd been forced to miss the first two years of his son's life. "I'm sorry," I said, attempting to empathize with his situation. "Donovan is such a charmer and a social prince. I didn't even take into consideration that he is going through some major life changes at such a young age."

Kelly reached over and lovingly patted the top of Donovan's head. "I'll admit," he began, "he's been adjusting well. It's like he's known me his entire life. It's crazy how we've bonded so fast. I don't know. Maybe I'm just being overprotective. I know anything can happen anywhere, but I would rather my son be with people I know and trust if he can't be with me."

"That makes sense," I agreed.

"I'm glad someone understands." He exhaled softly. "The school didn't, and they basically told me I had to choose."

"Choose?"

"Yeah, because I haven't completed my probationary period, they were only going to allot me a day off. I was willing to take time off without pay, but I was not willing to bring my son back here and just drop him off in any facility that had an opening, so I just…well, I quit."

I was less than thrilled about Kelly quitting his job, especially considering that it had taken him so long to get one, and now he had an additional mouth to feed.

"I know I'm responsible for another person now," Kelly said, no doubt sensing my disapproval, "and I know I need a job, but my son needed me more. I'm not worried though."

"You're not?"

"Nope. I'm a hustler, Octavia, and a hustler always finds a way to provide."

I nodded my head in agreement.

"Speaking of which," he said, leaning forward in his chair, "I have to slide out of town for a couple days on, uh, some business, and I was wondering if it would be okay for Donovan to stay with you guys while I'm gone. Contessa will be great with him, and you know how she loves kids."

"Ah, and now the truth comes out," I teased. "Did you convince Donovan to bribe me with those flowers?"

"Well, that depends. Did it work?"

"Possibly," I said, shrugging my shoulders. "When are you leaving?"

"Tonight," he said. "I know it's last minute and all, but I have a lead on a job, and I have to be there first thing in the morning."

At the mere mention of employment I was game to the idea. Last minute or not, I didn't care. The brother was trying to get a job, and I had to help him out. "I'll check with Damon," I said, "but I'm sure it'll be fine. We just need to make sure Contessa will be okay watching two little ones at the same time."

"I ran it by her already, and she said it's cool," Kelly advised me.

"Uh, okay. Well, I'll ask Damon at lunch." I smiled. "Where is it you're going?"

"Georgia," Kelly said. He hesitated slightly, and the instant change in his demeanor notified me that there was something more he was not telling me.

The mention of Georgia refreshed my memory, and I decided to ask Kelly the question that had been weighing heavily on my mind just days ago. "I need to ask you something," I said, sitting up straight.

"Yeah?" he asked, flashing his eyes at me.

"I saw you and Ilene together in my hallway," I began.

Kelly didn't so much as blink.

I continued, "The two of you appeared to be sharing, um…a very private moment."

"It wasn't all that private if you witnessed it," he said, laughing lightly.

I frowned, an indication that I was dead serious about it.

"My bad," Kelly said. "I can see you're concerned, but you have nothing to worry about. I hold a romantic interest in only one Whitmore woman." He laughed again.

"And *I* only hold a romantic interest in my husband," I said firmly, then paused for effect before continuing. "However, I want to know if there is something going on with you and my mother-in-law."

"Something going on? Like what?" Kelly questioned.

Are y'all fucking? I wanted to blurt out, but I chose to refrain. "You tell me," I said.

Kelly looked away for a brief moment, and I watched as his tongue flicked across the edge of his bottom lip. He was obviously stalling, and I was growing impatient. "Ilene and I made friendly conversation," he finally said. He looked at me with a seriousness in his eyes that could kill. "However, there is nothing going on between us."

"Kelly, her hand was on your chest, and there was this…look in your eyes," I reminded him.

"I understand how it might have looked, but things aren't always as they appear. The truth is, I was telling Ilene about my attack and showing her my injuries. Sometimes you can still feel where my ribs were broken. I was simply attempting to calm her down, to show her I am all right. You know how dramatic you women can be."

"Mm-hmm," I mumbled.

"What? You don't believe me?" he asked. "Would you like to see for yourself?" he questioned, lifting up his shirt.

I put my hands up in the air quickly. "No, I believe you," I said abruptly. The more I thought about his explanation, the more I convinced myself. Plus, the last thing I needed was him in my office with his shirt off.

"Well, we should get going," he said, standing. "Let Auntie know what Damon decides."

"I will." I smiled as I watched as Donovan climbed down from the chair, following his daddy's lead. "Bye, cutie pie," I said, looking at Donovan.

Donovan waved his hand at me and smiled.

"Oh, by the way," Kelly said, as the two of them stood at my office door, "I want you to think about something."

"Uh, okay. What?"

"Why were you so keen on knowing the truth about me and Ilene?" he asked, staring into my eyes.

"I don't have to think about that, Kelly," I said confidently. "I was just... concerned."

"But why?"

"Because Ilene is my husband's mother!" I said matter-of-factly.

"Ilene is a grown-ass woman Octavia," he said. "She doesn't need your protection. Even if she *was* having an affair with someone, it would be none of your business. I think you're more curious than concerned—maybe even jealous."

I cut my eyes at him but didn't say a word.

"You don't have to agree with me." He chuckled. "It's written all over your face, and you know it's true. I've learned that women are only curious about another woman's sex life for two reasons."

"Really? Enlighten me on that, Dr. Phil," I said sarcastically.

"One, if they don't have a life of their own," he said, raising his eyebrows.

I laughed out loud. "We know that's not the case here," I said, popping my lips slightly. "I have a very full life."

"True," he agreed, "which leads me to reason number two."

"Which is?" I was anxiously awaiting the second portion of Kelly's ghetto analysis.

"Jealousy," he said seriously.

"I have no reason to be jealous of my mother-in-law." I laughed.

"Laugh all you want, Octavia," he said, "but we both know it's the truth. The only time women are concerned about another woman's sex life is when they don't have a life of their own or whey they're jealous because someone else beat them to the dick they want."

I attempted to gather my words with the hope of a witty comeback, but I couldn't think of one. Kelly had won for the moment, and the smirk plastered across his face let me know he knew it. The tension between the two of us was so thick I thought I might choke on it. "Today at lunch I'll ask Damon if it's okay for Donovan to stay with us," I said, clearing my throat and changing the subject.

"Thanks," he said. He turned and exited my office with Donovan walking by his side.

Running my fingers through my hair, I exhaled. Kelly seemed to know exactly what to say and do to make me uncomfortable. I hated that about him, but what I hated even more at that moment was that I knew if he hadn't been talking about me, I would have agreed completely with his hypothesis.

"Hey, baby."

The sound of Damon's sexy voice made my kitty jump slightly. I had completed all my tasks at work, and he still hadn't made it for our date. I decided to give him a courtesy call just to make sure everything was okay. "Hey, love," I said. "Um, did you forgot about me?"

"That's not possible," he said sweetly. "I apologize, boo. I had a meeting with a client, and it ran over."

"No worries," I said cheerfully. "I just wrapped things up here. If you'd like, I can head that way, and we can go for lunch from there."

"Sounds good. Give me another hour to wrap this up," he said.

"Will do."

"How about the two of us catch a movie after lunch?" he suggested.

"You're taking the rest of the day off?"

"Yep," he said. "That is, if a very beautiful and talented woman agrees to accompany me for the rest of the day."

"You want me to hold while you call her?" I joked.

"That won't be necessary," he said lightly. "Jada just sent me a text to confirm."

"Send her one, courtesy of me, letting her know I'll whoop that ass." We both laughed.

"You've got yourself a date," I said happily.

"I'll see you when you get here."

"I love you," I said, smiling.

"I love you more."

* * *

I gave Tabitha specific instructions to call me if she needed me, told the rest of my staff to have a great evening, then exited my restaurant. I was super excited to spend some additional time with my hubby, and the two of us had not been to the movies in months. It felt like we were long overdue for a proper date.

I made it to the south side of the building, where I and my employees parked, only to find Kelly was still there, standing beside a black Ford Excursion, leaning over inside the back passenger side window. The car was parked behind mine, blocking me and the Armando I'd recently seen Kelly driving in. "What are you still doing here?" I asked, walking in his direction.

Kelly immediately stood up straight, looking in my direction. "Hey," he said. His voice was slightly elevated, and there was a strange look on his face as he flashed his eyes from me back to whomever was sitting inside the car.

"I thought you'd be long gone by now," I said, hitting the alarm button on my key fob.

"I...yeah, I was," he stuttered. I waited for him to further explain, but he never did.

"Where's Donovan?" I questioned.

"Right here," a voice answered from inside the car.

I watched as Kelly stepped back and the passenger door opened. A tall, light-skinned brother climbed out of the limo. The man had to be at least six-two and 200-plus pounds. He was well dressed in a dark designer suit with a white collared shirt and alligator shoes. He looked at me and gave me a slight nod of his head. "The little one was keeping me company," he said. "Come on out, li'l man."

A few seconds later, Donovan climbed out the back of the limo.

Kelly immediately lifted his son up into his arms and hugged him like he hadn't seen him in years.

"Forgive my friend's rudeness," the stranger said, facing me. "I didn't catch your name." He gave me a perfect smile—too perfect. There was something about the man's demeanor and the obvious tension circling in the air that just wasn't right.

"I'm Octavia," I said, hesitant to tell him my name. "And you are?"

"Octavia," he recited. "A lovely name for a lovely woman."

I didn't know if he was just giving me a compliment or if his statement was a failed attempt at flirtation. Either way, I was not going to play into it. "And you are?" I asked seriously.

"Leon," he said, extending his huge hand to me. "However, you can call me Gator."

"Gator? That's an unusual nickname" I said, shaking his hand. "Does it have anything to do with your choice in shoes?"

Gator threw his head back, laughing deeply.

I looked a Kelly, wondering if my question was really that damn funny. Kelly's expression was unreadable, but I could have sworn he looked nervous. *Something is shady with this shit,* I thought.

"If only it were so simple," Gator finally answered. "No, beautiful, they don't call me Gator because of my shoes. I'll spare you the details, but I will say my nickname—much like my respect—is well deserved." He kept his eyes locked on me while speaking to Kelly. "Isn't that right?"

"Yeah," Kelly said lowly.

Gator nodded his head.

I was more than curious to know what the relationship was between the two men, but the little female voice inside of me—better known as my institution—told me not to ask. I decided to listen to her. "Well, I have to go," I said.

"What's the rush?" Gator asked.

"My *husband* is waiting for me," I answered, putting added emphasis on the fact that there was a man looking out for me and expecting me.

"Your husband is a very lucky man, Octavia." Gator sighed. "Well, perhaps we'll see each other again. It all depends."

I was not the lease bit concerned about seeing the man again, but I still decided to question his statement. "Depends on what?" I asked.

"Kelly here," Gator answered. "How soon, how often, if we ever—all depends on him."

I looked from one man to the other while reciting my earlier notion. *Something is definitely shady with this shit*, I thought again. "Well, then, I…um, I guess we'll see," I said nonchalantly. "Well, if you don't mind, I have to get going…and you've got me blocked."

"Not a problem. My sincere apologies," Gator responded, winking at me. "AJ, back the car up so we can let the lovely lady out," Gator ordered, speaking to his driver. "Octavia, again, it was a pleasure meeting you."

"Thank you," I said, still suspicious about the men's connection. "Bye, Donovan," I said, smiling brightly at the little boy. I gave Kelly the once-over with my eyes and offered him a cool, "Goodbye," before opening the door of my Mercedes and sliding behind the wheel. I flashed my eyes up to my rearview mirror, giving the men one final look before I pulled out of the Ambiance parking lot.

Chapter 6

Kelly

"She's a beautiful woman, very beautiful." Gator said, staring at me. "Exactly who is she to you?"

"My former employer," I answered flatly. There was no way in hell I was going to divulge any other information about my relationship with Octavia to him. If things between Gator and myself turned from bad to worse, it could possibly put the life of anyone I was connected to in danger. I couldn't risk anything happening to Octavia. It was bad enough that Gator had caught me with my son. I'd never known him to harm a child, but I'd also never known him to pay a visit before a deadline either.

"Your former employer?" Gator questioned. "Interesting." The curiosity in his stare notified me that he felt there was more to the story with Octavia than I was telling him. I was thankful he didn't dwell on the subject. He instead walked back to the passenger side door of his car.

AJ instantly jumped out from behind the wheel and held the door open in true Benson style.

"Put your son in the car," Gator ordered.

I hesitated, fearful of what might transpire next.

"Now," he commanded. "I don't have all day," he expressed before sliding back into his vehicle.

I took a deep breath, then exhaled slowly before finally opening my car door and securing Donovan in his car seat. "Daddy will be right back," I said, before shutting the car door. A few seconds later, I sat in the back of Gator's car.

He sat across from me with a lit stogie in between his fingertips. "How long have we known each other, Kelly?" Gator asked, staring at me.

I knew his question was a moot one, in that he already knew the answer, but I also knew that when Gator spoke, he expected a response. "A few years," I answered.

"Almost twenty, to be exact," Gator corrected. "Two decades. You've known me longer than my own wife…"

I listened in silence as Gator reflected on our history. When I'd come out of the restaurant earlier and found Gator waiting for me, I'd felt like I could have shit a brick. When he hadn't showed up the night before or that morning, I began to feel slightly comfortable that I had at least two weeks to try and make something happen with his money. I should have known better, though, for Gator was nothing if not unpredictable. As it turned out, he'd had one of his goons watching me that night and following me that morning. I had given Gator the address to the apartment because I thought I would have his money in full, but I was wrong. I'd been caught slipping, and now my son's and Octavia's lives could be in danger. I hated that Gator had lain eyes on Octavia, but a small part of me was relieved that she'd made her appearance when she had.

After questioning me about Donovan, Gator opened his car door and told my son to climb inside. The only thing that flashed in my head at that time were visions of him riding off with my son and holding him for ransom. I didn't really think Gator would cause Donovan any harm, but I couldn't be sure, especially not with the amount of money I owed the man. I was sure I might never seen my son again, except for looking down on him from heaven or up at him from hell. I could only imagine what might have happened if Octavia hadn't come out when she did.

"Just give me a few weeks," I finally said, "and I'll have the rest of what I owe you." I knew it was easier said than done, since I still owed Gator close to $30,000.

Gator had put me on when I was hustling, and during my unemployment downtime, he was the one who'd tossed me back in the game. Gator and I did have a history, to be sure. Before my time in the penitentiary, I'd been one of his most loyal soldiers. I was convinced this was the only reason he'd been patient with me in my attempt to repay my debt. However, unlike Octavia, I knew how Gator got his nickname; I knew it was derived from one of the many methods he used to collect his money, and I also knew that no matter how much history I had with the man, his money was the only thing that mattered to him. I'd managed to drop him a $5,000 payment just to keep his people off me while I attempted to hustle up the rest, but I knew I was facing a grave ending.

"I meant what I said," he said. "Whether or not I see Octavia or your little man all depends on you." Gator's tone was smooth and light as the sounds of jazz coming through the car speakers, but I knew they were as deadly as playing on railroad tracks in oil-drenched slippers.

* * *

After visiting my weed supplier and swinging by my apartment to pick up a few odds and ends, I decided to pay the Whitmore household a visit. I knew I had some time before Octavia and Damon returned home from their little lunch rendezvous, and it was in my best interest to use that time to my full advantage. "Take Donovan and Jasmine outside to play," I ordered Contessa as soon as she opened the front door.

"Why?" she questioned. "What are you going to do?"

"Just do it," I snapped, readjusting the backpack I carried on my shoulder. I was not in the mood to play twenty questions with her, nor did I have time to waste.

Contessa's lips formed into two tight lines, I was sure from her urge to say something in return, however she made the smartest decision at that moment and kept quiet. The look she gave me as she took the children by the hand, walking away, leaving me standing in the foyer alone was evident of her disapproval—so much so that if her eyes had carried venom, I would have fallen dead at the door.

I have got to get her old ass in check before she puts my shit on blast, I thought as I headed upstairs. I stood inside Octavia and Damon's bedroom, staring at the king-sized bed. Thoughts of Octavia's lower lips against mine replayed in my head. I could still taste her, feel her grinding against my tongue, gushing all over my face. Shaking my head, I reminded myself why I was there in the first place. I had other things to focus on at the moment, but if things went according to plan, I would possibly have new, fresh memories to create with Octavia. After all, she would certainly need someone to break her off once Damon was dismissed. After searching high and low for cash I was sure Damon had stashed, only to come up empty-handed, I headed back downstairs to get Donovan so the two of us could depart. I thought about taking some of Octavia's jewelry from her dresser, but I decided against it. I needed a quick turnaround, and selling the pieces on the street or even to the pawn shop would not give me even half of what I needed or anywhere near their real value. I was becoming a man of desperate measures, but I didn't give a damn. If Gator didn't get what he wanted, I'd be dead; to be honest, I would take desperate over dead any day.

I was back to fulfilling Lena's request so I could secure the other half of the money she promised me. I knew Lena would deliver the cash on time, as long as the task was completed and everything played in her favor. Truthfully, I already had enough information in my possession to grant Lena's wish. I had proof that Damon had provided Nadia with her own credit card to fund Donovan's needs when he thought the boy was his son. I had an eyewitness, Nadia's ex-assistant María, that Damon was lying about his whereabouts when he was really visiting Nadia and our son. I was certain María would be onboard to help me twist my little tale in order to make things worse than what they really were, because she herself was one breath away from deportation. Dropping the dime on Damon and driving an unfixable wedge between him and Octavia was definitely a possibility. However, her hating me for being the bearer of the news was also a possibility. To be honest, I was growing quite fond of Octavia, and I didn't want to do anything that would make her hate me. I was becoming a desperate man, yes, but not so desperate that I would risk any chances I had with a real woman.

I walked into the kitchen to find Contessa sitting at the table. "Where are the kids?" I asked, stopping in my tracks.

"In the family room," she said, standing. The look on her face notified me that she was about to start some bullshit. "What were you doing upstairs?" she demanded.

I was getting more and more feed up with her behavior. "You never saw me upstairs," I informed her.

"Oh, but I did," she snapped. "Whatever you have planned, it's not going to work, and I'll tell Lena the same thing. Y'all aren't going to do this to these good people if I have anything to say about it. You won't win."

I looked at her like she had lost her damn mind. "When did it become. y'all?" I questioned. "What happened to us?"

"Us was before I knew these people and their families," she said. "Kelly, this ain't right."

That little humane part of me that could emphasize with the pain of others felt Contessa's words, but the bigger part of me that wanted to keep all ten fingers and toes and breath in my body wasn't trying to hear it. "It's not your place to decide what's right," I said. "You want this to be over?"

"Yes," she said, nodding her head.

"Okay," I said soothingly. "Then go pack your bags and leave, and it'll end for you right now. Start a new life. Do whatever the fuck you want to do. But here's the thing…the money you've earned stays here. Those clothes on your back stay here. Even the wig on your head stays here. You came into this thing with nothing, and you'll walk out with even less, because now you don't even have a clean conscious."

Her lips quivered slightly, and tears began to trickle down her cheeks from under the rims of her glasses.

"So, what? You're leaving?" I taunted. "Hmm? Are you? Back to rummaging through trash and collecting cans?" I waited. I knew the answer to each and every one of my questions was a resounding "no," but I believe in giving an individual a chance to respond.

"I…I'll go get your son," Contessa whispered before stomping out of the kitchen in a huff.

"Crazy bitch," I said, walking over to the refrigerator. All the drama had made me thirsty. I swung open the refrigerator door, on a search for something to quench my thirst, and I saw something that caught my eye. I knew right then what I had to do. I pulled the prize off the shelf and slid it in my backpack before closing the doors of the fridge. I was no longer thirsty; I was too busy making a list of ingredients inside my head. I'd managed to solve another little problem of mine even while I wasn't looking for that answer. *I guess it's true. Sometimes the solutions we need pop up where we least expect them.*

Chapter 7

Damon

Before my date with Octavia, I had several issues to contend with. The ones I felt were the most urgent involved Kelly. I still felt in my heart that there was more to his story than what he was telling me, and I knew I had to find out the truth immediately.

I had already called Bernice to offer my condolences. I decided this time to let her know I just wanted to make sure she didn't need anything. After asking her how she was holding up, I advised Bernice that I had met Donovan's father, Kelly. Surprisingly enough, Bernice confirmed—almost word for word—the story that Kelly had told me. Although I loved Bernice like I did my own grandmother, her words were of no reassurance to me. Kelly and Nadia had probably played the woman too. I told Bernice to let me know if she needed anything, and then I hung up.

I now sat behind my desk watching Lawrence process the information I had provided him. Last night, before Octavia joined me in our home office, I'd sent him an e-mail advising him that I needed to have a meeting with him ASAP. As usual, Lawrence had cleared his schedule to meet with me. Lawrence was arrogant and oftentimes a loose cannon, but I had to add loyal to his list of attributes. I had given him a play-by-play on everything that had happened at the gathering at my home, from me receiving the letter advising me that Donovan was not mine to Kelly's explanation of how he and Nadia had hooked up.

"There's something or someone missing in this equation," Lawrence said.

"I agree," I said. "The question is...what or whom?"

"Nadia didn't say anything?" Lawrence questioned. "She never gave you any hints or clues?"

"Nah. The majority of our conversations resulted in her asking for damn money," I told him, "or threatening to schedule family meetings with my wife."

"What about her granny?"

"Bernice? Hmm. Well, she could be involved, I guess, but if she was, she would have stood by the lie that I'm Donovan's father until the very end."

"Maybe she had a change of heart or got religion," Lawrence suggested. "You know how it goes. Death brings out the holiness in some folks."

I shook my head. "I don't think so," I told him. "Besides, she and my grandmother are thick as thieves. Even if Bernice would betray me, she wouldn't betray my grandmother."

"What's the other old lady's name again?" Lawrence asked, leaning forward. "Your nanny?"

"Contessa," I advised him. "She's Kelly's aunt."

"What about her?" he asked. "You think she knows anything?"

I hadn't considered her to be a threat, but she was related to Kelly. "Hmm. I don't know," I said. "It's a possibility, but what would she have to gain from it?"

"Money, plain and simple. Come on, D. You know old bitches get greedy just like young ones," Lawrence commented.

"I swear you have a way with words," I said, shaking my head at his bluntness.

"Shit! You don't keep me on the team because of my bedside manner." He laughed. "You keep me on the team because I'm real and I get shit done."

"Agreed."

"Anyway, what do we know about her, this nanny?" he asked.

I gave Lawrence the rundown on what I knew about Contessa, from her deceased husband to her locked-up son.

"Well, I'm gonna check her out," Lawrence advised me. "I'll also pay your boy Kelly a couple visits, see where he's going, how he gets there, and who he's doing it with. In the meantime, let me know if you think of anything else."

"I'll do that," I said, standing.

Lawrence stood and adjusted his tie. "You know, we could easily resolve this issue," he said as the two of us walked to my office door. "We could save you any additional problems or complications."

I knew Lawrence was suggesting murder, and although I wasn't a stranger to it, I would only use it as a final, desperate means; of course, Kelly sleeping with my wife would have been reason enough to act in final desperation. After my conversation with Octavia and Contessa about the earring I found, though, I was confident that hadn't taken place. "Let's make that our last option," I said.

Lawrence shook his head as he opened my office door. "Man, marriage continues to change you." He chuckled. "You've got such a hard-on for that wife of yours that you've gone soft everywhere else."

"Well, it's changed me for the better," I said as I followed him out my office door. I stopped abruptly when I saw Octavia standing in my office waiting room. I had hoped to be rid of Lawrence before she arrived, but she was early. "Hey, babe." I smiled and walked up to her. "When did you get here?"

"I just got here. I figured I would just wait until you finished your meeting." She smiled at me and gave me a light kiss on the lips. "I hope I'm not interrupting anything important," she said, looking a Lawrence, as if she was trying to remember where she'd seen him before.

"No, we're done," I said, turning toward Lawrence and extending him my hand.

Lawrence gave me a firm shake and nodded his head at Octavia before walking away down the hall, toward the main entrance doors.

"He looks so familiar," Octavia said, puzzled.

"Well, you know what they say. Everyone has a twin," I said, slipping my arm around her waist. "Maybe you've seen someone who looks like him."

"Maybe," she said, shrugging her shoulders. "I don't know."

"Are you happy to see me?" I asked, slipping my hand in hers. I wanted to change the subject quickly. The last thing I needed was for Octavia to remember where she'd seen Lawrence before.

"Always." She smiled, squeezing my hand softly and no longer looking like she cared about Lawrence. Instead, she stared at me with a look of love and desire etched in her honey-brown eyes.

I wasn't entirely proud of all the things I'd done to get Octavia, but when she looked or smiled at me like that, I was reminded of how worth it she was.

* * *

I treated my wife to lunch at Ol' Heidelberg, a cozy German restaurant in the city. We discussed our day and business while sharing a piece of carrot cake for dessert.

"Oh, I almost forgot," Octavia began. I watched her as she dabbed at the corners of her lips with the linen napkin. "Kelly has to go out of town for a couple days, and he wants to know if Donovan can stay with us."

"Kelly? When did you speak to him?" I asked lightly, curious about exactly how much contact the man had with my wife.

"Today," she said casually. "He and Donovan stopped by the Ambiance to visit."

I forced myself not to show any dramatic changes in my facial expression, but inside, I could feel my anger slowly churning in the pit of my stomach. It was bad enough that Kelly was connected to Nadia and knew about my involvement in their paternity mess, but now he was popping by Octavia's place of business. I was not going to allow it. I trusted my wife, but Kelly was another story—a major issue. "Really? Does Kelly visit Ambiance often?" I questioned.

Octavia's long eyelashes fluttered once, then twice. "What do you mean?" she asked, cocking her head to the side.

I loved the look of innocence and purity on her beautiful face, but I also knew she was playing naïve. I looked her in the eyes, sending her a nonverbal message that lovingly stated, *"Cut the bullshit, baby."*

The look of naïveté instantly evaporated from her face. "No, Dame, he doesn't," she answered seriously. "That was only the second time."

"The second time, huh? When was the first?"

"Right after his attack," she explained, "before he started on the garden.

He brought the sketches for his ideas and gave me a little present."

"A little present?" I probed.

"A porcelain angel figurine," she said. "It's really pretty, and it looks just like Jasmine. A guy he knew created it in Jazz's image, and…" Octavia stopped what she was telling me, I assume because of the frown that I could feel governing my face.

I tried to keep my emotions in check, but I could no longer hide my disapproval. I wasn't impressed one damn bit by what Octavia was revealing to me. I'd had my suspicions before, but with every word Octavia spoke in regard to Kelly, my concerns were confirmed: *Kelly is trying to get next to my wife.*

"You're…upset," Octavia concluded, observing my reaction.

"No," I said firmly. "I just feel that it was something I should have been made aware of."

"I failed to mention it because it was nothing," she said. "Besides, you've never been the jealous type before." She looked at me with raised eyebrows.

"I'm not the jealous type," I said smoothly. "But then again, I'm not a man who doesn't know and value what he has either."

She smiled a radiant smile.

I hadn't meant to stroke her ego with my comment; I was simply stating a fact. However, when it came to winning Brownie points with Octavia, I would take them whenever I could get them. "I just think I should be informed when another man bestows gifts on my wife, the same way you deserved to know about the assistance I bestowed upon Lena." It was a risky move, bringing up Lena, but I knew exactly what hand I was playing. On the one hand, it could have conjured up negative memories; on the other, it might have helped Octavia see things my way and lead to a mutual agreement. I was shooting for the latter.

Octavia's eyes lowered momentarily to tiny slits. It was written all over her face that she wanted to start a debate or at least bounce back with a sarcastic comeback, but she didn't. "Fair enough." She sighed. "You're right. I apologize for not telling you about Kelly's visits and the gift."

I smiled, reaching across the table for her hand. "Apology accepted," I said, stroking the back of her fingers.

"Should I have Contessa tell Kelly Donovan can't stay with us?"

"No," I said, shaking my head. "We can help him out this time," I said pleasantly. "I think Jazz'll like having a playmate around." In addition to that, I had bonded with Donovan during the time when I'd thought he was my son. Honestly, it would be good for me to have him around, too, even if it was temporary. "When is he leaving?"

"Tonight," she advised me.

"All right. I'm gonna pop in the men's room," I told her. "Why don't you call Contessa and tell her to let Kelly know it's okay, but make sure he waits until we get home before he brings Donovan over."

"Okay, love."

I excused myself from the table and pulled my Blackberry out of my pocket as I walked to the men's room. Kelly's out-of-town visit was going to make for the perfect opportunity for Lawrence to do some investigating. I quickly scrolled through my contacts until I found Lawrence's number.

"Talk to me," he answered smoothly.

"I've got something for you," I said lowly. "Be at my place tonight at 6. Park on the street facing the gate. Kelly's coming over to drop Donovan off before he goes on a trip."

"Enough said," Lawrence responded. "I got you."

Chapter 8

Lena

Taking another sip of my glass of Chardonnay, I stared at my laptop screen. I had over 100 e-mails, and not one of them was from Damon. *I bet Octavia had him block me! She is such a simple-minded trick!* I slammed my laptop closed and picked up my cell phone. I only got Kelly's voicemail again, but this time, I was unable to leave a message due to his mailbox being full. "I know, you stupid, whiny bitch!" I screamed, speaking to the prerecorded message. "*I'm* the reason his mailbox is full!" I felt like I was going to explode. Nothing was going as I planned, and it wasn't fair because I'd spent so much time and thought planning it all out perfectly.

I decided to attempt to reach Contessa on her cell phone, though I knew it would likely be a waste of time since she normally kept her phone off when she was at home, which was mostly all the time. Nevertheless, I was desperate and willing to try anything. Her phone didn't ring, so I assumed it had to be turned off. I again had to deal with the whiny prerecorded heifer, and I was beginning to hate people who didn't have a personalized message.

I tapped my manicured nails on the table in front of me. "I shouldn't," I spoke aloud as I scrolled through the contacts in my phone. Contessa had been kind enough to provide me with Damon and Octavia's home number when she'd first moved into their house. I had yet to use it, but desperate times were calling for desperate measures. I rose from the table and ran upstairs to my daughter's bedroom. She was sleeping peacefully as I tiptoed in to retrieve the phone I had recently purchased for her. At first, I'd been dead set against giving her a phone so early, but now I saw that the decision might be very beneficial to me. I returned downstairs to my spot at the kitchen table. I had Janai's phone set up so it displayed KJH on the caller ID of the party she was calling. I would have just blocked the number, but I was 100 percent sure Octavia's stuck-up ass had insisted that they have privacy director on their line. I picked up the glass from the table and tossed the rest of my drink back, hoping for a little liquid courage. *What if she answers? Will that mean Damon left her?* I thought as I slightly held my breath with each ring. *What if Damon answers? Will that mean he dropped Octavia's ass at the curb?* I was excited just thinking about the possibilities. The line rang several times, and I was starting to get nervous that I was going to hear another impersonal message.

"Hello," *he* answered.

My heart began to race a mile a minute. My love had answered. The voice I hadn't heard in weeks was on the other end of the phone, talking to me, of all people.

"Hello," he repeated.

I wanted to listen to him all night, but I knew at that moment that it wasn't possible. I lifted my hand to my mouth, covering my lips to muffle my voice. "May I speak with Contessa, please?" I also altered the sound of my voice slightly to add to my disguise.

"May I tell her who's calling?" Damon questioned, putting me on the spot.

I really should have thought this through more carefully, I said to myself. "Uh, Officer Snow...from the West Tennessee State Penitentiary," I lied. "I'm calling about her son, um..."

I had completely forgotten the name of the woman's son. When I'd first met Contessa, traveling to see her estranged son was her only request. Despite my better judgment, I had agreed to help her, but at first I was fearful that she'd divulge my plans to the man, and he'd influence her decisions. However, after her first visit with him, it seemed she was still dedicated to doing the job I had assigned to her. I figured she appreciated having money to travel to see her baby boy, and I didn't see what harm it could cause.

"Her son?" Damon questioned.

I could tell by the sound of his voice that he was concerned. "Yes... Jay," I said, finally remembering the name. "Her son Jay."

"Is everything all right?"

"Yes, everything is fine," I said reassuringly. "He just wanted me to give her a message."

"Okay, good," Damon said, sounding relieved. "One moment."

"Who is it?" I heard a voice ask in the background, a voice I instantly recognized as Octavia's.

She's still there? Damn it! I listened carefully to the dialogue between the two of them, hoping I'd pick up on some form of tension or an indication that the two of them were having problems.

"I'm going to take the kids upstairs and get them ready for bed," she said. "I'll take the phone to Ms. Contessa. Jazz, tell Daddy goodnight."

"Goodnight, beautiful girl," I heard Damon say lovingly.

"You know Donovan wants a hug too." Octavia laughed.

I almost dropped the damn phone. Not only did Octavia and Damon sound happier than a Hallmark commercial, but the whole crew was there: Damon, Octavia, Jasmine, *and* Donovan. *What the hell?* I waited impatiently until I heard Contessa's voice on the phone.

"Hello? Officer?"

"Officer my ass. I want to know what in the hell is going on there," I said angrily, "and I want to know right damn now!"

* * *

I found it incredibly difficult to focus at work the next day. I was lost in my thoughts, still thinking about the information Contessa had provided me. Kelly hadn't followed through with our plan. Instead, he'd covered Damon's ass by withholding the truth. I asked myself if he chose to do so because Damon was his brother and he had a sudden bout of brotherly love or if it was because he wanted to spare Octavia's feelings. Regardless of the reason behind his decision (which, for Kelly's sake, better had been the first of the two options), I should have been consulted.

Kelly and his antics were plenty to have to digest, but I also had a whole other can of worms to deal with involving Shontay. I had yet to speak with her, and I couldn't stop myself from wondering if she had called her best friend to get her side of the story and if she was still tripping about the kiss. If Shontay had called Octavia, I was sure the bitch had used her persuasion to sway Shontay's emotional vote in her direction, thus leading to me being the enemy again. *Ugh! That ratcheted wench!* I screamed loudly in my head. *I will not allow her to make me the bad guy again. I refuse to—*

"Ouch!" Jocelyn, my client screamed.

The woman's cry not only caused me to jump, but it also pulled my attention away from the thoughts of Octavia and brought me back to the task at hand. *Oh shit,* I thought, as I quickly unwrapped Jocelyn's singed hair from the flat iron I held in my hand.

"You burned me!" Jocelyn whined, jumping out of the chair.

I rolled my eyes in silence as I watched her.

She leaned against my styling station, staring at herself in the mirror, a mortified expression caked on her face. "What are you going to do about this?" she screamed, turning around to face me. She pointed at the spot on her forehead that I had accidentally touched with the flat iron. The spot was no bigger than a half-dollar, but on Jocelyn's light skin, it stood out like a neon green dress at a black tie affair.

"I apolog—"

"Apologize? Look at this!" she screamed, cutting me off. She pointed at the section of her silky black mane that was now shriveled due to the excess heat I'd absentmindedly applied. "What do you plan to do about this?!"

Out of all my clientele, I had chosen the most dramatic diva on the roster to have an effin' episode with. Granted, Jocelyn was a model, and her face was her job, but I was sure with the right amount of cover-up, her makeup artist could perform a miracle. I pulled out the top drawer of my station and removed the tube of Neosporin I kept in the unfortunate event of a burn. "Let me put some of this on it," I said, sulking while beckoning for Jocelyn to sit back down.

"I need ice!" she snapped, rolling her eyes.

You need to calm your ass down, I thought. I took a deep breath and exhaled lightly through my lips. "I'll get you some from the freezer in the break room," I offered.

"Just forget it!" she commanded, snatching the styling cape from around her neck. "Give me the damn Neosporin!"

I extended my hand and the tube to her and almost had a knock-a-hoe-out moment when Jocelyn snatched it from my grasp. *I'm a professional,* I reminded myself. *I am a professional.* "Jocelyn, I apologize," I said with sincere humility. "I truly don't know how I allowed this to happen, and—"

"Uh, hello," she said sarcastically. "You weren't paying attention to what in the hell you were doing and you burned me! Case closed. Period. I want my money back, and I want it back now! I didn't not pay $300 to leave here with a scar and a burnt-ass weave!"

"I'll have Joni reimburse you," I said calmly, pushing the small white button on the side of my station.

The button buzzed the front desk, indicating to Joni or whoever was sitting there that I needed help. A minute later, Joni came bouncing through the doors of the VIP area, smiling brightly. Her smile easily dissipated when she saw Jocelyn's face and hair. "Oh my," she said, looking at me. "Did we have a little accident?"

"What in the hell do you think?" Jocelyn barked, stomping past her and out of the room.

"It really doesn't look that bad!" Joni called behind her.

"Just give her money back," I grumbled, plopping down in my chair.

"No problem." Joni's smile and happy disposition returned.

I was thankful she left the room, for with the mood I was in, I was likely to take my frustration out on her in the form of an ass-whooping. I'm certain she would have been the first person in history to get beat down just for being happy. I closed my eyes and leaned back in the chair. While I was attempting to relax my mind, my cell phone rang, disrupting my moment of peace. "Hello?" I answered, not bothering to look at the caller ID.

"Hey, Lena. Are you okay?" Shontay asked from the other end of the phone.

"Hi, Shontay," I replied, sitting up in the chair. "I'm fine. How are you?" I forced the gloom from my tone urgently. She'd called me, and that was obviously a good sign. "I'm good," she said. "Listen, I just wanted to call and let you know that I'm on my way to the airport. I'm leaving."

"What? But I thought—"

"I know, but I need to get back to Huntsville. I've been gone far too long," she said.

"What changed your mind?" I questioned, beyond disappointed.

"Well, last night I called Savoy, and we agreed there are some things we need to work out. We can't exactly do that if I'm halfway across the country." She laughed lightly. "Plus, I miss my bestie and my goddaughter."

"I see," I said blankly. "Have you spoken with Octavia?"

"No. Savoy is the only one who knows where I am and that I'm headed home."

"Janai is going to miss you something awful," I said. "What would you like me to tell her?" I heard every detail about her and her man working things out, but it all sounded like blah-blah-blah bullshit to me. There was a voice inside of me that was pissed beyond measure, telling me Shontay was bailing on my daughter so she could go run up behind Octavia's ass. I was livid, but I told myself to maintain.

"Tell her the truth," she said. "Tell her I'll miss her, but she can call me or come see me anytime. In fact, we'll work a visit out once I get settled in the Ville or the A. It looks like I'll be living in one of those cities." She laughed lightheartedly.

I said nothing and didn't dare return her laugh; I personally didn't find a damn thing comical about the moment or the situation.

"Well, I'm here," she said quickly. "Take care, Lena, and I'll talk with you soon."

"Yeah, take care," I said before ending the call. I couldn't help but wonder if my actions had led to her hasty departure. I decided I should have been a little less aggressive, and maybe Shontay wouldn't have dipped on me. *But what about Janai? What kind of woman breaks her promise to a child?* It became evident to me at that moment that Shontay had changed. There was a time when she would have never even thought of breaking her word, especially not to an innocent child. I could only assume that having money had made her shallow, or maybe she always had been and had just had a great way of concealing it. I was becoming more and more fed up with people breaking plans and bailing on me. *What about what I want?* Standing, I stared at my reflection in the mirror. "You either make things happen yourself," I said, "or you continue to get pissed and shitted on waiting on others."

"Take care, Lena, and I'll talk to you soon!" Shontay's words echoed in my head.

"No, bitch," I said aloud. "You'll *see* me sooner than you damn well think."

Chapter 9

Kelly

Contessa was on my every move when I dropped Donovan off at their crib. I had barely shaken her long enough to slip Donovan's snacks, along with a few other goodies, back in the fridge. It was not that Donovan needed anything when he was with the Whitmores, of course, because they had enough to feed a small village or two, but I had to have a valid reason for going in their refrigerator—especially with King Damon on the premises. *How is he so lucky? He's got the money, the crib, the wife, and the wannabes, and I ain't got shit. No man should have all the damn luck like that.*

I'd told Octavia I was going to look for a job , but the truth was I was going to Georgia to pay Ilene a surprise visit. It was a gutsy move, or maybe a stupid one, but lately I'd been full of those, and with Gator waiting to collect, I needed to make sure my next move was my best move. I had managed to advise Ilene of how she could contact me when the two of us were alone during our first meeting, expecting her to reach to me, but she hadn't as of yet. I had given her the opportunity, but she'd chosen not to take it, so it was time to force her hand and pay her a visit.

I noticed as I was leaving my home in Atlanta that there was a dark sedan that appeared to be following me. After Gator had rolled up on me at Ambiance, I was sure I'd become more aware of my surroundings, but I had no clue how long that car had been on my trail. Nonetheless, I knew I had to shake it before I went to visit Ilene. I assumed it was another one of Gator's goons, and although I had no problem with him knowing where I laid my head, I couldn't allow him to find out about Ilene. I came to the conclusion that Gator had put some professionals on his team; whoever the pursuer was, he gave me hell when I tried to shake him, but after a few quick, illegal turns and a duck-off in an alley, I finally managed to lose him.

I stood on the doorstep of Ilene's home, waiting for someone to answer the doorbell.

When the door swung open, I was greeted by a plump older woman with fair skin and short, dark hair. "May I help you?" she asked in a heavy Italian accent. The gray and white uniform and Dr. Scholl's she wore were a clear indication that she was the maid, but the diamond earrings that graced her earlobes and the diamond teardrop necklace hanging from her neck was an indication that what Nadia had told me about my mother was true: As long as a person remained in her good graces, she'd take good care of them.

"I'm here to see Ilene."

"And your name?"

"Kelly Baker," I said.

The woman looked at me with one raised eyebrow, studying my face carefully. It was obvious to me that she knew who I was. "She's not expecting you, Mr. Baker," she said, stating the obvious.

"I know," I said, "but I still need to speak with her…right now."

The woman looked at me and mumbled something under her breath before telling me, "Wait here," and shutting the door rudely in my face.

A minute or two later, Ilene opened the door, looking like she was preparing to strut down the runway of a fashion show. She was dressed in a long, silk, charcoal-gray dress that hung slightly off her shoulders and whirled around her ankles, along with soft pink open-toe heels. The gray in the dress complemented her mocha complexion beautifully. Ilene shook her head as she looked at me. "You shouldn't have come here," she said immediately.

"I felt I had no other choice. I waited for you to call me, but—"

"I was going to call. I just needed a little time."

"How much time?" I questioned. "After all, you've had thirty-six years."

Ilene pulled her eyes from mine and briefly stared into space. There was a look in her face that I could only read as hurt.

I remained quiet, waiting for her response.

"Come in," she finally said to me.

"Thank you," I said as I stepped past her through the doorway.

"Follow me," she ordered, walking away.

I followed her through the foyer to the family room, taking in as many details as I possibly could. Nadia's description of the home had not done it one ounce of justice. I'd always thought Damon and Octavia's home was banging, but it was only a third of what my mom and her husband were working with.

Ilene led me outside to the balcony. "Have a seat," she said politely, easing down in one of four chairs surrounding a large iron table.

I selected the chair directly across from her so we were facing each other, eye to eye.

"So, to what do I owe this visit?" she questioned suspiciously.

"I wanted to see my mother," I said. It was only partially true. I did want to see her but I also needed something.

"I would ask how you knew where to find me," she sighed, "but I assume Nadia told you."

I shook my head. "Not exactly," I lied. "I found your name and address in her address book."

"And exactly what else did you find?"

"Well, she also had the days of the week and the times when your husband would be out. That was how I knew he'd be on the lake today." I couldn't tell her that everything I knew about her and the rest of the family had been provided to me directly from Nadia. After all, I'd already lied and told her I hadn't discovered our paternity until after Nadia's death.

Ilene laughed a throaty but refreshing laugh. "Your baby's mother knew how to keep tabs on the Whitmore men." She chuckled again. "Even when they were no longer a part of her life. I guess a true whore always does her research and keeps notes on her subjects."

I laughed slightly myself. I could already tell Ilene had a way with words.

"Excuse me," asked the maid, who had appeared in the doorway leading to the balcony. "Is there anything I can get for the two of you?"

"Water," I said, "or sweet tea if you have it." I looked at Ilene then past her at the beautiful, plush green landscape that made up her back yard. "What am I saying?" I said, shaking my head. "Of course you have it."

The maid cleared her throat loudly and mumbled something in Italian.

"Isabella, please bring us two glasses of iced tea," Ilene said courteously. "Thank you."

I waited until we were once again alone before asking, "*She* knows?"

"Yes," Ilene said. "I shared my secret with Isabella after I met you."

I felt it was interesting as hell that she would share such a secret with her maid, with the help, yet she'd failed to mention it to her own husband and son. *Or did she already tell her husband?* "What about Damon Sr.?" I asked. "Does he know?"

"No."

"So you plan to keep this a secret?"

"Yes," she said firmly. "That has always been the plan, and I would have done so successfully had it not been for your child's mother."

"Your *grandson's* mother," I corrected her.

She frowned slightly before looking away.

"Wait…you do plan to claim Donovan as your grandson, right?" I asked curiously, calling her bluff. I was perfectly fine with Ilene refusing to publicly acknowledge Donovan or me. If she did so, it would only put far too much pressure on me and lead to suspicion about my past.

"Kelly, you sprang on me at my son and daughter-in-law's barbeque that you are the child I gave up at birth." She frowned. "You also told me that you have a son by a whore." Ilene cleared her throat and continued, "with a woman who was once involved with not only my son, but my husband as well."

What the hell? My face must have sold me out.

"And finally," Ilene purred, "there is something you don't know." Ilene looked like she could taste the bitterness in her own voice. "The distaste I had for Nadia was not only because I knew Damon could do better or even from her snooping around in my things and discovering the pictures and birth certificate I'd hidden of my firstborn. Please understand that I take full responsibility for my decision to keep those things in the first place, but she had no right snooping through my shit. In spite of my knowledge that Damon could have done better and the fact that she chose to violate my privacy, I was able to overlook that." Ilene paused, shaking her head slowly. "However, one thing I could not and will not overlook is her little fling with my husband." She shook her head. "I still remember the look in Damon's eyes when I caught the two of them together. Nadia had dropped in for an unexpected visit," she continued. "She'd already discovered my darkest secret and managed to keep it on the hush, so I figured there was no reason for me not to trust her in my home. She had been around Damon Sr. several times, and I assumed he looked at her like a daughter, so I figured I had nothing to worry about in leaving the two of them alone, unsupervised, and I went ahead with my plans for the day. It was only going to be a couple of hours anyway, and I knew DJ would be home as soon as he got out of class." Ilene took a deep breath, then exhaled.

I waited, hanging on her every word.

"Isabella was out grocery shopping, so there was no one to interrupt them or to break up their little party until I returned home. I was headed to a fundraising meeting that morning, but I planned to go shopping after that. I figured Nadia would like to go shopping with me, so much so that she would find sitting through a hour lecture a minor price to pay. It was going to be my treat, so I turned around and went back home to get her, to surprise her." Ilene leaned forward, clasping her hands together on the table in front of her. "As it turned out, I was the one in for a surprise," she said sarcastically. "I found the two of them in my bedroom. Damon was on the edge of the bed with his pants down around his ankles, and Nadia was kneeling before him with her lips wrapped around his Johnson."

"You caught Nadia sucking your husband's…" I couldn't bring myself to say the word in front of her. I had always known Nadia was disloyal to a fault, but I never would have imagined that.

"His dick," Ilene said bluntly. "And yes, I caught her doing just that."

"Was that all that happened between them?"

"According to Damon it was." She smirked. "Of course, we will never know for sure, and to tell you the truth, right now I couldn't care less. I love my life, and my family is perfect, flaws and all."

"So where do Donovan and I fit into this perfectly flawed family of yours?" I questioned.

"Considering how complicated our situation is, I feel it's best that we keep this family secret between the two of us," she said. "Don't you agree?"

"I suppose you're right," I replied. I could see the word "relieved" practically unfolding in her eyes. "What I want to know is if you have intention of establishing a relationship with me? And what about Donovan? I mean, can you at least grant us that? I'm willing to keep things a secret, but I refuse to be excluded from your life. What do you plan to do about that?"

Ilene's expression changed dramatically, and it was clear I'd struck a nerve. "I can't answer that yet," she stated, running her fingers through her hair.

"When will you be able to answer?" I pressed. "You have two sons and two grandchildren. When will you be able to own up to that? Or is it your intent to make all of this go away?" Of course I was asking my mother—in not so many words—if she was planning to pay me off to keep me quiet. It wasn't like she couldn't afford a few hundred grand, and we both knew I wasn't above accepting it.

"I won't be able to make any decisions until—"

"Until what?" I asked, cutting her off.

"Until I have proof that you are who you say you are."

Isabella returned with two large glasses of iced tea. She set them down on the table in front us and asked if there was anything else we needed.

After Ilene advised her that we needed nothing further, I waited until Isabella excused herself again before continuing the conversation. "So what do you want the two of us to do?"

"I want to see a paternity test."

Ain't that some shit? I thought. I wasn't trippin' off the fact that she wanted confirmation, but Ilene's initial reaction to the news that I was her son had misled me to believe that our next step would include some bonding and getting to know one another, me getting closer and closer to my mother's fortune. Now there she was, demanding a DNA test to prove that I was her blood. I could only assume that she'd been caught up in an emotional moment at the barbeque, and that moment had passed. "Okay," I agreed. "When?"

"Well, considering you're here now," she said with a sigh, "I think now would be as good a time as any."

"Okay," I said, "but don't we need an appointment at the testing center?"

She looked at me and shook her head. "There are certain perks that come with social status," she said. "Not having to wait or making appointments is one of them." And with that, she excused herself from the table and stepped inside her home, leaving me alone.

* * *

An hour later, the two of us sat in her kitchen with a man Ilene had introduced to me as Dr. Jack, an older biracial man with gray hair cut close to his head and a salt-and-pepper beard. He was tall, with a muscular build, and Ilene had advised me that Jack was a licensed medical doctor whom their family had known for years.

"How soon can we expect the results?" Ilene asked.

"I can have preliminary results in forty-eight hours," he said. "The test is a little more pricey—"

"Cost is not a factor," Ilene interjected. "The sooner we know the truth, the better."

"Understood," Dr. Jack said, nodding his head in agreement. "Should I assume this visit and the things that have taken place here should be kept between the three of us?"

"That would be a wise assumption, Doctor," Ilene answered.

Jack looked torn between what she was requesting and what he was thinking. "Ilene, you know Damon and I are good friends. I really wish you would have gone to someone else—that you hadn't pulled me into this."

"Jack, I called you because you are a friend and because you're trustworthy," she said softly. "However, you are also a professional, and as such, there is a required vow of doctor/patient confidentiality. The law would back me up on this in expecting and encouraging you to stay true to that vow. Failure to do so would certainly mean the end—and I'm not just referring to our friendship." Ilene had found a way to politely tell Jack that if he breathed a word of our little secret, the demise of his career would soon follow the demise of their friendship. In that moment it became blatantly clear to me that Ilene was a boss bitch.

"Fine. I'll call each of you as soon as we have the results, and no one else will know," Jack said quickly. He lifted his black leather bag off the kitchen island and secured the strap on his shoulder. "Ilene, if you don't mind, can you please remind your husband that he has a physical coming up in two weeks."

"Sure." Ilene smiled. "That is, if I can keep him off that silly golf course and lake." It was as if she'd gone from Mommy Dearest to Snow White in less than sixty seconds. All of a sudden, everything was smiles and sugar again.

"Well, I hope you can," Jack said solemnly.

I couldn't help but feel bad for the man. Ilene had given him his own wood to suck, and now he was forced to act as if nothing had happened.

"It was nice meeting you," he said to me. "Ilene, I'll let myself out," he stated, moving quickly toward the kitchen exit.

"Talk to you soon, Doc," Ilene said. "Tell Marsha I said hello."

Jack didn't even bother responding. Instead, he continued to haul ass on his way out the door.

Once I knew the man was gone, I erupted in laughter.

"What's so funny?" Ilene asked innocently.

"You," I said. "You claim the man is a friend, but you threatened the hell out of him."

She sighed lightly and ran her fingers through her hair. "I am fond of Jack and his wife Marsha," she said, "but the painful truth is, at the end of the day, he gets paid to do a job. When it comes to getting paid, friendship goes on the back burner."

"So money trumps friendship?" I concluded.

Ilene smiled, batting her beautiful eyes. "Of course. In some situations, it even trumps love—as if you didn't know that already."

Chapter 10

Octavia

The Ambiance was jumping at lunchtime, filled to its legal capacity. The wait was well over an hour, but my faithful and dedicated patrons chose to wait. Not only was business doing well at Ambiance, but according to the calls I was receiving from my staff at my second location, business was booming there as well. I was short staffed due to sending Tabitha to Ambiance 2 to help out and Amel being away, which meant I had to do what any true boss would: I rolled up my sleeves and went to work. After the lunch rush finally died down, I sat at the back of the restaurant looking over the sales and stats for that morning. I was pleased; the numbers looked good, extremely good. Besides that, my staff always handled themselves with ease and grace, so I decided to reward each of them with a small bonus in their weekly paychecks. I sincerely appreciated and valued my staff, and I tried my best to let them know that at every opportunity.

"I thought that was you, sitting over here all alone," a familiar voice came from behind me.

I turned around to find Gator towering over the booth where I was sitting, dressed in another signature suit and yet another pair of alligator shoes. "Hello, Gator."

"Octavia, is it?" he asked, staring down at me. He was too damn tall and big to be hovering over me, taking up all my air, but I had no intention of asking him to join me in the booth. In fact, I was hoping he planned on keeping our conversation short and sweet.

"Yes."

"You come here often?" he questioned.

I couldn't tell if he was flirting with me or just being nosy. Either way, I didn't feel a good vibe from the man. "Uh, yeah," I said, "especially since I own the place."

In that instant, it literally looked like a light bulb began to glow behind Gator's eyes. "What? You own this beautiful establishment?" he repeated, nodding his head and having a look around. "Nice. Beautiful and successful. I like that."

"Thanks." I'd already told the gator-wearing Goliath that I was taken, so I couldn't imagine why he was there and why he insisted on talking to me. "Is there something I can help you with?" I questioned. "Looking for Kelly?"

"No. Kelly and I have a date to see each other in the future," he said. "I just so happened to be in the neighborhood and decided to stop by and check out the menu. Then I looked up and saw you sitting here."

"Oh, I see," I said. "Exactly how do you know Kelly?" I asked curiously.

"We go way back," he said. "He used to work for me too."

"Really? What did he do for you?"

Gator laughed. "Let's just say he did a few odds and ends that I needed help with."

What's so funny about odd jobs? I wondered.

"And what did he do for you?" he asked.

"He was my landscaper," I said.

"Landscaper?" Gator questioned. "I wasn't aware that landscaping is one of Kelly's specialties."

"Well, he's excellent at it. Our place looks great, thanks to him."

"Interesting," he said. "I guess we all have our names for it."

Names? Names for what? There was something in his tone that sent my radar up. I watched as he reached inside his jacket and pulled out a black business card.

"If you need anything," he said, placing the card on the table next to me, "feel free to call me directly."

"Thanks," I said, wondering why in the hell he'd think I'd ever need him.

"I should get going," he said. "Please tell Kelly I'm looking forward to seeing him sooner rather than later." he said, and he strolled off before I could respond.

I picked up the business card and looked it over. There was no logo, nor was there an address. All that was on it was a phone number, which I could only assume to be his. I crumbled it up and placed it back on the table, then got back to the work I'd been so rudely interrupted from.

* * *

I hadn't spoken to Shontay in weeks, and to be honest, I hadn't made any attempts to call her. It wasn't that I was mad at her or that I didn't love her with all my heart but I had been completely caught up in my own life and those actively involved in it. I knew in my heart that Shontay was safe and that we'd talk again when we had the time. But did that stop me from grabbing my bag, locking my office down, and throwing my staff the deuces when Shontay called and told me she was back? Hell no! Shontay was my bestie, my sister. We could go a month without talking, but when one reached out to the other, she was going to be there, no questions asked.

The two of us agreed to meet at El Mariachi, a Mexican restaurant that served some of the best margaritas in the city. I spotted my bestie sitting in our favorite booth, and I almost had to do a double-take. She looked gorgeous! She always looked beautiful, of course, but this time she looked runway ready. She was wearing a red maxi-dress that showed her toned chocolate arms and gave a seductive peek of her full breasts. There was an air of confidence surrounding her that was impossible to deny.

Shontay must have sensed me watching her, because she looked up, directly at me, then smiled. It took her less than twenty seconds to slide out of the booth and strut proudly up to me, meeting me halfway. "Octavia!" she practically screamed, throwing her arms around me.

"Look at you!" I was practically screaming myself.

The two of us stood in the middle of the restaurant, hugging and exchanging compliment after compliment.

"I love your hair!"

"You've lost weight!"

"You are killing that dress!"

"That suit is banging!"

We were in engulfed in a cornucopia of compliments, completely oblivious to those around us. It had been a year since we'd seen each other, but like true family, we were ecstatic about our reunion. After having our sister moment—truly worthy of a Kodak commercial—we finally sat down. We ordered our traditional favorites: chicken enchilada platter with yellow rice and two ultimate strawberry margaritas.

"I've missed you, girl," Shontay said, smiling.

"And I you," I replied honestly. "How are you? I mean, you look un-freakin'-believable, but how are you?"

"I'm good now," she said, nodding her head. "How is Damon?"

"He gets better as the days go by," I said, beaming with pride at the thought of my perfectly perfect husband.

"And my goddaughter?"

"Beautiful and getting bigger and bigger every day."

"Mama Charlene and Charles?" Shontay quizzed. "I imagine Charles is still fine."

I gave her my don't-play look and laughed. "Yes, he's good, and he's still very much in love with Mama."

"I wouldn't expect anything less." Shontay giggled. "How is your mama?" she asked seriously.

"She's doing well, considering—"

"Considering what?"

"Mama was diagnosed with breast cancer a while back," I told her. Although my mother was doing well and her mastectomy had gone better than expected, it was still difficult for me to say the words. I could feel the tears surfacing in my eyes as I looked at Shontay. I fought to keep my tears under wraps, but hers trickled slowly down her cheeks.

"When? How? I mean…how is she doing?" Shontay stuttered.

"She looks great," I said, "and she says she feels good. She had a mastectomy, and the doctors say the cancer hadn't spread beyond her left breast. It's apparently in remission, which is good news."

"I'm sorry, Tavia," Shontay cried. "If I had known…I should have been here. I should have been here."

I reached across the table and took her hand in mine. "Mama waited a month before she told me," I confessed. "When she finally did, I broke down completely, but Mama was just like herself—brave, bold, and beautiful. She told me she accepts it, and she's going to win."

"That woman has always been strong as a damn ox," Shontay commented, dabbing at her eyes with her free hand.

"Yep, she sure is."

"At least you're here so you can be with her throughout her journey," she said sadly. "I wish I'd had that chance."

Shontay's mother Josephine had passed from cancer. The two of them had been estranged for years, thanks to Kenny blocking Josephine's calls and hiding the letters she had written Shontay. However, in Josephine's last few days, Shontay and her made up, so at least Shontay was there to help make her comfortable and express her love at the end.

"I'm thankful to have that chance," I said honestly, "but if I could change it..."

"I know you would," Shontay said, giving my hand a light squeeze.

The two of us took a break from our conversation to sip on our drinks and dig into the food our waitress had just set on the table.

"At first I was hesitant about returning here," Shontay said, striking our conversation up again, "but I'm good now."

"Hesitant?" I asked curiously. "Why?"

"I didn't think there was anything left here for me."

"What?" I inquired. "Why would you think that?" I took a sip of my drink while waiting for her response.

"The life I established here was based on having a good ol' 9-to-5 job and being married to Kenny. For so long, that seemed like my only option, and that was all I knew how to do—work, be a wife, and put up with his shit. Now everything has changed."

"For the better," I reminded her.

"Yes." She smiled. "But sometimes when you've had such a shitty journey on the road to happiness it's hard to revisit the places that hold the crappy memories."

We both laughed.

"I completely understand," I said, empathizing with her.

"But I have a lot of beautiful memories that took place in this city." She sighed. "Like all the times you and I have shared, my goddaughter, whom I can't wait to see, and Savoy."

"Speaking of Mr. Breedwell," I said slowly, "where is *the* man?" The last time I had spoken to Shontay, she'd told me that the two of them were together but that she was keeping her options open. I was curious to know if she still felt that way.

"He's in Atlanta," she said.

"So the two of you flew into two different cities?"

"Yes. Two different cities, three months apart."

"Explain."

"Savoy has been back from Africa for three months now," she explained.

"He left you there alone?"

"I suggested it."

I listened closely as she explained that Savoy had been pressuring her to make a decision on where their relationship was headed and to make a permanent move to Atlanta. Her things were already in Atlanta, but she had yet to finalize where she wanted to live. She said that although she loved Savoy deeply, she was not ready to make another serious commitment, so she had suggested that the two of them see other people.

I gave her a blank stare, letting her know I thought she had lost her mind.

"What?" she asked, looking completely innocent.

"You don't give a man as fine as Savoy permission to date other women," I said seriously, meaning every word. Savoy had pecan-brown skin and pretty gray, cat-like eyes, as well as full, kissable lips. In addition to his beautiful facial features, he was tall with large biceps and the build of an athlete. He was the second finest man I knew.

"What was I supposed to do?" she questioned. "Have him wait for me."

"I don't know what you do in that situation," I said honestly, "but what you don't do is tell him to go out there and find some new coochie to play with." I said it jokingly, but I meant every word.

"At the time, it felt like the best solution," she said. "Thing is, Savoy decided he didn't want to share or be shared. He told me it was all or nothing."

"And you chose nothing?"

Shontay nodded her head in agreement. "I did at the time, but then I came to my senses and reminded myself that a good man is what I've always prayed for. I didn't want to miss my blessing."

"I never prayed for a good man or a man at all, but I know I'm blessed to have Damon," I said sincerely, "and please believe I know and understand all about almost missing your blessing." Of course I was referring to the time when I'd first met Damon, back when I'd had that fling with Beau. "So anyway, you came to your senses and caught the first flight out of Africa and decided to stop through on your way to the A?"

"Well, not exactly," Shontay said, sounding dramatic. "I actually made a stop in LA. I had planned to spend a week there, but then I had my epiphany and broke down and called Savoy. He agreed that we have some things to work out, and I agreed that the only way for us to do so was if we're in the same city, or at least in the same country."

"Well, I'm just glad the two of you could come to an agreement." I smiled.

"Me too," she said. "Now I just have to deal with that mama and those sisters of his."

"What do they have to do with your business?" I questioned.

"They feel some kind of way about me," she said. "When I met them and they found out I was married when Savoy and I started dating, they didn't approve. Then, when I chose to stay in Africa, they didn't approve of that either. I keep doing things they don't approve of."

"Who cares? They don't have to approve," I reminded her. "You're not sleeping with them." I could tell that despite Shontay's transformation, there was still a small part of her that demanded the approval and acceptance of others, and that made me sad. "So what were you up to in LA?" I asked, changing the subject.

"I went to see Lena." She made her statement so quickly I *almost* didn't catch it.

"You went to see...Lena?" I asked, staring at her like she'd lost her mind.

She threw both of her hands in the air, telling me to hear her out. "She told me about your run-in," she said, "and I told her I can't blame you for how you reacted when you found out she was friends with Damon. I can't blame you for putting your foot down and demanding that Damon have no further contact with her."

I appreciated Shontay providing her approval and support of my feelings toward Lena being friends with my husband, though her affirmation was not necessary. Any real woman would have done the same thing in my shoes. I wasn't about to suggest that people couldn't change, as I was living proof that they can, but I knew there are some repeat offenders, and my natural instinct told me that, given the chance, Lena would have been one of them in a heartbeat. She'd be guilty of being a home-wrecking whore on multiple counts. I was just keeping it real. "So, how exactly did you end up in her company?" I questioned, eyeing my friend suspiciously. I loved Shontay, but I knew that when birds of a feather flock together, they can sometimes get sick together. If I had one inkling of suspicion that my bestie had caught the home-wrecking hoe bug, I would have no problem cutting ties and burning bridges. I loved my man that much.

"Before I left for my trip, Lena and I were on good terms," she said.

"First of all her name wasn't Lena then," I said sarcastically. "It was *Alicia.* Remember? Hmm? You know—the hood-rat who was sleeping with your husband? Yes, that bit—"

"Of course I remember," Shontay said, cutting me off, "but for conversation purposes, can we refer to her by her new legal name?"

I was perfectly fine with referring to her as "that bitch," but I decided not to let my emotions take over the conversation I was having with my best friend. "Fine. I'll grant you this one wish," I said, leaning forward in my seat.

"Thanks."

"But don't ask for anything else," I teased.

"I'll try not to." She sighed deeply before moving on. "Anyway, before I left, Lena and I were on good terms, and I told her to stay in contact, mostly because of my relationship with her daughter. Well, she called me and said Ki…er, Janai wanted to see me."

"Mm-hmm," I said, grunting while I listened.

"It was a perfect excuse for me to come back to the States without having to admit that I *wanted* to come back. I flew in and spent the day with Lena and Janai, but I realized after talking about you and thinking about how you've always been here for me that I miss the good people from my old life." She looked at me with raised eyebrows and a look in her eyes that was slightly begging for my understanding.

"If I was as accepting as you are and as forgiving," I began, "I could see why you went to visit. After all, you did accept Janai as a part of your family, and the death of her father does not change the bond you had with the daughter. I do feel some kind of way that you went to California before you came to Alabama to see me, your best friend, your sister," I said, playing the family card—my way of inflicting guilt on my bestie.

The dramatic eye roll she gave me was evidence that she was aware of my intentions.

"However, I also understand that you have been on a journey to rediscover yourself and find your inner happiness."

Shontay nodded her head in agreement, then smiled.

"Now, I just have one question," I said, pausing for effect. "Do you know who the hell you are yet?" I stared her directly in the eyes until we both erupted in laughter.

"Yes, sis, I do," she said, catching her breath.

"Whew! It's about damn time." I giggled. "It only took you what? A year?"

"Seven months. It's a slow process for some of us," she retaliated.

We both laughed again. It felt good to laugh and talk face to face with Shontay. I was slightly jealous that she'd visited Lena first, but at that moment, none of that mattered. I didn't express my thoughts to Shontay that day, but I couldn't help but wonder if there was a hidden agenda behind Lena's invitation to visit.

Chapter 11

Damon

Octavia and Shontay were enjoying what they referred to as "a much-needed girls' night out" while I sat in our home theater watching the Magic tap the Lakers' asses on the court. Contessa was looking after Jasmine and Donovan, which allowed me a much-needed man-and-his-TV night in. I was comfortable in a white T-shirt and blue basketball shorts, and I had an ice-cold Heineken in my hand. It was a rare occasion for me to take the time to do absolutely nothing all by myself, but it felt good.

I was in the process of screaming at the Magic from the comfort of my leather recliner when my Blackberry beeped, indicating that I had a text message. If it wasn't my wife or Dwight Howard hitting me up to let me know what in the hell was the problem with his defense at that moment, I did not want to be bothered. "Oh, come on!" I screamed, looking up at the screen. "You just gave the damn ball away!" I picked up my device while flashing my eyes back and forth between it and the television.

The message was from Lawrence, asking if I was free to talk. I hadn't spoken to him since I'd put him back on Kelly's case, and now that he was hitting me up, I knew he had some information for me.

I turned the volume down with my universal remote before calling

Lawrence.

"Sorry to disturb you so late, probably during family time," Lawrence apologized, "but, well, this couldn't wait."

"No problem," I said, sensing the urgency in his voice. "My wife stepped out with her girlfriend tonight."

"Okay. Well, who's there with you?" Lawrence questioned.

"Contessa and the kids are here, but they're upstairs," I said, wondering where he was headed with his questioning since it was clearly urgent. "What's up?"

"Well, D., I was over here on your boy's ass," he said.

"Was?"

"Yeah. 'Fraid I lost him," he said solemnly

"What?" I couldn't believe my ears. In all the years I'd known Lawrence, no one had ever given him the slip while he was trailing them. "You're slippin', old man."

"I ain't slippin' on a damn thing," he said defensively. "That muthafucka was driving all paranoid, like he knew he was being followed."

"Why would he think that?" I asked, certain that Lawrence was just in denial. It was obvious that he was slightly losing his touch.

"I don't know!" he said loudly. "Maybe he has something to hide or maybe he was just spooked. Either way, I'm damn sure gonna find out."

"All right." I exhaled. *Lawrence may have a point. The only people I know who constantly check to see if they're being watched either have money or something to hide.* I wondered which was Kelly's case. If I'd have been a betting man, I would have put money on the latter. "Just get back on him ASAP."

"I'm on it," he said. "He dropped his bags off at his baby-mama's old spot, so I figure that's where he's planning to lay his head. I scooped up another vehicle the slippery li'l fucker won't recognize, so I'll be ready."

"Good deal," I said. "Just keep me posted."

"No doubt," Lawrence said. "But listen, that's not really why I called."

"Why then?"

"Well, it's about your nanny dearest."

"Contessa? What about her?"

"First of all, there is no Jay Baker on the inmate list in Tennessee," Lawrence advised. "Do you know another name this alleged son of hers might be going by?"

Jay was the only name Contessa had provided me, and it was also the name that the correctional officer that had called for Contessa had used. "That's odd. An officer called a couple nights ago," I said. "She said she was from the prison and that she had a message for Contessa from her son Jay." I glanced at the silent TV for a moment, but I was no longer interested in the Magic and the Lakers, as Lawrence had succeeded in rousing my suspicions.

"An officer from the prison? Really? Hmm. What number did she call from?" he asked. "Give it to me, and I'll find out who it really belongs to."

"Give me a second," I stated, climbing up out of my recliner. "The handset I answered her call on is in the other room. I'm sure the number's still on the caller ID, since we don't get that many calls on that line. Hold up." I walked to the family room and removed the cordless handset from its charging station. I scrolled through the names and numbers on the caller ID, only to find that the number had been deleted. The only call from that day was at 10 in the morning, from Octavia's cell phone during her usual morning check-in on Jasmine. "Damn."

"What?"

"That number's just…gone," I told Lawrence. "That ain't right. Why would anybody bother deleting it?"

"I don't know, man, but this shit is looking shadier and shadier by the moment, D.," Lawrence stated, expressing his valid concerns. "I'm telling you, I've got a bad vibe about that sitter of yours and this whole deal with her alleged locked-up son, her so-called nephew, the whole nine yards."

"Hmm. Lemme double-check and make sure the phones didn't get switched," I said calmly, still somewhat optimistic that there was a simple explanation. "I'll also talk to Contessa."

"Be careful with that, D."

"Yeah, I will. I'll hit you back."

"Bet," Lawrence chanted before hanging up.

I thought about the information Lawrence had given me about Contessa's son—or lack thereof. I didn't want to jump to any conclusions just yet, as I knew it was possible that Jay was just short for Jeremiah or any number of names. Plus, I'd never confirmed her son's last name and had always just assumed it was the same as hers. I checked the other two cordless handsets just to be sure I had the right one; there were no calls for that day on either of them. With the mystery still unsolved, I decided to quiz Contessa about what I'd learned.

I knocked on her bedroom door and waited. After a minute or two of no answer, I let myself in.

Donovan and Jasmine sat on the floor, watching cartoons on the television. Jasmine immediately ran up to me, reaching her little arms up.

"Where is Ms. Contessa?" I asked, lifting my little girl up into my arms.

She kissed my nose and pointed toward Contessa's closed bathroom door.

I placed my baby girl back down on the carpet next to Donovan and called for Contessa. "Ms. Contessa!"

No response.

I walked over to the bathroom door and knocked three or four times while calling her name again. I couldn't hear any movement coming from the other side of the door, so I turned the door handle and slowly pushed it open, not really wanting to catch the old woman on the toilet or coming out of the shower. "Ms. Contessa?" I called again, staring at her.

She didn't respond, and I really didn't expect her to, considering she was lying on the bathroom floor wearing nothing but her plush purple bathrobe, staring blankly at the ceiling with her eyes wide open, white and not blinking. There was vomit on her chin and between her lips. Beside Contessa's right hand lay one of her insulin injection needles, but it was empty.

I dialed 911 and pressed my fingers to her neck to check for a pulse, but I found none. She was dead, and I still had questions.

* * *

Octavia took the news of Contessa's death hard. I assumed she'd be upset about it, but it had never occurred to me how tight their bond was until Octavia broke down in my arms. It seemed I was seeing the softer, more vulnerable side of my wife lately, and to be honest, I kind of liked it.

For the sake of my distraught and heartbroken wife, I was grateful to learn that Shontay was going to stay with us until she left for Atlanta. Although I could hold my wife down and comfort her better than any man on Earth, I understood that some words of comfort just sound better coming from a home-girl. I put the kids to bed and left Octavia and Shontay alone before slipping in the office to return Lawrence's phone call.

"Damn. I thought you forgot about me," Lawrence answered. "What'd Super Nanny have to say about mommy's li'l criminal?"

"Not a damn thing," I informed him.

"You couldn't get her to talk?"

"Nobody could have—not even you. She's…dead."

"Damn! You killed her?"

"No," I said with a sigh. "It looks like she had a diabetic coma."

"Are you shitting me?"

"You know I don't joke about that type of stuff."

"Damn." Lawrence exhaled. "Of all the times to kick off, that old bitch picked now."

"First, I don't think you need to speak so disrespectful of the dead. And second, I don't think she had a choice," I reminded him. "When it's our time—"

"It's our time…yeah, yeah," he finished. "Well, we still have nephew over here."

"Has he made it back?"

"Just pulled into the garage a few minutes ago," he said. "I'm gonna see if anything pops off tonight, and I'll call ya if it does."

"All right," I said quickly, hearing Octavia call my name. "Stay up."

"You too."

Chapter 12

Kelly

Nadia had been one pair of stilettos away from being broke when she died. She didn't even have life insurance. *What kind of selfish bitch brings a child into this world and doesn't make sure there's something waiting for him or her in the event that something happens to the child's parents?* It wasn't as if Nadia couldn't have afforded the premiums. The truth was, she was just too busy keeping herself laced in the finest garments to care about what would happen to Donovan if something happened to her. The only half-decent and responsible thing she'd ever done was to pay the rent up on the properties she'd been leasing. The one in Huntsville had gone up in smoke when I'd taken her life, but the one in Atlanta was still standing, paid up for a year. I was thankful for that since it saved me from having to fork out cash to rent a hotel room whenever I was in the city. The three-bedroom, two-and-a-half-bath home was not only cozy but also well decorated with leather and glass furnishings. Nadia had personally coordinated every detail and accent.

I walked through the front door of the home, locked the door behind me, then plopped down on the sofa. My day had been productive but not to the extent I'd hoped. I couldn't read Ilene, and when a man can't read a woman he's dealing with, it's a problem—even if that women is his own mother. I knew there was much more to her than the designer labels she wore and the model-like elegance she presented herself with. I just didn't know how much more. I was anxious about hearing from Ilene once she had the results back from Dr. Jack, but I also wondered what her next move would be and how my son and I might fit into her financial equation.

The leather sectional I sat on housed a small console between the center cushion, the perfect hiding place for my stash. I reached down inside the console, only to discover that the sack I'd placed there when I'd first arrived in Georgia was gone! The box of Swishers was still there, but my green was gone. "What the hell?" I spoke aloud, standing. I lifted each cushion, thinking and hoping my bag had fallen between them somehow, but I found nothing. I dropped to my knees and felt along the floor under the sofa.

"Looking for this?"

I quickly jumped to my feet, an uncontrollable reaction to hearing Lena's unwelcome voice.

She stood with one hand on her hip, the other holding up the half-ounce bag of marijuana I'd purchased before leaving Huntsville.

"How'd you get in here?" I questioned.

"Through the back door," she said, stepping toward me. "Oh, and you may want to have that replaced." She dropped the bag on the coffee table and just stared at me.

I could see the anger infused in her pupils, so I thought it was wise to keep my mouth shut.

"Why haven't you returned any of my calls?" she questioned. "I know you got my messages."

Yeah, I thought, *and much like right now, I didn't wanna be bothered by your ass.* "I've just been busy, that's all," I said. "I been meanin' to hit you up."

"Before or after you decided to change our plans?"

The mere fact that Lena knew where to find me told me she'd spoken to Contessa, which meant she knew that things between me, Damon, and Octavia hadn't gone according to her plan. "I decided to take an...uh, alternate route," I said, plopping back down on the couch. I grabbed one of the Swishers and began breaking it down.

"What route would that be?" she asked. "Are you talking about the one involving Damon and Octavia adding your son to their family? Seemed to me like they were one big, happy, fuckin' unit when I called their house."

I was not in the mood to argue. All I wanted to do was roll my blunt, get lifted, and possibly go out and prowl for a thirsty chick who'd let me take out my frustrations between her thighs. *That's it. I just wanna bang a bad chick, then kick her ass out and get me some rest.* But I couldn't do that because Nanny Save-a-Ho just had to intervene and let Lena know my whereabouts. "They sound that way for now," I said, dumping the tobacco out of the cigar, onto the table in front of me. "But soon—very soon—that's all gonna change."

"Soon? It should have already changed!" she barked. "Why can't you understand that?!"

"You wanna do this shit your-damn-self?" I asked, looking up at her. "Do you?" I could see the dilemma in her eyes. "That's what I thought. You don't want to because you can't. If you could, you would've never enlisted mine and Contessa's help. Am I right?"

Silence.

"Thought so," I said, redirecting my attention to the task at hand.

After a few minutes of heavy breathing without comment, Lena finally sat down. "Well, you should have at least consulted me first," she said calmly. "Your failure to do so left me questioning your loyalty."

My loyalty? That never has to be questioned, I thought. *I will always and forever be loyal to me and mine, first and foremost.* Still, I knew I had to calm her down. "I got you, baby," I told her. The moment wasn't right for the harsh truth. Besides, I still needed her to have my back via my wallet. I lit the end of the blunt, remembering that Lena had my stash in her hand when she'd entered the room. Thoughts of her lacing my green with something began to flock my mind. "Here…hit this," I said, holding the el out toward her.

"I don't smoke anymore," she said, shaking her head.

You do today, I thought. "C'mon. Hit it with me, Lena," I insisted.

Lena looked at me and could see that I was stone-cold serious. She blinked several times, then shook her head and erupted in laughter. "Wait a minute. You think I did something to your shit?" She chuckled. "Wow." She took the el from my hand and then shook her head again. "Trust me, if I wanted you dead, you'd be dead already." She took a long pull, inhaling deeply, then slowly exhaled. "Believe *that.*"

I laughed myself. "Well, the feeling's mutual baby," I warned her. "The feeling is mutual."

* * *

Once Lena and I finished getting lifted, I treated her to a home-cooked meal consisting of stuffed chicken breast, veggie medley, and brown rice. Cooking was one of my specialties, and there was nothing like cooking for a beautiful woman, even if said woman was hung up on another brother. Hell, I didn't mind, and I was hoping she didn't either, because at that very moment, I had my head between her thighs, my lips latched on her clit, and my mind on Octavia. After playing with Lena until she was soaking wet, I slid in and pounded her down until I was satisfied and she was screaming. Fifteen minutes later, the two of us lay in bed in silence.

Lena was a beautiful woman, and I'd been thinking about breaking her off from day one, but now that it had actually taken place, I was a little disappointed. She had to be the stiffest broad I had ever been with. It wasn't that she didn't have the potential to be good in bed; she just didn't know how to use her potential. It's true that money can't buy you everything, because it sure couldn't buy her good sex skills.

I was debating whether or not to give her another chance to prove me wrong, thinking maybe she was having an off moment, when my cell phone rang. "Hello?"

"Kelly, it's me, Damon."

"Damon, what's up?"

At the sound of Damon's name, Lena immediately sat up in the bed and looked at me.

I ignored her desperate stares. "Is Donovan all right?" I asked, sitting up against the headboard.

"Donovan's fine," Damon said, sighing lowly. "I'm sorry, man, but it's your aunt."

I tossed the covers back and climbed out of bed, standing on the cold wooden floor. "Is Auntie okay?" I asked, concerned.

Silence.

"What's going on, man?" I pressed.

"Kelly, I'm afraid Contessa has…uh, she passed," he informed me. "She's gone."

"What? She's *dead*?" I repeated, staring at Lena.

Her eyes were wide as she watched me, and I could tell she was hanging on my every word.

"H…how? Wh…when?" I stuttered.

"I'm not sure exactly, but I found her earlier," Damon continued. "The paramedics said it looked like a diabetic seizure."

"Fuck!" I screamed. "Come on, man. Tell me this is some kind of sick-ass joke."

"I wish I could," he said solemnly. "Again, I'm sorry. She seemed to be a wonderful woman, and she was so great with the kids. She'll be missed here."

"I appreciate that," I said, swallowing hard. "I'll get on the road first thing in the morning. Man, I can't believe this shit. Damn!"

"I'm so sorry," Damon said sympathetically. "We'll see you tomorrow."

"Contessa's dead?" Lena asked as soon as I hung up; I barely managed to end the call before she began questioning me. "What happened?"

"Yep, dead." I exhaled, climbing back on the bed and stretching my legs out in front of me. "Diabetic seizure, they're saying."

"But…how?" Lena was obviously shocked, and she looked somewhat saddened. "She sounded fine last time we spoke to each other."

"I'm sure she did." I yawned, propping my arms up under my head. "Then again, when insulin is contaminated by household products, it can cause all kinds of side effects. Death is obviously one of them."

"*What?*" she asked slowly.

"Lie back down," I instructed her. "We'll talk about it in the morning."

"But I…huh? I just don't understand…" Lena stopped abruptly. Staring at me as if a light bulb suddenly went off, she frowned. "You?"

"We're better off without her," I said frankly.

"When did *we* decide to off Contessa?!" Lena whined.

She was being far too emotional about the situation. Granted, she'd pulled Contessa off the streets and cleaned her up, but the fact remained that Contessa had become a liability; she could no longer be trusted. I hadn't planned on taking the woman's life and had only wanted to teach her a lesson and put her out of commission for a while, but things didn't go as I expected. When I'd snatched one of the insulin vials she'd stored in Octavia and Damon's fridge and then put it back, I was holding my breath, hoping that when Contessa got ready to give herself her next shot, she wouldn't notice it had been tampered with. Now, I could breathe freely. My problem was solved, and it had happened a lot earlier than I'd thought it would.

"Look…the old broad started talking shit about wanting out and how much she loved Damon and Octavia, etcetera and so on. She'd become a liability, so I handled it."

Lena's mouth was wide open, but no words came out.

"She was a problem, and I solved it," I said. "Besides, we don't need her."

She shook her head, then hesitantly lay back down next to me.

I closed my eyes, yawning lightly. "Don't worry. I've got it all under control."

Chapter 13

Kelly

The next morning, I saw no signs of the car that had been trailing me the previous day, but I knew I had to get Gator's flunkies off my ass, one way or another. I decided to ask Lena for another advance. It was bad enough having asking her for the money, but her shitload of questions and the lecture that followed did not make the task any easier. I finally told her about Gator and the bind I was in. After bitching and whining about my helping her secure Damon, she finally agreed to front me another payment so I could try to get Gator off my ass. I thanked her by knocking her back out before hitting the road. I had to give her credit; she was better the second time around, but she still wasn't good. Nonetheless, pussy's pussy and a nut's a nut, so I took whatever I had access to at the moment.

I was pushing seventy MPH on Interstate 65, just crossing the line into Madison County when my phone rang. "Hello," I answered.

"Jack was going to call you, but I told him I would," Ilene said. Her voice didn't carry its usual extravagant tone. In fact, she sounded troubled.

"What's up?"

"It seems you and I have a…uh, a little problem," she said slowly.

I knew instantly that she was referring to the paternity test. "I told you,"

I said. "You could have saved your money and just listened to me, but I'm glad you got the confirmation you needed…Mom."

"I am glad for that as well," she said dramatically. "We need to talk, and I prefer that we do so face to face," she said. "Can you meet me around 6 this evening?"

"Unfortunately no," I told her. "I'm back in Huntsville."

"So soon?" she questioned. "What was the rush? I was certain you would be *hanging* around a *little* longer." She put emphasis on the words "hanging" and "little," and there was something odd about her choice of words.

"Uh, well, unfortunately, leaving wasn't by choice," I said. "My aunt died."

"Contessa?" she asked.

"Yes."

"I'm sorry to hear of your loss," she said. "I enjoyed meeting Contessa. She seemed like such a sweet woman."

"She was," I said softly. "But then again, death is something we all have to deal with. We're born. We live. We die."

"You make it all sound so simple," she stated, sounding slightly surprised. "Losing someone you love is really that cut-and-dry for you?"

"I deal with death and love the best way I know how," I answered. "It's the way I was taught."

There was silence between the two of us for a moment.

Finally, she spoke again, sounding rushed. "I have to go now. My husband just walked through the door. Take care. We'll talk soon." She hung up without saying goodbye and before I could respond.

I hit end just to make sure my line was clear, then called the number Damon had called me from.

"This is Damon," he answered.

"Damon, hey, it's Kelly."

"Hi, Kelly. How you doing?" he asked, actually sounding concerned, and I respected that.

"Still in shock," I lied, "but listen…I'm back in the city."

"Glad you made it safely," he said. "Royal has Contessa's body. If you want, Octavia and I can meet you there."

"Sounds good," I said, thinking of Octavia.

"If you're up to it, we'd like to go ahead and start making burial arrangements while were th…" He paused. "Hold for just one moment," he said.

A few minutes passed until he clicked back over. "Sorry about that," he said. "My mother. I hope you don't mind, but I told her about your aunt."

I was 100 percent sure that *our* mother had called Damon just to see if I was lying about Contessa. I laughed silently, shaking my head. It was a move I would have made, and I wouldn't have expected anything less from the woman who'd brought me into the world. "No problem at all," I answered.

"Good," he continued. "As I was saying, if you're up to it, we can go ahead and work out the funeral arrangements."

What arrangement? I thought. *Cram her ass in a box, crate, or even a plastic bag and dump her somewhere.* I didn't care, as long as she was no longer going to be an issue or problem for me. "You're right. The sooner the better," I said. "We can take care of everything while we're there."

"Sounds good," Damon said. "Why don't we meet you there in a half-hour?"

"I'll be there."

* * *

"I can't believe it," I said sadly, rushing out the doors of the morgue in dramatic fashion. I placed my hands on the lobby wall, pretending to use it for balance. I could see Octavia and Damon out of the corner of my eyes. They sat on the small leather bench against the wall opposite of where I was leaning, watching me. "No," I panted. "Why?!" I grabbed my chest and turned around until my back was against the wall. I took a couple short breaths through my mouth, mimicking hyperventilation.

"Kelly, are you okay?" Octavia asked, the first to come to my rescue.

Continuing my Oscar-worthy performance, I leaned forward then rocked back, taking another round of shallow breaths. I reached out and gently grabbed her wrist. "Whhhhy?" I repeated breathlessly.

"Damon," she said, looking back at her husband, then back at me.

I looked up into her honey bedroom eyes and saw concern and compassion. Even with fear etched in her face, she was beautiful—too beautiful. "I'll…I'll be…all right." I gasped, putting my free hand up in the air to let Damon (who was now heading in our direction) know that he could slow his roll; his intervention was not necessary. "Water. Damon, can I have…can you get me some water?"

"Baby, can you grab him a cup of water?" Octavia asked him.

"Of course," Damon replied. He looked at me briefly before turning to hurry down the hall.

I slowly straightened my back, sliding my hand from Octavia's wrist down to her palm. "Sit down," I said. I continued to fake my attack, a little less dramatic this time.

"Here. Lean on me," Octavia suggested. "You're shaking."

I let go of her hand and slipped my arm around her shoulder as she slipped hers around my waist, trying to offer me innocent support. I could smell the sweet fragrance of her hair as the two of us moved slowly in step toward the bench she'd occupied with Damon earlier.

"Sit," she ordered. "Slowly."

Obeying, I dropped my arm from around her shoulder, then eased down on the bench.

Octavia eased down beside me. "Calm down and try to take a slow breath in through your nose," she instructed.

I did as she said, looking at her the whole time. "I can't believe she's… she's gone," I repeated, closing my eyes tightly. I squeezed as tightly as possible, willing myself to tears.

"I know," Octavia whispered.

I opened my eyes, and a second later, a single fake tear trickled down my face. I looked at Octavia. She sighed lightly, then brushed away her own tears with her fingertips; I knew her tears were genuine. It wasn't the first time I'd seen her cry, and much like the last time, it did something to me. I pulled her into my embrace, wrapping my arms around her shoulders. I could feel her resistance. I felt her fighting against the weight of my body.

"I loved her so much." I pretended to cry. "She was all Donovan and I had." I was playing a ho card, and it was working. I felt Octavia's hands pressed against my back.

"It's okay," she said soothingly, patting my back. "It's okay."

I inhaled, turning my face toward her neck. The luxurious scent of her airy, floral perfume penetrated my senses. I could feel my dick growing hungrily between my legs. The feel of her breast pressed against my chest, making me even harder.

"She's in a place of peace," Octavia stated. She was completely unaware of the cravings flowing through me like the blood in my veins; oblivious to my desire to kiss and touch every inch of her body; clueless to the fact that Damon stood behind her, clenching a bottle of water and watching our every move.

"Is everything all right?" he asked.

"Yes," Octavia said, pulling away from me. She looked at Damon and smiled, wiping her face, then looked back at me. "Are you going to be all right?"

"Yes," I said, looking at Damon. "I'll be fine."

"Here you go," Damon said, extending the water to me.

"Thanks, man. I really appreciate it," I said with forced gratitude.

He turned his attention to Octavia, ignoring me. "Don't cry, baby," he said, pulling Octavia against his body. "Contessa would not want you to be unhappy."

He had that right. The old woman was so adamant that the entire Whitmore clan remain Norman Rockwell perfect that it had cost her, her own life.

"I know," Octavia mumbled. She hugged Damon tightly.

He stroked the length of her hair. "I love you," he said.

"I love you more," Octavia replied.

I watched as Damon's lips formed an arrogant smile. He stared directly at me, and if his eyes could have talked, I would have sworn they were saying, *"You heard her, bitch. She loves me. She's mine."* I turned my head, breaking our stare-off, then opened the bottle of water. I guzzled down half the bottle while listening to Damon console Octavia. I was sure his voice was soothing to her, but it was making my dick limp.

Octavia and Damon volunteered to pay for all of Contessa's funeral arrangements. I told them I wanted to have a graveside service only— something simple, basic, and quick. I explained that it was what Contessa would have wanted, but the truth was that I just wanted to get it over with as soon as possible.

Our entire time at the funeral home, I played the role of grieving nephew perfectly. I was sucking off Octavia's sympathy like a newborn baby on his mother's tit. Damon didn't interfere with the sympathy she was showing me, but I could tell I was working his last nerve. *Good*, I thought.

We wrapped up the details and prepared to leave. Damon volunteered to let Donovan stay for a couple more days to give me time to deal with Contessa's death, but I told him I'd pick my son up in the morning. I didn't want Damon bonding with Donovan any more than necessary. The only reason I didn't take him home that night was because I needed to meet up with Gator, and that was no place for a kid.

"Oh, I forgot to mention it," Damon said, looking at me as the three of us walked through the parking lot to our cars. "We were unable to locate Jay."

"Who?"

"Jay," Damon repeated with his eyebrows raised. "Your cousin. Contessa's *son.*"

I'd had so much going on in my head that I'd forgotten some of the basic shit. "I'm sorry," I said, shaking my head. "I'm still thinking about Auntie. Anyway, you tried to get in touch with Jay and you couldn't?"

Damon stared at me suspiciously. "Yes," he said. "We checked every prison in Tennessee, and none of them have an incarcerated Jay Baker on their rosters."

"When did you check?" I questioned. My gut feeling was telling me it was far too much of a coincidence that Damon had already tried to contact Contessa's son. *Why would he take it upon himself to contact my family?* Granted, we weren't really family, but he didn't know that. Something wasn't right with the entire situation.

"Damon checked as soon as they pronounced Contessa dead," Octavia clarified.

"Wow. Fast results," I said slightly sarcastically.

"Money talks," Damon said blankly.

"He may have been moved to another facility," I suggested. "I remember Auntie mentioning that they were considering sending him a little further west due to overcrowding."

"That makes sense," Octavia said pleasantly. "We thought maybe we had the name wrong."

"No, it's Jay," I said, "but you guys don't need to worry about that. I'll track down the relatives and let them know. I'm sure he'd rather hear it from me anyway."

Damon remained quiet for a moment, then said, "You're probably right."

"Well, I should go," I said, quickly changing the subject. "I'll be by first thing tomorrow morning to pick Donovan up. Thanks for looking after him."

"Take your time." Octavia smiled. "He's a doll, and Jazz loves having him around as a playmate."

Damon nodded his headed in agreement.

If I could have been a fly on the wall of one man's brain, I definitely would have landed on Damon's. When you don't know what a mofo like him is thinking, you've got serious cause to be alarmed.

We said our goodbyes and went our separate ways.

* * *

Twenty minutes later, I was annoyed as fuck as I maneuvered through traffic. My first thought as I switched from the left lane to the right was that the brown Chevy Lumina with tinted windows, riding three cars behind me, just happened to be going the same direction as I was. I wanted to be sure, so I whipped into the Walmart parking lot and waited. The vehicle crept by slowly, then pulled into the parking lot of the Wendy's located right beside Walmart. I waited to see if anyone would exit the vehicle, but when no one did, I knew I was once again being followed. I hadn't realized it before because I'd been followed by a different car. I didn't know if it was a different driver or same driver different vehicle, but hell, I didn't care. Either way, it was nerve-racking. *Damn Gator and his clever car-switching muthafuckas.*

"I wasn't expecting to hear from you so soon," Gator answered on the second ring.

"I have something for you," I said, relaxing against the leather seat. "Another payment." I wanted to make sure he understood that I didn't have it all yet so I didn't let him down again. Leading him to believe otherwise would have been a major no-no. "Would you like me to meet you at your office or just give it to the mofo you assigned to escort me for the last two days?"

"I don't run an escort service," he said firmly, "so why don't you leave the bullshit out and tell me what the hell you're talking about?"

"I'm talking about whoever it is that you've got following me," I said, irritated. "I thought you said you were going to tell your people to fall back?"

"Are you calling me a liar?" he asked.

I wanted to blurt out *"Hell yeah!"* but I knew better.

"If I told you I told my people to fall back, that's what they did. I don't know what you're snortin', but you're starting to piss me off."

"So you don't have anyone tailing me?" I asked.

"No! Now why are you wasting my time?" he snapped.

I sat up, looking out my driver side window. *If Gator didn't send my unwelcome guest, then who did?* Lena popped into my head first. *Naw. It would make no sense for her to put a tail on me. If she wanted to know where I'm going, she'd have just followed me herself.* "Sorry. Looks like I've got a little problem," I said. "I apologize. I'm trippin'."

"You said you have something for me," Gator said, disregarding my apology. "I should expect my package when?"

"You can get it right now," I said, "but I was also hoping for a favor."

"I've granted you enough favors," he said. "You're still breathing, aren't you? Considering what you owe me, don't you think that's some kind of favor?"

"I appreciate your patience," I said as pleasantly as possible through my clenched teeth. "This will be the last one. I just need a little help with…"

There was silence on the other end of the phone.

I was losing his attention, and I knew I had to recapture it quickly. "Look, I can get all the money I owe you plus interest today," I lied, "but it requires some assistance."

After what felt like an hour but was actually only a few minutes of silence, Gator finally said, "Despite everything, I've always liked you, Kelly." His voice held a bit of nostalgia in its tone. "That's why I've shown you more care and consideration than I've ever shown anyone else."

I couldn't deny that, for Gator had been his version of generous with me. I'd gotten my ass kicked and a few broken ribs, but I'd lived to tell about it. Others were not so lucky.

"I hope you remember my generosity," he continued.

* * *

After I spun a web of lies explaining to Gator that I had come up on a lick that would clear my debt with him, he finally agreed to have one of his henchmen meet me. The selected location was an empty house located in the heart of the city. There was an all-white Mercedes-Benz parked by the curb outside the home, which I assumed belonged to Gator's crew.

The home was located in the middle of an older neighborhood, home to mostly older retired couples. There was little to no traffic on the street, giving the neighborhood an abandoned feel.

I checked my rearview mirror to make sure I could still see the Lumina creeping around back there. Sure enough, the car was still hanging behind me. I arrived at the house just after 6, pulled inside the garage, then shifted into park. The garage door immediately began to lower once I was inside.

There was a brother standing inside the garage, waiting for me. As I stepped out of the truck, I noticed that the man looked no older than sixteen. He was a tall, lanky kid with big eyes, low-cut hair, and buck teeth. He wore an oversized Polo shirt and baggy jeans and held a cell phone in one hand and small garage door opener in the other. I stared at him, thinking to myself, *Damn, this kid can't possibly be the so-called henchman Gator promised to send.*

He looked at me, shook his head, and said, "I'm gonna need that down payment first."

I reached back inside my car and pulled out the envelope that held the money Lena had given me. It had become obvious that Gator had written me off as me being soft, or else he just didn't take me seriously. *Why else would he send Baby Snoop to handle grown-man business?* I handed the kid the envelope and waited impatiently as he counted the money and then counted it again. I shook my head.

"What?" he asked, sounding slightly offended.

"Nothing, kid." I laughed.

"So what's next?" he asked, slipping the envelope into his back pocket. After a quick briefing of what I needed him to do, he said, "Let's do this." He handed me the opener and reached into his pocket to retrieve a set of keys.. "Don't scratch my shit," he instructed, tossing the keys to me.

"And don't scratch mine," I ordered, watching him as he climbed behind the wheel of my truck.

"I got this." He laughed.

I hit the button in my hand, and the garage door opened up. I watched as the kid slowly backed down the driveway, out onto the street. Five minutes later, the Lumina zoomed by. Gator's boy led it out of the neighborhood, through the back entrance. After a few turns, we ended up on an unevenly paved road. The street was dimly lit by one single streetlight, the bulb flickering repeatedly. There were no houses on the strip—nothing but large oak trees that shadowed the surrounding sidewalks. I stayed a good distance behind the Lumina to prevent drawing attention to myself and to give myself enough room to see my truck in the distance ahead of him. I watched carefully until I saw the taillights of my truck flash twice, indicating that the driver was tapping his breaks. I watched as my truck came to an abrupt stop, followed by the car that was trailing it. I moved forward, closing the distance between the three of us and placing the pursuer right in the middle of our vehicle sandwich. A minute later, I saw Baby Snoop climb out of my car and jog back to the driver side of the Lumina. He waited for the driver to roll down the window, exchanged a few words, then handed him the cell phone Gator had advised him to bring. Then he ran back to my truck and hopped in. I watched as he made a U-turn in the road and zoomed past me. I dialed the number Baby Snoop had given me earlier.

"Talk to me."

I didn't recognize the male's voice. "Why don't you talk to me instead?" I said firmly.

"Where you wanna start?" He laughed. Whoever he was, he was arrogant as hell.

"Why are you following me?"

"What do you have to hide?" he retaliated.

"Answer the fuckin' question," I said bluntly, flashing my eyes up to my rearview mirror.

"You answer this, muthafucka," he said, "who is the *real* Kelly Baker?"

"Who wants to know?" I asked, processing my next move.

"Me," he said arrogantly.

"You got a problem with me?"

"My people do," he said, "and, see, I'm their problem-solver."

"So where are your people now?" I questioned.

"You're worried about the wrong thing," he said. "I'm your only problem right now."

I shifted the Benz into reverse and backed up slightly, then put the car in drive. I was done with the conversation, for it was getting me nowhere. "You're right," I agreed, "but I'm a problem-solver, too, and now my problem is solved." I flashed my headlights quickly, and the sound of gunfire erupting played in my ear through the phone.

"Mutherfuck—" I heard my caller scream.

His reaction was too late. Baby Snoop had been hiding behind the shadows of one of the trees lining the street, and he'd already opened fire on the car. In spite of his baby face, the li'l fucker came out like a trained assassin. I saw glass cascading like rain and sparks illuminating the night sky.

I watched as the driver side door opened on the Lumina and a tall brother fell out on to the street. He struggled, stumbling over his feet, then finally stood up straight. "Son of a bitch," I mumbled.

He held a gun in one hand while clutching his bloody neck with the other. He looked in my direction, and I could see in his eyes that his thought was to put a bullet right between mine. In that moment, I realized that Baby Snoop was lying on the ground, clutching his chest while he attempted to pull his young self up off the sidewalk. I watched motionless as the man in front of me turned and faced the boy, raised his arm, aimed his weapon, and let off a single shot before falling in the street. The one shot was all he needed; it fatally struck the young man, and he collapsed face first on the sidewalk.

I quickly climbed out of the Benz and rushed to Baby Snoop's side. He lay in a puddle of blood his brains seeping out of the back of his head. Things had gone terribly wrong, and I'd just added another pound to my shitload of trouble. I walked over and checked the other man's pulse but found none. I snatched the envelope out of Baby Snoop's back pocket and took off on foot, running through the grass and past the trees until I reached the place where the kid had parked my truck for me. I burned rubber, almost losing control of the truck as I broke the speed limit to get as far away from the crime scene as I possibly could.

* * *

An hour later, I sat in the dark in my living room, getting lifted. I knew I had to make a move before Gator reached out to me. I had lied my way into that mess, and I was now about to try and lie my way out.

"Business handled?" he answered.

"Naw," I said. "I went by the spot and waited for around an hour. There was no sign of your man."

"What do you mean there was no sign of him?"

"I peeked in the garage, but there were no cars inside or outside of it, and nobody was around. After an hour, I left. I thought maybe you hadn't taken me seriously, so I came back to my spot. Look, Gator, I know I've been fucking up, and I'm thankful to you for keeping me in your good graces. I was serious about that come-up, and I thought you were too, but your man didn't show up. But look…I can understand, and I still have that payment for you." My mouth was running a mile a minute, trying to save my life.

There was an unsettling silence on the other end of the phone that made my heart beat erratically. "I'll get back with you," he finally said before hanging up.

Chapter 14

I couldn't believe Kelly had gotten his dumb ass caught up with a damn dope supplier and that he actually expected *me* to bail him out. I transferred the money from my business account to give to him, but I meant every word I said about the money being a loan. I had to commend him for the good loving he gave me before he departed to handle Contessa's burial arrangements. In all honesty, he deserved some props for that, 'cause he was a beast in bed.

I hated the way things had gone down between Kelly and Contessa though. I'd really liked the woman, and I'd thought she was loyal, but according to Kelly, she was one breath away from selling us out. *I guess you can't even trust a sweet little old lady.* Hell, my mother Gloria was proof of that. That woman could only be trusted with money, and the only way to retain her loyalty was to break her off plenty of bread. That was why when Damon offered to give me a new start, I packed up my daughter and threw caution to the wind. My mother said I'd thrown up my middle finger and given her my ass to kiss, and I guess she was right about that, but I didn't owe her a damn thing. The two of us were barely on speaking terms during the time when I'd been seeing Kenny, and those rare moments when we were okay, it was only because she was willing to babysit Janai—believe me when I say I had to pay the selfish bitch for every single minute, whether she was the child's grandma or not.

Once I established myself in Los Angeles, she began to call and check on me, stating that she'd found Jesus and was now a new woman in Christ. I didn't believe a word of that shit, but I did appreciate the fact that she seemed to finally be showing some concern about my wellbeing. It was nice that she could actually hold a conversation with me that didn't involve her calling me a worthless bitch, which had been one of her favorite taglines for me. As our conversations progressed and we began to grow close, I grew willing to send my mother allowances from time to time. I never sent her more than a couple hundred dollars because I didn't want her to know how successful I really was. In the event that she might revert to her old ways, I didn't want to have to deal with her outrageous demands for money.

See, before I left for California, my mother lived by a you-owe-me policy. She seemed convinced that I, along with my younger sister Felisha, was responsible for repaying her for everything she'd ever done for us since birth. She even wanted compensation for the time we'd lived in her womb! "You worthless bitches owe me for fucking up my body!" she often said. My mother hadn't always been like that though.

When I was younger and Damon and I were high school sweethearts, she'd been a kind, caring housewife, but after my stepfather Vernon ran off and left her, my mother became a bitter, desperate woman who would sell herself—and her children, if necessary—just to make ends meet, literally.

I never knew my biological father, and I was taught not to ask any questions about him, so Vernon became my male role model when I was six, and he eventually married my mother. He was the only man I'd ever known whom I actually looked up to, and he was good to us. He went to work every day and brought home a check every payday. My mother was catered to and, to be honest, slightly lazy. All Vernon ever asked for was a clean house and a hot meal, but she didn't provide that. That was where Felisha and I stepped in. We cooked, cleaned, and washed *her* man's drawers. We never complained because she gave us freedom, and we had free reign to do whatever we wanted. As long as Vernon was around, my mother showed us love and attention, so we made her look good.

One day, though, Vernon didn't come home from work, and everything about her changed. In an instant, she became cold and callous. A week after

Vernon's departure, my mother packed us up, and we left Atlanta in the middle of the night. My mother explained that we were leaving because we could no longer afford to pay the bills without Vernon. When we got to Huntsville, she became an entrepreneur of sorts—a whore, running different men in and out of our home in exchange for cash.

When I hit eighteen, I hauled ass to get out of her home, out from under her reign. I won't lie and say I didn't take her bad habits and dirty lessons with me, as I used my own sexuality to gain what I wanted, resulting in my relationship with Kenny. My only error was that I developed feelings for him and got pregnant, two rules that can never be violated if you're trading sex for money.

I hated the things my mother did, but I loved her for being my mother. She always had a way of manipulating others' feelings and making her ideas—no matter how twisted—seem golden, like fresh rain in a drought. My mother was a user. She used me, she used my sister, and she used Vernon. I'm sure he left because he finally got fed up with it. However, now that she'd been *born again,* my mother proclaimed to be a new woman, and she even had a real job working at the church she attended. I was a changed woman myself, so I was willing to give her a chance.

I pulled up in front of my mother's three-bedroom home and parked, then climbed out of the truck. I double-checked my reflection in the driver side mirror before strolling up the driveway with my keys in hand. I intentionally left my Louis bag on the floor of the car, not wanting to draw any extra attention to myself.

The home looked exactly as I remembered it: the same dirty red bricks and the same crooked white shutters. There was a white Lincoln Continental parked in the driveway with a personalized Jefferson County tag that read "Blessed." The car was parked behind my mother's green two-door Toyota Camry.

I ran my hands down the front of my dress, smoothing out wrinkles that were all a figment of my imagination. I knocked once, then again on the front door.

"Who is it?" I heard my mother call from the other side.

"It's Lena," I replied.

"Whatever you're selling, we don't want none."

"Mama, it's me!" I exhaled loudly. "Alicia."

"Who?"

"Alicia," I repeated.

The door swung open, and I was standing face to face with the woman who'd given me life. Gloria didn't look a day over thirty, and she carried herself as such. Her hair, which was normally covered by a wig, was cut close to her head and highlighted blonde. My mother stood at five-one and was approximately 125 pounds, and her skin was the color of toasted bread. She and my sister were almost the splitting image of one another, but I'd apparently taken after my father. My mother was dressed in a bright yellow maxi-dress that flowed down around her ankles and hung slightly off her shoulders—a dramatic change from the tight-as-a-glove dresses she wore before my departure to LA.

I waited, practically holding my breath, anticipating her response to my showing up unannounced.

"You should have called," she said with a straight face.

"I'm sorry," I said, clearing my throat. "It was a spur-of-the-moment decision. I can come back if you want. I'll just—"

"No you can't," she said bluntly.

"Should've known," I grumbled, turning to walk away. *I don't know why I wasted my time,* I thought. *She's still a bi—*

"Alicia!" she called behind me.

I continued to walk, ignoring her call.

"Alicia, baby! Come back!"

My mother has never called me baby. Even when I was a child and my stepfather was around, I was never called that. The only person she'd ever referred to by that term of endearment was Vernon or whatever man she was dealing with.

I stopped my stride and turned to look at her.

She held her arms open. "Baby, I was just playing," she said lovingly. "Please come back."

In all the things I had accomplished, all the strides I made, I still could not resist the feeling of warmth and joy such a simple expression of love from my mother provided. I hurried back, walking in her direction. Within seconds, I was nestled in her embrace.

"It's good to see you, baby," she said, pulling away. "You look..." She smiled and shook her head. "Beautiful!" she added. "I barely recognized you."

"Thanks." I smiled. "That's a good thing."

She laughed.

"And you look great, Gloria."

"Gloria? Call me Mama," she said.

I tried to contain my shock, as I hadn't called her that since I was fifteen, and she'd always advised me and my sister that calling her that in public was bad for business. So we always called her by her government name, even in private. "Um, okay. Mama, you look great," I said sincerely.

"Good, clean living will do that for a person," she said, taking me by the hand. "Let's go inside."

"You have company?" I asked, looking back at the Lincoln in the driveway.

"No, baby. That's mine."

"It's nice," I said honestly, wondering how she could possibly afford such a ride.

"Just another blessing." She sighed. "The good people at New Joy Church gave it to me. I guess they got tired of the little green machine breaking down on me."

I felt an ounce of guilt as I flashed my eyes at the rusted-out Toyota. I had given Kelly a damn car while my own mother was receiving donations from strangers.

Inside, my mother had new furnishings, including a nice plush sofa and loveseat. The furniture wasn't extravagant, but it was nice and clean. The house smelled of fresh Pine-sol, and the wooden floors shined like new money. There were beautiful black portraits adorning the walls, pictures of happy families, and I saw framed pictures of my sister and me on the coffee and end tables.

"Where is Kiya?" she asked as the two of us sat on the sofa.

"Janai," I corrected.

She hesitated, then shook her head. "Forgive me," she said humbly. "I have to get used to calling her that. How is Janai?"

"She's great," I said. "She's in school, so she's staying with one of my friends while I'm visiting." I had actually asked Joni to look after my daughter while I was away taking care of business.

"Oh. How long will you be here?"

"Just for a few days," I said.

"Where are you staying?" she asked. "You know I have an open-door policy. You're welcome to stay with me."

An open-door policy? Since when? I thought. I was still having a difficult time accepting the new woman sitting next to me. "Thanks," I said appreciatively, "but I'm staying with a friend."

"Would this friend happen to be...a man?" she asked with raised eyebrows. There was a pleasant look of excitement on my mother's face.

"Yes, Mama, but we we're just friend," I said, referring to Kelly. Granted, Kelly had completely put it on me when the two of us had sex. We both agreed that we were merely satisfying our carnal needs.

"So there is no man in your life?" she probed. "You look too good to be all alone, sweetie."

I smiled proudly. "Well, there is someone I *want* to be with," I advised her, referring to Damon, "but our situation is...complicated."

"The only complication there is when it comes down to getting a man is death," she said, matter-of-factly. "Is he dead?"

"Of course not!" I laughed lightly. "He's alive, healthy, and...married."

"Another Kenny?" She exhaled loudly.

"No," I said quickly. "He is *nothing* like Kenny. He's the exact opposite. In fact, being married is the *only* thing the two of them had in common." I studied her expression.

She frowned, then clasped her hands together. "How does he feel about you?"

"He loves me," I said confidently.

"Where did you meet this man?" she questioned.

My mother seemed genuinely interested, so I told her everything, even how Damon had helped me open my salon.

"Wow, baby! I had no idea you were doing such good things!" she commented. "A salon owner? Wow."

"Yes, and I couldn't have done it without Damon," I said, reminiscing about the kindness he'd shown me. "I know I've been in this type of situation before, but—"

"Every situation is different," she said, much to my surprise. "Certainly if this man went through so much for you, he must have genuine feelings for you. Maybe you should go for it."

"I am," I said proudly. "I've already set the wheels in motion."

"That's great, baby girl," she purred enthusiastically. "All I want is the best for you, but setting the wheels in motion doesn't mean you're moving forward. If you want this Damon, you'd better make some moves that'll get you somewhere—that is, if he's worth it."

"Of course he is," I answered, slightly defensive. "He's Damon Whitmore."

"And he loves you?"

"He said so."

"Then why aren't you with him already?"

"I haven't had the chance to show him what I have to offer," I said honestly. "We never got our chance. I told you he's married now."

"Then I guess you better create a chance," Mama said firmly.

I didn't reply. Instead, I let her words sink in, digesting their meaning. I knew all I needed was a chance to show Damon how good the two of us could be together—just one chance. My mother was right: I hadn't had the chance, but I needed to create one, and I needed to do it immediately.

Before leaving my mother's home, I gave her a big hug and a little something to put in her bank account. She begged me to stay in touch and to bring Janai to visit, and I assured her I would, as soon as I got myself and my daughter settled in; I'd decided the two of us were moving back to Huntsville.

Chapter 15

Damon

I had been a couple of days since I'd spoken to Lawrence, and when I'd attempted to make contact, I either received his voicemail or no response to my e-mails. It wasn't like Lawrence to be MIA, and it had me concerned. I decided to give him a few more days, assuming he'd gotten caught up trying to locate Contessa's son before I considered trying to locate him. I needed to know what progress he was making on the case, and I needed to know immediately. I remembered him saying he'd had a bad vibe about the whole situation with Contessa, and I was beginning to feel the same way. For one thing, there was something completely wrong with Kelly's explanation of the location of his cousin. For another, when Kelly came to pick up Donovan earlier that morning, something in his eyes didn't sit well with me. I knew he was mourning the death of his aunt, but some extra shit in the way he looked at me caught my attention.

I decided to clear my head and settle my nerves by taking the day off and treating my beautiful wife to a shopping spree. That night, I made her a home-cooked meal, which the two of us enjoyed by candlelight. After that, I ran her a warm bubble bath. I turned the lights off and surrounded our tub with her favorite vanilla-scented candles, turned on her favorite Maxwell CD, and left her alone so she could enjoy her private time.

After playing the part of Jasmine's pony and crawling around on my hands and knees until *I* was tired, I gave my daughter a bath and put her to bed.

I decided to check on a few foreclosure leads I'd received earlier via e-mail. I hated that there were so many people—good people—who were losing their homes, but I loved the opportunity to help others on their journey to home ownership and independence. I pulled up the MLS listings for the properties that interested me. One was a three-bedroom home in Malibu. From the pictures on the Internet, the home looked to be in good condition, but I knew pictures don't tell the whole story behind a property. I decided to shoot an e-mail to Julian, my property manager, asking him to do a walkthrough with our personal home inspector. There was a nice three-bedroom condo in Huntsville that also caught my eye, and I decided I'd check that out as soon as I had a free moment.

Julian responded to my e-mail quickly, letting me know he'd view the home within the next twenty-fours hours.

I completed my property search and then checked the rest of the messages in my inbox. The only other message of interest was from "LJW." I opened it only to discover that it was from Lena, advising me that she wanted to add Joni as her new point of contact for anything relating to her lease or business. She provided Joni's number and e-mail address, then ended the message with a courteous, "Thank you." I sent her a reply stating that I was in complete agreement and forwarded her message to Julian.

* * *

I tightened my embrace around Octavia while stroking her bare back with my fingertips. The two of us lay naked in the comfort of our bed, after making what I could only describe as sweet love. Now there was silence between us as she lay with her hand on my chest and her head resting above my heart.

"I don't want to hire another nanny," she said lowly.

I was pleased with her statement. I had been against hiring a nanny in the first place, but I'd given in to Octavia's request and agreed to open our home and our lives to a stranger. In the end, I was happy with her choice, as Contessa was good with Jasmine and was an incredible help around our home, but I still would have preferred an alternative to childcare for our daughter. "Would you like to reconsider daycare?" I asked.

"I still think it's better if Jazz receives one-on-one personal attention."

"Another in-home babysitter?"

"No." She sighed. "I was thinking about working from home for a little while."

"Are you serious?" I questioned. In the time the two of us had been together, Octavia had never had the slightest desire to be a stay-at-home mom. In fact, she had been adamantly opposed to the idea when I'd brought it up. Now, hearing that she was considering my first suggestion made me even more happy than I had been just seconds earlier.

"I am completely serious," she said, sitting up beside me in the bed. "It doesn't make sense to put Jazz through another transition. Besides, it will only be for a couple months, until she starts pre-k. I'll have to hire an extra person or two for the restaurants in the event we have a rush when I can't be there, but I think it'll work."

"What can I do to help make the change easier on you?" I asked sincerely.

"Well, prepare to share the office downstairs." She laughed lightly.

"I've got a better idea." I smiled. "Why don't we do some renovations and expand the office so you can have your desk and I can keep mine?"

"His and hers?" she said.

"Yes, and we can set up a network so the information from the restaurants are linked to your PC."

"Hmm...yeah, I'd like that," she said appreciatively. "I was thinking of installing cameras in my offices—not that I think any of my employees are thieves or anything, but I just wanna make sure everyone stays on the up and up. You know how it is when the boss is away."

"We can do that," I reassured her. "I'll have the guys who did our system here install it and set it up so you can monitor it here, from the house." The mention of cameras reminded me that I needed to check on the one I'd had installed on the outside of our home. I had noticed that the picture was somewhat fuzzy weeks earlier, but considering everything that had been going on with Kelly and Donovan and Contessa, it had slipped my mind.

"I like that idea, baby." Octavia smiled sweetly before leaning down and kissing my lips. "I figure on the days when I want to go in to work, I'll just take Jazz along."

"Or she can come to work with her daddy," I suggested. I wanted to be sure that Octavia knew I was happy about her decision and also that I was willing to do anything I could to make things easier for her.

"That sounds good too." She smiled.

"I'll holler at Savoy and see what he's working on," I told her. "If he doesn't have anything in the works, we can contract him to do the renovations on the office." I hadn't seen Savoy in a while and had barely spoken to him, but he was my boy, and no matter when the two of us got together, it was all love.

"That would be perfect." Again, she smiled. "Plus, it'll give Shontay an excuse to stay in the Ville a little longer." She continued to smile as she climbed on top of me and began straddling my waist. "You always have the best ideas," she purred, brushing her nails over my chest lightly.

"Really?"

"Of course you do," she said sweetly. "It was your idea to marry me, was it not?" She giggled lightly.

"It was," I said, staring into her eyes, "and it was the best idea I've ever had."

Octavia's eyes shone brightly, like stars in the night sky. "I love you, Damon Whitmore."

"I love you more, Octavia Whitmore."

She pressed her lips to mine and gave me a kiss that would have made the world's strongest man weak in the knees; my man instantly began to rise. "Hold up," she said, patting my chest lightly.

I watched her as she climbed off the bed and hurried into the bathroom. I admired her naked backside, thinking to myself that I was a very lucky man indeed.

It sounded as if she was rummaging through a drawer, and a minute later, she returned with a small box in her hands. She lay the box on my chest, cocked her head to the side, and stared at me.

"And what is this?" I asked, pulling myself up against the headboard.

"Open it," she said, standing by the bed.

I stared at the box. It was the same Grogan's Jewelers box I'd used to give her a new pair of diamond earrings. "Isn't this the box I gave you a few weeks ago?" I teased.

"Yep," she said, batting her eyelashes. "It's called recycling. Give wifey a break."

"My bad, boo." I chuckled lightheartedly. "It's the thought that counts, right?"

"Yes."

I laughed again while opening the box. Inside was the pink plastic case where Octavia usually stored her birth control pills. I was slightly confused and assumed it was some kind of prank—a joke I wasn't quite getting. "What does this mean? What are you saying, babe?" I asked with raised eyebrows.

"Don't look so terrified," she teased, sitting on the edge of the bed.

"Never scared, beautiful," I said seriously. "Just curious."

She took the case and the box from my hands and set them on the nightstand. She stroked my cheek lightly, staring into my eyes. "Do you know how perfect you are?" she asked.

"I'm not perfect," I said honestly. "Far from it."

"You're perfect for me," she said sweetly, "and truthfully, that's all that matters."

"Is it?" I asked.

"Yes," she said. "You are the yang to my yin, the Clyde to my Bonnie, the die to my ride, the—"

"I get it, I get it." I laughed.

She smiled. "You're my partner," she said, "and what make you happy makes me happy. I know how happy being Jasmine's daddy makes you, so I was thinking we could multiply that happiness times two."

"You *want* to have another baby?" I asked.

"If you still do."

I pulled her up on my lap. "Of course I do."

"Good," she whispered, wrapping her arms around my neck, "because nothing would make me happier than having a son who's just like his daddy."

I thought about the lies I'd told her in the past, and I felt a surge of guilt. "No, baby," I said. "Our son will be *better* than me. I'll make sure of that."

Chapter 16

The only thing better than waking up in the morning is waking up in the arms of the man you love. When I opened my eyes and realized I was still in Damon's arms, I couldn't suppress my smile or stop giving thanks. Despite the tragedy that had taken place in our home with the loss of Contessa, there was love and happiness in the air—the kind of love and happiness that only comes around once in a lifetime, true love and true happiness. After getting Jasmine and myself dressed for the day, I led my little girl downstairs so the two of us could make Daddy breakfast.

Shontay was already up and sitting by the pool, with the morning edition of *The Huntsville Times* in her hands.

I lifted Jasmine up into her highchair before opening the patio door to properly greet my friend. "Good morning!" I smiled, admiring how Shontay seemed to glow under the sunlight.

She looked rested and refreshed in a pair of fitted jeans and a plain white T-shirt, and she was wearing her hair up in a large afro puff. "Morning." She smiled and looked over at me. "How are you?"

"I'm un-freaking-believable," I said happily. "And you?"

"I'm good." She smiled brightly. "Went for my morning run and talked to my man. By the way, he'll be here this weekend." Her smile seemed to radiate at the mere mention of Savoy. It was so compelling that I was forced to smile too. "Life is good," she said.

"That it is," I agreed. "I'm getting ready to make breakfast. Would you care to join us?"

"No thank you," she replied. "I've already eaten. I have to get back into my workout routine now that I will be back in the company of my man."

"Damon and I work out too—several times a week," I said devilishly.

Shontay raised her eyebrows. "You are such a freak."

"No, I'm freaky, and there is a difference." I laughed.

"One has a Y." She laughed. "To me, that's the *only* difference."

"Maybe or maybe not." I laughed. "Speaking of your man," I said seriously, "do you know if he's busy with any projects right now?"

"Not that I know of," she answered. "What's up?"

I brought Shontay up to speed on mine and Damon's conversation from the night before, including my decision to work from home and Damon's desire to expand our home office. I also shared with her our plans to conceive another child.

"Wow." Shontay looked utterly speechless upon hearing my news. "I would have never imagined in a thousand years that you'd take on the role of stay-at-home mom."

"Me neither, but things change," I reminded her. "I mean, I never thought you'd become the bold Foxy Brown suga you are today, but look at you."

"I didn't either, but I must say I wear it well," she said, smiling proudly.

I loved Shontay's newfound confidence; it suited her, and it was long overdue. "Exactly," I said to my friend. "So you get my point."

"I do, and I would love to have another godchild. I promise I won't miss almost a year of the next one's life."

We both laughed.

"Good," I told her.

Shontay joined me in the kitchen so the two of us could continue our conversation while I prepared breakfast: poached eggs, turkey bacon, grits, and homemade biscuits. When Damon came down, she gave each of us a hug and Jasmine a kiss before departing.

Damon looked handsome, as always, in his dark suit, shirt, and silk tie. Standing next to him, I felt underdressed in my fitted sundress, but I was comfortable as hell. "So what do you ladies have planned for today?" Damon questioned as we sat at the breakfast table. He had a full plate in front of him and the "Sports" section of the newspaper lying next to him.

Jasmine sat beside him in her high chair, feeding herself Cheerios.

"Jasmine and I are going to see Mommy and Daddy," I told him, while I skimmed through the "Local News" section of the paper. "Also, Shontay wants me to run her over to get her car out of storage sometime today."

Shontay had purchased the Lexus before she and Savoy had departed for their trip around the world, and it had been in storage every since. I was hoping and praying she still had a car to pick up.

"Well, let me know if you have any problems with the car," he said. "Why don't you take Shontay to that spa you like? My treat."

Although, I made good money, it was always Damon's treat. He spoiled me, and I loved him for it. "I'll check and see what else Tay has planned for the day. I'm sure she has some preparations to do before Savoy touches down this weekend, but I don't know any lady who'd pass up a free trip to the spa." I continued to scan the paper until I saw something that caught my eye. "Whoa! Our city is getting just as bad as some of the bigger ones," I said, as I continued reading the article about the men who'd been found dead.

"What's up, babe?" he asked between bites of food.

"They found two men dead the other night," I said, glancing up at him. "Both suffered from multiple gunshot wounds," I explained, paraphrasing the article. "Says here that one man's been identified as Victor Henson and the other as Emerson Bailey." I could feel Damon's eyes on me. I looked and watched Damon as he wiped the corners of his mouth slowly.

"May I see that?" he asked, pointing to the paper.

"Sure." I handed him the section that contained details of the crimes. According to the article, the men had shot each other over some sort of dispute, but HPD was still looking for any witnesses to come forward. "Isn't that sad?" I said, shaking my head. "It's like Huntsville's become the Old West."

Damon looked horrified as he scanned the article. He looked extremely disturbed by the information, and he didn't say a word.

"Baby, are you okay?"

"Um, yeah, boo, I'm fine," Damon recited slowly. "Just thinking about how short life is." He folded the paper over and pushed away from the table before standing up. He kissed Jasmine on the top of her head before walking around to me. "I better get going," he said. The look in his eyes was distant and troubling.

I stood and wrapped my arms around his neck.

He hugged me tightly and slowly pulled away.

"Are you sure you're okay?" I asked, concerned.

"Yes, baby, I'm fine," he said. Then he leaned down and kissed me softly on the lips with a tender, short kiss. "Talk to you later, boo," he said.

"Bye, babe."

* * *

Shontay followed me to my parents' home after we picked up her car from Public Storage.

Mama greeted us at the door with a smile on her face and open arms. She looked gorgeous in her sky-blue, off-the-shoulder, above-the-knee dress and matching sky-blue, open-toe heels. I had to be the proudest daughter in the world when it came down to my parents. They were my heroes, my inspiration.

I listened as Shontay brought them up to speed on her travels and the countries she'd visited while she was away.

After that, Daddy took Jasmine outside with him, leaving the rest of us ladies alone.

"So where are the pictures?" Mama asked, as we all sat around the dining room table, me on Mama's left and Shontay on her right.

"I took plenty, but unfortunately I don't have them with me," Shontay explained bashfully.

I hadn't bothered to ask her for photos; I'd been too busy celebrating the fact that she was home.

"Did something happen to your camera?" Mama asked with raised eyebrows. My mother had a way with words that commanded attention and the truth.

"No. I mean the pictures are with Savoy," Shontay said.

"And where is he?" Mama probed.

"In Atlanta, *but* he'll be here this weekend," Shontay replied quickly.

"I see. The two of you flew into different cities?" Mama questioned.

"Yes, ma'am," Shontay replied politely.

"Why?" Mama asked.

"It's a long story." Shontay laughed lightly. For the first time since her return, she appeared nervous. Mama had that effect on people.

"I have time," Mama said matter-of-factly.

"Well, we kind of had a temporary breakup," Shontay said slowly, "but we're back together now—or we will be when he gets here."

"What led to the breakup?" Mama quizzed, folding her hands together in front of her on the table. "Did he cheat? Lie? Lay his hands on you?"

"No, ma'am. Nothing like that," Shontay answered slowly.

"So what then?" Mama asked again, looking from Shontay to me.

I shrugged my shoulders and looked at Shontay. I could have sworn I saw signs of perspiration on her forehead.

"Well…" Shontay began.

I listened as she explained to my mother, word for word, what she'd explained to me about her refusal to commit to Savoy and his refusal to share.

"Savoy is a good man," Mama said, shaking her head. "Is he not?"

"Yes, ma'am," Shontay answered.

"So why play games?" Mama asked. "Why not love and enjoy every waking second the two of you have?"

"Whew. That's a good question, Mama," I sighed, shaking my head. "I mean, for the life of me, I don't understand why women always try to mess up a good thing, and—"

"I don't need your help with this one," Mama said, cutting me off, "and like you're one to talk!"

Oh, no the hell she didn't, I thought.

Mama lowered her eyes at me and looked at me with an expression that said, *"Yes the hell I did. And what about it?"*

I decided to back down gracefully by giving her an innocent smile. I loved my mother, and she was one of my heroes, but I would fear her ass-whoopings until my dying day.

"I guess I was just caught up in being me," Shontay confessed. "New money, new look—"

"So you wanted to keep your options open to look for something new?" Mama concluded. "Something better than the gentleman who went out of his way to sweep you off your feet and love you through your mess? Something better than a man who is not only extremely handsome but also a hardworking, talented businessman?" Mama looked at me when she said it.

I couldn't help but feel she was throwing some of her words of wisdom at me. "I married mine!" I said loudly, holding up my left hand and waving my ring finger in the air in front of me. "I think I've made up for any error or omissions."

"Lower your voice and put your hand down, young lady," Mama ordered.

Grown or not, I exhaled softly and did exactly as she requested.

"I'm not fussing," Mama said. "I just want my girls to be happy for as long as possible, which means neither one of you have a minute or even a second to waste when it comes to the ones you love. If I could take back the time Charles and I lost, I would. I'd pay for it. Don't get me wrong, because I love every moment we share now, but to take back those years and add them to the years to come would be wonderful. I can't and won't dwell on it, but I also won't pretend I don't long for every wasted second now." Mama's eyes were filled with warmth and passion as she spoke.

I could see in her face that she was concerned about how many minutes she had left. I reached over and placed my hand on hers. The two of us interlocked our fingers tightly. I tried not to focus on the negatives associated with my mother's illness, and having a mother who was so strong and resilient made that easy. Mama made everything seem like a walk in the park, but in moments like those, I was reminded that she was human. Under all her armor, she was just like me: a fragile being, vulnerable in the game of life.

"It won't happen again, "Shontay said, smiling. "I know who I am now, and I know what I want. I will never let him go again," she spoke confidently, holding her head high.

"Good," Mama smiled, taking one of Shontay's hands in hers. "I want you to always remember that...*both* of you," she said, looking at me.

I smiled and nodded my head in agreement, and Shontay did the same.

* * *

I offered Mama a trip to the day spa along with me and Shontay. She declined but volunteered to babysit her granddaughter for the night. I was not one to miss an opportunity to run naked through the house with my hubby, so I naturally accepted. I felt refreshed and revived after Shontay and I left Terrame Day Spa, for full-body massages, manicures, and pedicures will do that to a girl, especially when they didn't cost me a dime.

After getting the star treatment at the spa, Shontay and I decided to go our separate ways so she could do some house-hunting and I could treat my husband to a lunch date. Damon had seemed so down when he'd left for his office earlier that morning, so I decided I'd pay him a visit in an attempt to help lighten his mood.

I still remember one of our very first lunch dates. Damon had planned a picnic for the two of us at his office. That was long before he'd hired his staff, back before Nomad Investments was a household name in Huntsville. I decided to re-create that date by treating my husband to an indoor picnic. I stopped by Publix and purchased strawberries, whipped cream, and two submarine sandwiches, then stopped by our home to wash the fruit and take a quick shower. I slipped on my pink, fitted, strapless, above-the-knee wrap dress and pulled my hair up in a classic but sexy bun. I wore just the right amount of soft pink lip gloss and stepped into a pair of pink five-inch stilettos. I packed our picnic basket, complete with silverware, glasses, and a bottle of champagne from our liquor cabinet, grabbed a blanket, and was ready to seduce my man all over again.

"Come in," Damon answered from the other side of his office door.

I opened the door and stepped inside. I had a blanket draped neatly over my arm and was carrying the basket, and I closed the door behind me.

Damon sat behind his desk, staring at the screen of his PC. When he looked up and saw me, his smiled stretched from one side of his face to the other.

"Hey, handsome." I smiled and walked up to the desk. I set the basket and blanket down before extending my open arms to my man.

"Hello, gorgeous," he said, standing and then walking around the desk.

The two of us embraced like it was the first time we'd seen each other in forever.

"And to what do I owe the honor?" he asked, stepping back and looking at me. It was obvious that my husband appreciated what he saw.

"I thought I would surprise my sexy boyfriend for lunch," I said, batting my eyes.

"And what a surprise this is!" he said, kissing me softly on the lips.

"I think the best husband in the world deserves a nice surprise once in a while," I said sweetly.

"Thanks," Damon said solemnly. "You don't know how much I appreciate hearing those words."

"It's the truth," I said sincerely.

Then, there was an awkward moment of silence between the two of us, and it was not something I was accustomed to. I chalked it up as Damon having had a long morning and decided to continue my quest to lighten his mood.

"Do you remember one of the very first lunch dates we had was here?" I asked. I picked the blanket up and spread it out on the floor in front of Damon's desk.

"I remember," he said. His tone seemed to lighten as he reminisced along with me. "That was before I opened the office, before I had a staff. Remember, it was in the room we now use for client consultations?"

"Yes," I smiled. "I loved that room."

Damon's original office was located in what I considered to be a high-traffic area. He later relocated, but both rooms were huge, equipped with wall-mounted flat-screen televisions, surround sound, private baths, and glass and wood furnishings. His original location had French doors that opened into the room, whereas the current location had a solid wood door. Although Louisa's desk sat only a few feet away, I still felt the new office was more secluded and private; for me, that was a plus.

"If I remember correctly, it was your idea for me to switch rooms," he reminded me.

He was correct about that. Granted, I loved the room he had before, but it was too close to all the action at Nomad Investments. As part of my vow to keep my marriage interesting, I liked to stop by occasionally and break my man off. This had come to a halt one day when the two of us were in his office getting hot and heavy and he received a call from Louisa informing us that although we had the blinds drawn, she and all the employees passing by could still see the silhouette of my naked ass. Those weren't Louisa's choice of words though; if I remembered correctly, she'd said, "What the good Lord blessed her with." However, the point was, everyone could see my ass. I was thankful that on the particular day, many of Damon's employees had stepped out of the office for a group lunch date, but from time to time, I could still see the admiration in the eyes of the ones who were present.

"If I remember right, you still had your clothes on when Louisa called us," I reminded him.

He laughed. "Baby, you know how to put on one hell of a show."

"Uh…thanks," I said, grabbing the picnic basket. "I'm glad you're pleased."

"Always." He smiled and helped me down onto the blanket. Damon grabbed the remote for his sound system and put on one of my favorite tracks, "Fortunate" by Maxwell, before joining me on the floor.

"I know you still have business to handle today," I said, opening the basket, "but I brought one of our old favorites." I pulled out the bottle of Rosa and two champagne flutes.

"I do have work to do, but a glass won't hurt me."

"But I plan to…" I said suggestively.

"And I plan to let you." He smiled.

The two of us laughed and talked, reflecting on our first date and the journey that life had taken us through. After we enjoyed our lunch together, I was preparing to serve Damon dessert when I heard a knock on the door.

"I should have told Louisa not to disturb us," Damon mumbled. He gave me a sweet peck on the cheek before opening his office door.

Louisa stood at the door with two men standing behind her. One was short, with olive-colored skin, a pot belly, and a receding hairline. The other was tall, a pale, older-looking man with blond hair.

"Sorry to interrupt you," Louisa said politely, "but these two men are detectives, and they would like to speak with you, Damon."

"I'm Detective Cruz," said the short man, holding up a badge. "This is Detective O'Connor."

The second man also displayed his badge.

"Thank you, Louisa," Damon said. "That will be all for now."

Louisa excused herself, leaving Damon and the men standing face to face.

"Gentleman, can this wait?" Damon asked coolly. "As you can see, my wife is here to join me for lunch, and—"

"This won't take long," the short man interrupted, looking a me. "We just have a few questions about Victor Henson."

I remembered the name from the newspaper article, but I had no idea why they wanted to talk to Damon about it.

Damon looked back at me. He didn't look the least bit concerned or surprised that the men had come to his office. "Sweetheart, do you mind?" he coaxed.

"Not at all," I said, shaking my head. I thought for one brief moment that Damon was going to invite the men in, but he didn't. Instead he told me he'd return shortly, and then he exited the office, pulling the door closed behind him.

Two glasses of Rosa later, I was itching to know what was going on. I decided to go locate my husband and the detectives. I found the three men outside in the parking lot, talking at the side of the building. I decided to stay within earshot but out of sight for the moment.

"We checked the phone records, and your number was the last number he called," Detective Cruz said, his tone was overflowing with accusations. "Did he tell you of any problems or issues he might have had with anybody?"

"As I explained to you before, Detective, when I spoke to Victor, he seemed to be in good spirits, as always, and he didn't mention any problems or issues."

"And Victor was a client of yours?" Detective O'Connor interjected.

"Well, he was looking to become one," Damon said. There wasn't an ounce of fear or nervousness in his voice, though he did sound more than slightly annoyed.

"Where were you the night Victor was murdered?" Detective Cruz questioned.

"I was with my wife and daughter that night," Damon answered.

"And your wife can corroborate that?" Cruz asked.

"Yes," I said, stepping out of the shadows.

The men all turned and looked in my direction.

"He was with me, and I'm also willing to vouch for the fact that my husband and I had our phones off that night for *intimate* reasons."

"I see," Detective Cruz said blankly. "Well, I guess that's all for now.

Thank you for your time, Mr…and Mrs. Whitmore. If you think of anything that might help our investigation, feel free to contact us." He reached into the front pocket of his suit jacket and handed a small white business card to Damon.

"Mr. Whitmore, Mrs. Whitmore," the men said as they walked off and headed toward a black Crown Victoria with tinted windows.

"It seems everyone is guilty by association these days," I said, watching the car as it drove off. " It's sad."

"Octavia, I've, uh…I have something to tell you, baby," Damon said, and the seriousness in his voice captured my full and undivided attention.

"What is it?" I asked.

"There is something I haven't mentioned, about the man who was killed."

"What is it?" I asked, nearly in a shaky voice because he was making me slightly nervous.

"Walk with me," he said, taking me by the hand.

I watched Damon carefully as the two of us walked hand in hand down the sidewalk. I was concerned and anxious to hear what he had to say.

"His real name is…er, was Lawrence. Victor was an alias he used for work. I'd known him for years," he began. "He wasn't just a potential client of mine. I was a client of his."

"What kind of work did he do?" I asked. There were several different scenarios running through my head. As much as I hated to admit it, one of them involved my husband confessing some gay love affair he'd had with the man. Damon had never given me any indication of such tendencies, but my mother had warned me to always be prepared for anything.

"Lawrence was a man of many talents and…skills," he said.

Aw, hell, I thought. *Here it comes.*

"He worked undercover for me," Damon continued.

"What do you mean he worked undercover?" I asked slowly.

"He was a private investigator, of sorts," he said.

"A PI?" I questioned, relieved.

"Yes."

I was happy and one the verge of smiling until I remembered that my trail hadn't been so clean recently. The first thing that popped in my mind in light of that news was the kiss I'd shared with Kelly. The second was our failed attempt to have sex. I could feel a knot developing in my throat and what felt like an ocean gushing in my stomach. *What if Lawrence was investigating me? How long had he been on the case? Why in the hell is Damon so calm? This must be the calm before the storm.* "Damon, why would you need a private investigator?" I asked cautiously.

"I had him following Kelly," he said.

Oh shit! I stopped walking and squeezed his hand tightly but chose to look away. I couldn't look him in his eyes, for I was too fearful of what was coming next. "Why would you have someone following Kelly?" I asked.

"Because I don't trust him," Damon confessed. "Something about him seems too good to be true."

"You trusted him at first, right?" I asked, forcing myself to look at him. "What happened to change that?"

This time, he looked away.

Oh hell! He knows, I thought.

"It's just a hunch, a feeling I have," he finally answered.

I focused on his answer. "A hunch? Is that how you knew Ms. Contessa's son wasn't where she said he was?" When Damon told me he had tried to locate Jay, I had wondered how he had done so with such impeccable timing. Now things were starting to make sense. "What are you, psychic?" *God, I hope not!*

"I'm not psychic that I know of, but I did have a feeling, and Lawrence was checking Contessa out, too, because of her relation to Kelly."

"And just what did he discover?"

"Besides the fact about her son," he said, shaking his head, "I don't know. Lawrence was murdered before I could find out anything more."

"Well, what did this PI of yours find out about Kelly?" I was still skeptical, but I needed to know if Damon knew.

"I don't know." He exhaled deeply. "But what I do know is that Lawrence was working Kelly's case when he was murdered."

"How do you know? Couldn't he have moved on to another case? Or maybe he was working more than one at a time," I said, sounding skeptical. I knew what Damon was insinuating about Kelly, and I found that hard to believe. *Did I actually allow a killer in our home? Near our daughter?*

"Because I knew Lawrence," he said. "If he was going to change his game plan for any reason, he would've called me. That was just how he was, a true professional. He wouldn't go against the plan without contacting me first."

"What about the man who was found dead with him? Do you think Kelly had something to do with that?" I asked.

"I don't think so," he said. "Whoever killed Lawrence was a professional, a hired gun, and that takes money. Not only that, but Lawrence was a professional himself. Whoever took him out had to have help. There was no way one person could have taken the man down alone. It was a setup." Damon seemed passionate about his hypothesis.

"But you don't trust Kelly, right? In that case, we should be cautious," I concluded.

"Definitely. We need to put some distance between him and us," he said. "The memorial service is this weekend, and now that Contessa is no longer with us, we have no real reason to associate with him."

I nodded my head in agreement, and I felt a surge of guilt about the entire situation. "I'm sorry," I said sincerely, staring into Damon's eyes.

"About what, baby?"

"I brought him into our home," I said lowly. "I should have never…" I was not only referring to the possibility that Kelly had something to do with the murders, but also to my hidden indiscretions, even if I didn't have the courage to speak of them aloud.

"Shh," Damon said, pulling me into his arms. "What's done is done. I just think it's best that we disassociate ourselves with him as soon as this weekend is over."

I thought about all the lines I'd crossed with Kelly, and I had to agree. "Me too," I said. I wrapped my arms around Damon's shoulders, and as he held me tightly, his words echoed in my head. I knew in my heart that there was more to his story, more behind his decision to investigate Kelly, more that he wouldn't—or couldn't—tell me. I just couldn't stop wondering how much more.

Chapter 17

Kelly

I hadn't heard from Gator, and I was relieved about that. When it came to dealing with that lunatic, no news was usually good news. The media stated that the man who'd been following me was Victor Henson, a factory worker from Opelika, Alabama. Whoever the man really was, he was good—damn good. He was so good that he maintained his cover, even in death.

I listened as Octavia's pastor recited a scripture as the casket that held Contessa's body was lowered into the ground. I had to give it to Damon; he put the bitch away nicely—from the dress Octavia had picked out for her to the long-stemmed white roses surrounding her grave, to the coffin I playfully named "the Cadillac of caskets." I pulled my collar up around my neck and tried not to concentrate on the cold rain that insisted on making the day even more miserable.

"Please bow your heads," Pastor Davis said.

I bowed my head but chose to keep my eyes open as the man began to pray. I lifted my head slightly and looked across at Octavia. She stood leaning close to Damon, with her eyes closed and her head bowed. Damon held a dark umbrella with his left hand and had his right arm around Octavia's shoulder. His head was bowed, too, and his eyes were also closed.

I wondered what his ass had up his sleeve. I knew there was more to him than his exterior, a clean-cut, throwing-his-money-around, white-collar sellout. I just didn't know what else was lying beneath. I looked around at the others gathered around the gravesite, and I had to admit, I was impressed with the small crowd of supporters who'd come out to show Contessa some love. Octavia's mother Charlene and her father Charles, and even Ilene and Damon Sr., had managed to make it into town for the service. I didn't know if Ilene had chosen to attend because she liked Contessa from their one encounter of if she was there to support me, the alleged grieving nephew. Whatever their reasons for being there, everyone had only good things to say about Contessa. It was amazing that a woman whose entire identity was fake still managed to make an impact in such a short period of time.

I turned my head, focusing back on Octavia, and watched as she dabbed at her eyes with a handkerchief. The woman was beautiful, even when she shed tears. I scanned my eyes over her physique, admiring the jacket and skirt that clung to her so well in the damp weather. The jacket revealed just a glimpse of the top of her breasts, while the skirt hugged her hips and stopped just above her knees. *It should be a crime for one female to be so sexy,* I thought.

As I thought of all the things I wanted to do to Octavia and all the places on her body where I wanted to travel with my tongue, I suddenly developed a nagging feeling that I was being watched myself. I turned my head slightly to the right and locked eyes with Ilene. She cut her eyes from mine to Octavia, then back to me. *Is that disapproval?* I wondered. It was obvious that Ilene had been watching me watch her daughter-in-law, looking like a hungry dog, and she didn't like it one bit. I shrugged my shoulders before turning my head and closing my eyes.

Once Pastor Davis finished what had to be the longest prayer in the history of religion, I began to make my way back to my vehicle. As I sloshed across the wet grass, I noticed Octavia's parents walking hand and hand next to me. I nodded my head in their direction as a way of acknowledging their presence, then continued toward my car.

"I'm sorry again about your loss," Charlene said, looking over at me.

"Thank you," I said lowly. "She's in a much better place."

"Yes she is," Charles agreed.

"Listen, we've invited everyone back to our home for dinner." Charlene smiled. "You're more than welcome to come."

"Thank you," I said sincerely as we reached my truck. "That's very sweet of you."

"Charlene went all out, Kelly," Charles said, looking at his wife. "Turkey, ham, dressing, greens, pinto beans, mac and cheese…mmm, mmm, mmm." Charles licked his lips like he could taste the food already. "There's even dessert!"

"You're making me hungry." I laughed lightly.

"Good," Charlene said happily. "So you'll come?"

"Come where?"

I knew my mother's voice before I turned around.

She stood behind me with her husband hovering over her with an umbrella. She looked like royalty in her blue, sleeveless dress and high heels.

"Charlene just invited Kelly to join us for lunch," Charles informed her.

"Really?" Ilene said, casting me the same look she'd given me when she'd caught me eye-fucking the man's daughter.

"Yes," Charlene said. "Charles was just telling Kelly that I have a full meal prepared."

I listened to the women discussing the menu while I watched Octavia and Damon approach.

"And I think my lovely daughter prepared dessert," Charlene said once the two of them were standing within earshot.

"I did." Octavia smiled sweetly. "It's just my cheesecake though."

"The recipe from your restaurant?" I asked, staring at her.

"Yep. That's the one," she answered quickly.

I had noticed even before the service that her words with me were short and blunt. I decided to brush her slight rudeness off and considered it her way of dealing with the death of Contessa, whom she clearly adored. "I think I'll take you up on that offer, Mrs. Ellis." I smiled. "I could use a good home-cooked meal…and some company."

"Please don't let us interfere with any plans you've already made," Ilene interjected. "We completely understand if you have somewhere else you have to be."

I looked around the circle while wondering if I was the only one who'd picked up on the desperation in Ilene's voice. It was obvious that she was hoping, wishing I'd change my mind about attending their family dinner. "Trust me," I said, "there's no place I'd rather be right now."

* * *

After enjoying the meal Charlene had prepared, I knew where Octavia got her culinary skills. Her mother had put what I liked to refer to as her foot in the meal, and I could confidently say there wasn't an unhappy palate in the house.

Throughout the meal, the conversation was light and mostly geared toward current events, the weather, and random bullshit. Occasionally I looked up and caught Damon watching me. I kept waiting for him to say something, but he didn't speak a word.

It wasn't until after Octavia served her Better Than Sex cheesecake that he addressed his concerns. "Kelly, were you ever able to locate Jay?" he asked, cutting his eyes in my direction.

I had forgotten all about Contessa's son, whom I'd promised to look for. "Uh, not yet," I said. "I've been so busy trying to deal with Auntie's death that I haven't been able to accomplish much."

"That's understandable," Charlene said.

"I'm retired from the force," Charles added, "but let me know if you need me to reach out to some of my old connects."

"I appreciate that, but I'd rather handle it on my own," I said, looking across the table at Damon.

There was a smug look of satisfaction on the man's face—the kind of satisfaction one only feels from throwing someone under the bus.

"But if it becomes too big for me, I'll let you know, Charles."

"Good deal," Charles replied.

"If all else fails, I'll just hire a detective," I said, laughing lightly. "I mean, surely a good PI can locate a brother in prison." I glanced at Damon, looking for any reaction that might indicate he'd put Victor on my ass.

"I agree," Damon said coolly, "if there is one to be found. Charles had several years in the private sector as well."

"Sure did," Charles said, shaking his head. "Saw the best and the worst while I was working undercover."

"I'll keep that in mind," I said.

Damon's eyes locked with mine, and I knew his ass was secretly gloating, I could just feel it. The invisible tension between the two of us was mounting by the second, making me hotter under the collar than I'd been in a long time.

I knew Octavia's parents' home was not the place to let out the aggression I felt toward my half-brother, but at that moment, I didn't give a damn. "Charles, I don't know if Octavia mentioned it to you, but my son's mother also passed recently." I looked at Damon again; the expression on his face had now changed, and he looked a little like Bambi, preparing to be run down by a semi. His eyes were wide, and his eyebrows were pushed back. He seemed to be hanging on my every word, and I loved that.

"Yes, she did mention something about that," Charles said. "I'm sorry to hear of yet another loss for you."

"Thank you," I said, rubbing my hands together slowly. "I guess that's part of why I'm so slow to take care of things. I imagine if Nadia were here to help me…"

Octavia was the first to catch the name. "Nadia?" she asked.

"Yes, Nadia, Donovan's mother," I said nonchalantly.

"It's such a small world," she said, shaking her head. "Damon use to date a Nadia. Remember her, boo?"

I looked at Damon, daring him to come clean and tell Octavia the truth, but he said nothing.

"She was a professional dancer," Octavia continued.

"Wow. Really?" I said. "That's interesting. My baby-mama was also—"

"Damon, darling where did I put the card for Kelly?" Ilene asked, cutting me off.

"It's in the car, I'm sure, honey," Damon Sr. advised her.

"I need to find it," Ilene said hastily. "Now."

We all looked at her like she had lost her mind.

"I put a little something inside for Donovan, and I'm sure he'll appreciate it," she explained.

I stared at her. The grayness in her eyes was compelling, damn near begging me to be quiet, and I chose to obey.

She pushed away from the table then stood. "Damon, are you sure it's in the car?" She didn't wait for him to answer. "I'll go look. Octavia, darling, would you like to help me?"

"I'll help you," I volunteered before Octavia could respond. "I need to get some fresh air and walk off that good meal Ms. Charlene hooked up." I looked over and smiled at Octavia's mother.

She blushed slightly. "It was my pleasure, Kelly," she said sweetly. "I'm glad you enjoyed it."

"I did," I said, standing up. "I see where Octavia gets her kitchen skills from." I ignored Octavia's and Damon's stares as I walked away, following Ilene out of the dining room and to the front door.

Ilene marched on her heels until she reached her Jaguar. Once we were several feet away from the front door, she began to vent. "What in the hell is wrong with you?" she snapped, spinning around to look at me.

"What do you mean?"

"What was that back there?" she questioned. "What kind of game are you playing?"

"I'm just playing the cards I've been dealt," I said.

"By telling Octavia about Nadia?" she questioned. "By causing her pain?"

"So your concern is for Octavia and *her* feelings? Are you saying your overprotective apron strings for Damon Jr. has nothing to do with this?"

She blinked several times before answering. "Damon is my son,"

"Need I remind you that you have two sons?"

"You don't have to be my son," she said with a straight face.

I watched as she unlocked her car door, reached inside, and pulled out an envelope.

"Here," she said, extending it to me.

I didn't have to take it to know it contained what was probably a healthy sum of hush money. "How much?" I questioned her.

"Twenty-five," she answered.

I had been wanting to know how Donovan and I were going to fit into Ilene's perfect family or how much our secret was worth, and she had just provided me an answer. The woman who wore $1,000 shoes and whose ring finger carried at least $50,000 had just told me I was worth a measly $25,000 to her, and she did so without saying a word. I laughed, trying to suppress my anger. "You know, you and Nadia had a lot more in common than your husband's dick," I taunted. "I used to look at her and wonder how something so beautiful could be so vile inside. Now I have to ask myself the same question about you."

Ilene stared at me with no emotion whatsoever. She was rock solid, but I was determined to break her.

"I really should thank you for what you did for me thirty-six years ago. I would have rather made my bed in the piss-covered streets than to be raised by someone like you—a shallow, simple bitch."

"Kelly, I could have easily lied about the results," she advised me, "but I chose to tell you the truth, so—"

"You didn't do that for me," I snapped. "You did it for yourself, to help clear your conscience."

"My conscience is perfectly clear, dear. I have no reason to feel guilty about the decisions I've made in life. There is always a reason why people give their children up, Kelly," she said bluntly, "and it's usually because they feel it's the right thing to do. They don't expect the child to pop up thirty-six years later and turn their world upside down. Granted, I know it isn't your fault that our paths have crossed, but I don't see why we can't go back to the life we knew before."

"If you don't want me in your life, that's fine," I said, "but don't insult me with $25,000. The ice your maid wears in her fat lobes and around her chunky neck cost that much."

She remained quiet for a moment, an indication that I'd struck a nerve and that it was a good one. "Well, then tell me how much do you want," she questioned, staring at me. "Thirty? Forty?"

"Is this how your family works?" I asked, laughing lightly. "Money makes it all go away for you?"

"I'm not sure, but it certainly does help," she said.

"That's not how Octavia works," I told her.

The mere mention of Octavia evoked anger and emotion in Ilene. "You listen to me," she said. " Leave Octavia out of this."

"She deserves to know what type of people she's dealing with," I said.

"She already knows," Ilene snapped. "She is dealing with people who love her."

"I'll let her be the judge of that."

"Kelly, darling, you poor fool. It doesn't matter what you do. Octavia will never leave my Damon—especially for the likes of you."

"We'll see about that," I threatened.

"Oh my." Ilene looked at me with a stunned expression on her face. "You're…you're falling in love with her."

"You don't know what you're talking about," I said defensively. After all, the conversation was about how trifling and dirty she and her damn family were, not about me and what she thought she knew about me.

"I see they way you look at her," she said. "You really love her."

I chose to remain silent.

She laughed. "Allow me to give you some motherly advice for the first time in your life. You have to get over whatever it is you think is going to happen with Octavia," she instructed, "and you need to understand that no matter what you do or what they may have done, those two will stay together…forever."

"Who are you trying to convince?" I questioned. "Me or yourself?"

She looked at me with a softness and a gentleness in her eyes; if I didn't know any better, I would have mistaken it for love. "I don't need convincing," she said sternly. "The truth is and always has been the truth, and it does not need justification."

"We shall see," I said. "In the meantime, you can keep your dirty money."

Chapter 18

Damon

Despite my run-in with Kelly at my in-laws' home and my thinking I was going to have to lay him on his ass, the rest of the weekend turned out well. Savoy made it into town, and the two of us spent all day Sunday in front of the flat screen in my home theater, watching our favorite teams hammer it out on the court, eating wings, and talking trash. My brother was back in town, and he and my sister-in-law looked happier than ever. Life was good, and I was thankful.

My decision to tell Octavia the truth about Lawrence hàd been a difficult one, but it was necessary. It also helped with my plight to keep her contact with Kelly at a minimum. Before and after Contessa's memorial service, she barely acknowledge Kelly's presence and I liked that.

To date, there were still no explanation of what had taken place between Lawrence and Emerson, and it looked like it was going to end up in the cold case files. I hated not knowing the whole story. I knew the possibility existed that somewhere along his journey of following Kelly, Lawrence had made a detour and gotten caught up in some very bad shit. However, I couldn't go off possibilities or assumptions. Considering everything that Lawrence had done for me—especially that he might have lost his life working for me—I needed the facts. I felt I owed him that. I reached out to Detective Jennings, my connect with the Huntsville PD, and asked him what additional info he could find out about the man who was found dead with Lawrence.

I had a full schedule and several meetings planned throughout the day, including one with the security company about installing cameras in Octavia's restaurants. After hosting an office meeting with my team to commend them for their hard work, I headed out to Ambiance 2. I had purchased the land and paid for the construction of the place as an anniversary gift for Octavia, and although I was fond of her first location (where we had our first date), I loved the architectural layout and design Savoy created when he built the second one—from the elevated dance floor, lounge, and Grecian columns downstairs to the glass private dining room, lounge, and additional dance floor upstairs. I'd offered to have Ambiance remodeled so it would look exactly like its counterpart, but Octavia declined. The Ambiance was her first baby, and she wanted to keep everything as it was. I understood, but I left the offer open and on the table in the event that she might someday changed her mind.

When I arrived at the restaurant, Ryan, our representative with Stanley Security, was already present and sitting upstairs with Octavia in the private dining room, going over our various monitoring options. I greeted my wife with a kiss, shook Ryan's hand, then sat down at the table next to Octavia.

"I've already selected the package I want," she said enthusiastically. "All you have to do now is cut the check, boo."

"I got you covered." I laughed lightly and looked at the informational material she had spread out in front of her.

The system she'd selected was the latest, most advanced of all of them. It even included the option to receive the monitoring feed via her Blackberry. It was also the most expensive, but my baby was gonna get whatever she wanted. In fact, I'd have selected the same one myself. After setting a date to have the systems installed for both restaurants, I wrote Ryan a check.

"I almost forgot," I said. "I need a technician to come out to our house and check out one of our cameras. I noticed a couple of weeks ago that the picture is fuzzy."

"Not a problem. I'll call you as soon as I get back to the office to set up a date and time," Ryan advised me.

"Sounds good," I said, extending my hand to him again. "Thanks again,

Ryan."

After Ryan's departure, Octavia and I continued to sit at the table, discussing our plans for the rest of the day.

"I have an interview, and then I'm going home to start packing up Contessa's things," she said.

"Are you sure you're okay doing that?" I questioned. "If you prefer, I can do it for you."

"No, it's cool, babe," she said. "Besides, something tells me she would have preferred me to do it. I'm sure she wouldn't have wanted you rooting through her drawers."

We both laughed.

"But thank you for being so considerate."

"Anytime, my love."

"If you want to help out, though, you could swing by Mommy and Daddy's place and pick Jasmine up on your way home," she suggested.

"I'd be happy to."

Shontay was glad to look after Jasmine until Octavia had everything set up to work from home, but since Shontay and Savoy were still playing catch-up, Octavia and I had decided it was best if Jazz stayed with her grandparents for the day.

The two of us were saying our goodbyes when Kaitlyn, one of Octavia's hostesses, came up and announced that there was a gentleman downstairs who was asking to speak with my wife.

"Thank you, Kaitlyn." Octavia smiled.

"Your next interview?"

"If so, it's an hour early," she said, looking down at her watch. "Also, the person I'm supposed to be interviewing is a woman, not a gentleman." She shrugged her shoulders. "Oh well. That'll just give me the opportunity to escort my handsome husband downstairs and make all the girls jealous," she said, slipping her hand in mine.

"I'm always glad to be escorted by a beautiful woman," I said, leaning down and kissing her cheek.

"*A* beautiful woman? I better be the *only* woman," she ordered, as the two of us headed toward the elevator.

"I can't promise you that," I teased. "There is this gorgeous little shawty I allow to accompany me to places from time to time."

The steel doors opened and the two of us stepped on together.

"Is she around two feet tall and enjoys taking naps after watching cartoons?" she asked.

The doors of the elevator opened up, after delivering us to the first floor.

"Yep."

"Goes by the name Jasmine, Jazz, Baby Girl, Li'l Mama, and Princess, just to name a few?"

"That'd be her." I laughed.

"Well, I guess I can deal with that, but she better be the only other woman escorting you anywhere, mister, besides my mama and yours," Octavia advised me as the two of us stepped off the elevator hand and hand. "I would hate for a ho to come up missing."

"Baby, you're no killer," I reminded her playfully.

She looked up at me and smiled. "Well, not yet, but I am a woman, and women never know what they're capable of doing until they're forced to do the unthinkable."

There was a look of truth and honesty in her eyes, so strong that it not only turned me on but also sent a chill through my body. The two of us had a second of nonverbal communication with our eyes before we located Kaitlyn at the front of the restaurant.

Kaitlyn advised us that the man requesting to speak with Octavia was at the bar in the downstairs lounge. "He says he just wants to commend you on the food and the service," Kaitlyn said.

Octavia beamed proudly. Her reputation for good food and friendly service was improving daily, and word-of-mouth meant more business. She was continuing to build her brand and make her establishments a household name, and I was as proud of her as she was of herself.

"Well, baby, I'm going to go so you can go talk to your fan club," I told her. "I'll see you later."

"You most certainly will." She smiled sweetly. "I love you."

"I love you more," I replied.

We hugged again and went our separate ways.

I was halfway down the street when I remembered I wanted to surprise my hardworking team and grab some lunch for myself before heading back to the office and all those meetings. *What better way to thank my people than with some of the best dessert in town?* I thought. I came to the traffic light and made a U-turn to head back to Ambiance 2, on a quest for cheesecake.

Kaitlyn advised me that Octavia was still speaking to her guest, and I told her I would wait for her in the dining room. I scanned my e-mails while I waited. A minute later, I looked up and saw Octavia walking in my direction, strutting on her heels, rocking the soft yellow fitted jacket and pants to the very last thread. As she approached, I knew something was wrong. The smile that had graced her lips earlier was gone. Her soft facial features were hardened, obviously by whatever it was she was thinking. I immediately stood, ready to handle whatever and whomever had managed to brush away the smile from my wife's lips, but as she got closer, I realized it was worse than I expected. Not only was her smile gone, but there were tears escaping her eyes when she locked with mine. She was holding something in her trembling hand, but I couldn't tell what it was.

I moved quickly across the floor, stepping in her direction to meet her halfway. "What happened?" I asked as the two of us stood face to face.

She shook her head as she looked at me. "Damon, tell me he's wrong," she whispered, handing the letter to me.

"Who, baby? Who's wrong? And about what?"

She stepped back and turned to look in the direction of the lounge. I followed her eyes and saw Kelly, standing by the bar, just watching us. I pulled my eyes and attention away from him and redirected both back to Octavia and what she had given me. It was a copy of my American Express bank statement and a credit card bearing the name "Nadia Jones." The statement was for the charge cards on one of my business accounts, which is the account I'd once given Nadia access to. It was an old, outdated statement, of course, but it was something Octavia knew nothing about, so naturally the information was new to her. There were dates and purchases highlighted in neon yellow; Kelly had gone all out to deliver the incriminating news to my wife. I looked at Octavia, and although there were probably a million different things I should have said at that moment, I couldn't conjure up a word.

Octavia's eyes grew wider as she stared at me. "Dame..." she whispered, shaking her head. "Oh, Dame."

Chapter 19

Octavia

I stepped out of my car with my bag on my arm, then slammed the door. I was so upset that I called and canceled my interview and went straight home. With all my heart, I wanted to believe that what Kelly had told me about Damon was a lie, and even though there was physical proof, I still wanted to believe in my husband. However, when I'd looked into my husband's eyes, they had confessed the things he could not say with his mouth. *The truth told with a man's eyes is one no woman can deny.*

I had barely gotten the front door unlocked when Damon's Range Rover came zooming up the driveway. I left the door open and headed straight upstairs to our bedroom. I threw my bag on my dresser and kicked off my heels. I pulled of my jacket and pants before retrieving a fitted tank top and a pair of yoga pants from my armoire. I was angry and hurt at the same time. It was the second secret I'd learned about Damon in the last six months, and I couldn't help but wonder how much more there was that I didn't know about the man I'd married. I was on an adrenaline rush, moving from one spot in the room to the other. I feared that if I slowed down, I would reach my breaking point. I snatched the first pair of sneakers I came across in my closet and plopped down on the edge of my bed to put them on.

"Baby, can we talk?" Damon questioned, standing in the doorway of our bedroom.

"Oh, so now you want to talk?" I asked angrily. "Why now, Damon? You didn't have shit to say earlier at the restaurant." I slipped my feet inside my shoes, then stood up and headed for the bathroom. I pulled the top drawer of my built-in vanity so hard I heard the hinges crack. I ransacked the drawer until I found a scrunchie and my paddle brush. I pulled my hair high up on my head and secured it in a sloppy ponytail, not even caring how I looked, and marched back into the bedroom.

"Octavia, I'm sorry about that," Damon said. "I was just...it caught me off guard."

"*You* were caught off guard?" I snapped, staring at him. "Oh, you poor baby. Imagine how I felt when I saw that, Damon! Kelly comes to my place of business and tells me he's been keeping a secret he can no longer hide. In my head, I'm thinking it's something about his life and his issues, something that would justify those so-called hunches you had that made you send a PI after him." I shook my head. "But then he tells me his baby-mama, this Nadia, was your ex-girlfriend. I admit that at first, I didn't see the relevance, but then I remembered one important factor about the story of Donovan's mother." I paused. "There was another man in the equation, one she originally tried to pin Donovan on. So I looked at Kelly and asked him what he was trying to tell me, and he said the man who was helping raise his son was you!" I took a deep breath, then exhaled slowly. "He told me it was you, Damon! And not only that, but you were breaking Nadia off too." I shook my head and began to pace back and forth along the floor like a caged animal. "I knew better than that. It was obvious that someone had their lies crossed, because one thing I know is that *my* man would not take care of that bitch.." I stopped pacing and stared hard at him. "See, that would be disrespecting his home...this home," I said, pointing to the floor. "That would be disrespecting his wife...me. So I told Kelly he could kiss my ass because there was no possible way that *my* husband would trick out like that for his ex-tramp." I closed my eyes, attempting to block the tears that were starting to surface. "But then? Then he showed me the credit card statement, Damon," I continued, still staring at him, "for your account, in your name, and an American Express card with that whore's name on it, linked to the same account. What were you doing, baby? Treating her to shopping sprees while you lied to me about your whereabouts so you could be in her face? Missing quality time with our daughter so you could spend time with her and her son? Is that it?!"

"Octavia, that's not how it happened," he said, raising his voice.

"Then you tell me how it did happen, Damon," I demanded. "Tell me!" I waited, watching him closely. I needed to hear from him how things had transpired. I needed to know from him—my lover, my friend, my husband—what had happened to bring us to that very moment. "Tell me the truth, Damon," I pleaded. "Please."

He looked at me and nodded his head in agreement. "Have a seat."

I eased down on the edge of the bed, never taking my eyes off him.

He walked over to the bed and sat down next to me. "This is what happened…"

* * *

After hearing Damon's sordid tale of how he was practically living a double life up until Nadia's death, the pain I'd been feeling moments earlier intensified by three times. I was hurt because he'd lied. I was hurt because I hadn't caught on to those lies. I was hurt because he'd felt he had to lie. *What does that say about our marriage? What does it say about our love? What does it say about him? About me?* "I can't believe this," I said, standing. "Damon, did you sleep with her during those trips?"

He looked offended that I would even ask, but I needed to know.

"Well? Did you?"

"Of course not!" he said. "I'm sorry for what went on, Octavia, but—"

"Sorry for what, Dame?!" I asked, cutting him off. "For not telling me or for getting busted? Which one?!"

"Both," he declared strongly. "I should have never given another man the opportunity to tell you what I should have confessed from the very beginning."

"So now you're being honest," I said, throwing my hands in the air.

"I've been honest, baby."

"Really? When?" I asked.

"Every time I've told you I love you," he retaliated. "Don't act like you don't know our love is real. If you don't know anything else, you know that much."

I remained silent.

"I know my methods may not have been the smartest, but I did what I did because I love you, Octavia. Everything I've ever done, right or wrong, has been because of love. I thought I was protecting you by not telling about the situation with Nadia. All I've ever wanted to do is love and protect you. I fucked up by not considering how the truth would affect you if you ever found out. For that I apologize, but I refuse to apologize for love or for wanting to protect you." Damon's stare at me with enough passion that I could have sworn he was looking into my soul.

"Is that the real reason you had Lawrence following Kelly?" I questioned. "Because he knew your secret?"

"I had Lawrence do a background check on Kelly when you advised me that you had offered to let him stay here," he informed me. "I wanted to know who would be living in our home, with my wife and daughter."

The thought of Damon investigating me popped into my mind, but I told myself I was tripping and immediately dismissed it.

"Then, after he told me who he was—or, better yet, when he showed up at our home with Donovan—I couldn't shake the feeling that there was more to the story with him and Nadia than he was telling me. I still feel that way."

"There may be more to *his* story," I said with attitude, "but at least he told me the truth about yours—the truth you should have told me long ago." Yes, I was pissed off with Kelly for withholding the truth as long as he had, but the fact remained that Kelly had no obligation or commitment to me. Damon did, and my husband should have been man enough to step forward. "I need a break right now," I said, grabbing my bag off the dresser.

"A break?" he asked, watching me carefully. "What do you mean?"

Up until that moment, I'd been making each and every move second by second, but when the words came out of my mouth, I knew what I had to do and when I had to do it. "I don't know who you are right now," I said honestly, "and if I don't know who *you* are, then I sure as hell don't know who *we* are."

"What are you saying?" he asked, standing. "Octavia, you know me! I am your husband, the man who loves you, the man who has always loved you."

"The man who looked me in my eyes and told me lie after lie," I reminded him. "Where was the love when you were lying to me, huh, Damon?!"

"You show me a man who says he loves his woman but won't do for her the things I've done for you, and I'll show you a liar!" he yelled.

"You don't have to show me a liar," I snapped. "There's no better example than the one whose ass I'm looking at right now!"

Damon looked at me and shook his head. "We can fix this," he said. He reached out and pulled me into his arms. "We can fix this, Octavia, and we can move on."

It was so easy for me to lose myself in the comfort of his embrace, to allow myself to succumb to his strength and the safety I'd always felt when he held me, but I wasn't going to let it happen this time. I pulled away and stepped back, putting distance between the two of us. "Maybe we can, but what if we can't?" I said.

Damon looked shocked and slightly hurt by my response.

Good. Now he knows how I feel, I thought.

"Baby, what are you saying?"

"I'm saying I think it's best if you and I separate for a little while—just until I can figure some things out."

"I will not allow my wife or daughter to leave their home," he said firmly. The look in his eyes was cold and dark as he stood with his arms crossed. "The two of you *will not* leave your home."

"You're right," I agreed with him. "Jasmine and I are not leaving." I paused before taking a deep breath and exhaling. "But you are."

Damon looked at me with wide, bright eyes. He shook his head and exhaled. "Octavia, I love you," he said, "and I understand your wishes right now...but if you think I'm going to leave my home, you're right about not knowing me." He ran his hands across his head before adding, "I'm going to get our daughter. I'll see you when I return."

Before I could protest, he slipped out of our bedroom, leaving me alone, standing with my mouth wide open. I walked over to the bedroom window and watched as his Range made its way around and down our circular driveway. *Ain't that some shit?!*

Chapter 20

Kelly

I couldn't help wonder how things were going for Damon. I hated hurting Octavia, but I knew she would eventually overcome the pain of hearing that her man was full of shit and had lied to her on multiple occasions. I knew it was a risk—that things could have backfired and Octavia could end up hating me for concealing the truth from her in the first place—but thankfully, it didn't go that way. She'd actually thanked me for keeping it real with her.

I hadn't heard from Ilene, and that was fine with me. She'd made her decision, and it was up to her to live with it.

I had just tucked Donovan in for the night when I received an unexpected visitor. I opened the door and instantly cursed to myself.

Gator's driver, AJ, stood at my door with hands cupped in front of him. "Gator would like you to step outside."

"For what?" I questioned.

"Why do you think?" He smirked, staring mockingly at me.

"I've got the money," I said. "I can just give it to you," I offered, assuming he was there to collect on my debt to Gator.

"Gator would prefer that you give it to him yourself."

"But my son…" I began. "He's sleeping, and I can't just—"

"It'll only take a moment," he said, "or maybe it would be more convenient for you if Gator comes inside, hmm?" He raised one eyebrow and gawked at me, as if daring me to keep arguing and making excuses.

"Fine. Tell him I'll be out in a sec," I said. I knew I was done for either way, and Gator would get what he wanted, one way or another. The last thing I wanted was to have that crazy man inside my home, so I decided to take my chances outside with him.

* * *

Five minutes later, I sat in the back of Gator's truck. He sat beside me, and a tall, thin brother with dark skin and low-cut hair was in the second row on the passenger side in front of us.

"Here you go," I said, holding up the envelope that contained the five grand. "I'll have the rest shortly." I waited for Gator to take the package from my hand, and when he didn't, I opted to lay it on the seat in between us. I had a very bad feeling about the situation, but I decided to remain calm. If the man had planned to have me killed, I'd have been dead before I left my apartment.

"We have a…uh, a slight problem," Gator said, looking out the window.

"What kind of problem?" I questioned, knowing all too well what he was talking about.

"One of my employees was found murdered." He spoke slowly and calmly, which made him seem even more intimidating.

"I'm sorry for your loss," I said.

"Well, that's all fine and good, Kelly, but the problem is, he wasn't just any employee. He was the one I assigned to accompany you several nights ago, at your request."

I knew I had to be cautious with my response. If I seemed too anxious, it would be an admission of guilt. Then again, if I didn't show enough curiosity and concern, I would be in the same boat. "Wow. I'm sorry to hear that," I said. "What happened?"

"That's my question," Gator said, rubbing his hands together. "I sent him out to meet you, and the next thing I knew, his father was being contacted to identify his body." Gator paused before continuing. "Now, normally, I would not take such matters to heart. We all live to die, and in this business, death comes quicker for some than it does for others. But, see, E. was not just any employee."

I contemplated responding but finally decided to remain quiet.

"You see, Kelly, E.—Emerson—was my nephew as well as my godson."

If my heart could have spoken at that moment, I'm sure it would have screamed out, "*Fuck!*" "Damn, Gat—"

"E. was my only son," said the man sitting in front of us, finally breaking his silence by cutting me off. His voice was deep and brash and filled with what I could only describe as pain. "Seventeen fucking years were all that I had with him. Seventeen fucking years, and then he's gunned down in the street, lying dead next to the stranger who killed him—some random son of a bitch none of us have ever heard of."

"Emerson?" I repeated, pretending to try and remember where I'd heard the name.

"Yes," Gator said. "The cops found him and some muthafucka named Victor Henson lying cold over on Oakwood Road."

"I think I may have seen something about that," I said, rubbing my chin. "Yeah, I did—on the news a few days ago. I thought they said they took each other out."

"That's what they say," Gator said blankly, "and that may very well be true, but what I want to know is what led to the so-called dispute in the first place. Who was the Victor fucker, and how did he end up in the presence of my nephew? Hmm?"

"Those are all good questions," I said, nodding my head.

"*Unanswered* questions," Gator emphasized. "Surely you understand the importance, the urgency of finding out the missing pieces to this crude little puzzle."

"Yeah," I said lowly.

"I mean, you have a son of your own, don't you, Kelly?" Gator quizzed, looking over at me. The man's pupils were as dark as the night sky just before a storm.

"Yeah," I answered.

"Imagine how you would feel placing your son's life in the care of someone, only to see him cut down like nothing, bloody and dead in the street," Gator stated. "How would you feel?"

There was no need for me to answer, but the pressure I was receiving from Gator's stare compelled me to reply.

"Angry," I said honestly.

"Would you allow yourself to go on without knowing each and every detail, right up until the moment he took his last breath?" Gator continued.

"No, but Gator...really, what does any of this have to do with me?" I asked cautiously.

The man sitting in front of us turned in his seat and glared at me with tears in his eyes. At that moment, he was likely far more deadly than Gator ever had been, because the pain of a parent losing a child carries more ammunition than an arsenal of weapons.

Gator raised his hand, as if telling the man to relax.

The man climbed out of the car and slammed the door behind him. I watched him as he walked around the front of the vehicle and took a stance next to Gator's driver, who stood by the driver side door.

"You have to understand my position," Gator said. "See, Terrance is looking for answers about what took place the night his son was murdered. He's a good man and a close friend, and I feel obligated to provide those answers. Surely someone knows something about that night. One thing I know for sure is that E. would never ventured off or strayed from what he was instructed to do. He was a good boy, and he always followed orders and plans to a tee."

"Listen, Gator, I'm sorry to hear about what happened to your nephew," I said quickly. "If I hear or see anything in the streets, I swear you'll be the first to know."

Gator laughed dramatically. "I'll hear about it in the streets quicker than you," he said sarcastically. "Kelly, I'd like to make you a proposition."

This caught me by surprise. "A proposition?"

"Yes. I am desperate to find out what really happened that night," he said. "See what you can find out on this Victor character, anything you can dig up on his life. Did he have a wife? Kids? Anything that'll help fill in the gaps for us. I'm offering you the opportunity to repay your debt in full... and to redeem your standing with me."

"Gator, I'd love to help, but I'm not exactly a PI," I said politely. "It sounds like you need a professional, and—"

"Considering all you have to gain—or lose—I trust you will come up with something," he said.

"And if I decline?"

"I sent my nephew off to meet you," he said, "and he came back in a body bag. You asked me for what should have been a simple favor. You promised I'd receive all of my money and my man on the job—in this case, my brother-in-law's son—would return home in one piece, but that wasn't what happened. I know you to be a halfway respectful man, and I couldn't imagine you wanting to do anything that might threaten that opinion of you."

"I see."

"I hope so, Kelly. Your life may depend on it."

Chapter 21

I couldn't make Damon leave the home he'd purchased for us, and at that point, I was so pissed off that I refused to leave my-damn-self, so I took pleasure in walking around the house half-naked in my stilettos, taunting my husband. Yes, it was childish, but I didn't give a damn. I couldn't believe the nerve he had to lie to me for so long, about so many things. It was a good thing Nadia was no longer alive, because I would have made that bitch wish she was dead. Granted, Damon was wrong for not telling me, but she was wrong for orchestrating the lie in the first place.

The thing I still could not come to terms with was the fact that Donovan favored our little girl so much. I expressed my concern about this to Shontay while we sat on the carpet in the room Contessa had once occupied. The two of us had sorted through all of Contessa's clothing and were placing it in storage boxes. I'd had every intention of boxing her things up sooner, but after the fallout with Damon, I was thrown off course.

"Maybe Nadia *wanted* Damon to be the father so bad that he came out looking like him," Shontay suggested.

"Right. Or maybe he fed them so damn long the boy started to look like him," I suggested bitterly.

Shontay looked at me and rolled her eyes. "You know very well that was not the case. Besides, that's just an old wives' tale."

To my surprise, Shontay remained very supportive of Damon, even after I told her about Nadia and the paternity drama. She had even taken his side in the matter, stating that he was trying to protect me and that I'd probably given him the impression that he couldn't communicate certain things to me. Imagine that! Now, granted, she'd tried to clean it up by stating that Damon was dead wrong for lying, but I'd already tuned the rest of what she was saying out when she failed to say the words I wanted to hear: *"Octavia, you're right, and he's wrong."*

"Being with Savoy has made you far too understanding," I teased.

"Right, and having a man cater to your every need, worshipping the ground you walk on, has made you forget that you're not perfect," she said.

"Hey! I'm not the one who lied," I said defensively. "Damon went above and beyond with his BS, giving her access to his credit card and sneaking off to see them. And what if Donovan did turn out to be his son? Did he just plan to hide that from me for the rest of our lives? Who does that?"

Shontay gave me a blank stare. "Um, Kenny did that," she reminded me, "until we busted his ass."

I'd been so lost in my own thoughts and feelings that I'd forgotten about Kenny. "That's right. He did, didn't he?" I frowned. "Well, at least he didn't give her free range to the Amex card."

"That was only because Kenny's credit stank worse than shit on the pavement on a sunny day," Shontay reminded me.

We both laughed.

"If you'll recall, I was bearing all the financial burden because his sorry ass couldn't hold it down."

"That's right. I forgot about that too." I sighed deeply. "So you're telling me I married…a Kenny?"

"Hell no!" she blurted loudly. "Have you taken a look at Damon lately?"

"Yes," I said, sucking my teeth, "but I'm not talking about looks, girl."

"Or finances?" she added.

"Or finances," I agreed. "I'm talking about…dishonesty."

"Octavia, Damon is cut from a different cloth than Kenny was," Shontay said, shaking her head. "Look…I'm not condoning what he did or didn't do. All I'm saying is that you can't put that man in the same category as my ex-husband. It would be foolish and downright morally wrong to do so." She laughed. "It's an abomination of the code."

"A liar is a liar," I said. "It doesn't matter how beautiful or how ugly the liar may be, or how big or ridiculous their bank account is. Trust me, your ex was tore up. Savoy is a major come-up. Major!"

Shontay laughed lightly, shaking her head. "Get on with it," she smiled.

"My bad," I said. "No matter how many differences we can think of between Damon and Kenny, the fact still remains a liar is a liar—and they were both liars." I shrugged my shoulders and continued to stack Contessa's clothes in the box.

"What if Damon had come to you in the very beginning?" she asked. "How would you have reacted?"

Something told me it was a trick question, but I decided to roll with it anyway. "I suppose I'd have been a little bothered," I said calmly, "but it wouldn't have been as bad."

"Really, Octavia?" Shontay asked, smirking at me. "Really? Are you saying you wouldn't have snapped? You wouldn't have questioned every word Damon spoke to you and made him feel like shit after that? You're telling me you wouldn't have hopped in your car and headed straight to the A or wherever Nadia was at the time to confront her and light her ass up?"

I looked at her like she'd lost her mind—or read mine. "Of course I would have," I confessed. "Damon's ears would have been ringing, and if Nadia had chosen to get jazzy with me during our conversation, she would have had a well-whooped ass. But that's not the point. The point is I didn't get the opportunity. Hell, I wouldn't have ever found out the truth if it hadn't been for Kelly."

"Tell me again this Kelly's supposed reason for telling you?" Shontay asked.

"He said he felt guilty for keeping the secret from me for so long, for lying to me after we'd helped him out so much," I explained. "He said he should have told me from the very beginning."

"Um..." she said.

"Um? What the hell does that mean?" I asked, staring at her.

"I don't know the man, and at this time I don't care to," she said, "but what I do know is that he didn't stir up all this drama just because of a guilty conscience. I know it, and whether you're willing to admit it or not, you know it too." Shontay dropped the last of the items she was folding into the box and stood up. "Anyway, I'm going to check in on Jasmine and Savoy. I'll be back."

We'd left those two downstairs in the home office earlier. Although Savoy was working on the drafts for the office renovations, he wasn't actually going to start on the renovations for another two to three months. He explained he had another project lined up to start in the upcoming weeks that would require the majority of his time. In the meantime, I'd made our home office all mine. I had my home network synched with both my restaurants so I could easily access inventory and keep up with sales and even my employees' timesheets. I also had my security cameras online, streaming directly to my home PC. I decided against cameras throughout the restaurant and had them placed only inside my offices and near the registers.

When the technicians came out to our home, they noticed that one of the wires on the fuzzy camera Damon had mentioned looked as if it had been cut. The camera in question faced the garden Kelly had built for me and panned out over the guesthouse. I shrugged it off as a coincidence and kept going. My new employees, Summer and Bridget, were doing an excellent job, and my new venture of working from home was running smoothly.

I folded the flaps of the box over and sealed it tightly with clear packaging tape as Shontay's words echoed around in my head. I thought about the kiss I'd shared with Kelly and the night he set his tongue out for my pleasure. I hadn't told Shontay about those scandalous events, and in all honesty, I'd pushed both incidents from my mind. It was easy for me to do, since I was too busy focusing on what Damon hadn't done or wasn't doing right. But then I suddenly felt something I rarely admitted to: guilt.

I finished sealing the other boxes and sat down on the bed. While cleaning out Contessa's closet, Shontay and I had discovered a shoebox tucked away on the top shelf. I opened the box, expecting to find pictures or other memorabilia that Contessa wanted to keep safe, but to my surprise, I found a stack of twenties and a few hundreds, rubber-banded together, along with a small piece of paper. The paper contained the name of a website, "www.jpay.com," along with the numbers "0289756." I also found information on Contessa's savings account and a short, handwritten Living Will. In the Will, she named me as her sole beneficiary and asked that I continue to send money to her son. I was honored but shocked that she hadn't mentioned Kelly or even Donovan. It didn't make any sense, especially considering how close she was to her nephew. I decided it was the perfect opportunity for me to break the silent treatment I'd been giving my husband. We finally had something else to talk about besides our troubled past.

"This is Damon," he answered.

"Hey."

"Hi," he said flatly, followed by a cruel silence.

"Uh, did I catch you at a bad time?" I asked.

"Of course not." His tone seemed to lighten slightly. "I always have time for you."

I smiled like a little girl in a room full of Barbie dolls. "Okay. Well, Shontay and I were packing up Contessa's things today, and we found a box. It has a Living Will in it, and the Will says she wanted to leave everything—including the money she'd been saving—to me."

"You? I know you were close and very good to her, but why not Kelly? He was her nephew, right, and he obviously needs it more than we do."

"I know," I said. "Her only other request was that I continue to put money on her son's books."

"Easier said than done," he said, "considering we can't find the guy. Was there anything else in the box?"

"Yeah," I said. "There was some cash I haven't counted yet, her bank account information, the name of a website, and some odd number. I'm going to log on later and check out the website."

"Sounds like a plan," Damon said. "We definitely have to locate her son now so we can fulfill her wishes."

"I agree," I said. "I even asked Daddy to look into finding him."

"Your dad? When did you ask Charles?"

"Last week, when I went to visit." I said.

"Why didn't you tell me, babe? "Damon questioned.

"Um, because I wasn't speaking to you last week," I said as sweetly as I could muster.

"Oh, right. How could I forget that?" He laughed lightly, followed by another awkward moment of silence on the line.

"I love you," I finally said.

"I love you more."

"See you when you get home."

"Can't wait," he said. "I have a potential tenant I'm meeting for a showing at the condo in Madison, and then I'm headed that way."

"That's great,," I said sincerely.

The condo Damon was referring to had been empty for a little over a year. He'd originally put it on the market to be sold, but after several walkthroughs with people he presumed to be serious buyers, he still hadn't received an offer. Damon finally decided to rent the condo out so he'd at least reap some kind of income on the property.

"Well, I'll be here when you get here."

"Can't wait," he said before hanging up.

* * *

As it turned out, the domain name Contessa had written down was a site used to communicate and send money to those in prison. I was slightly shocked that Contessa even knew how to use the Web, since she struggled to even operate the TV. I could only assume that living with Damon and me in our modern home had opened her eyes to the world of possibilities technology had to offer.

I did a search on the number that she'd written down; as it turned out, it was an inmate ID for Stephen Garrison. I contacted my daddy and asked him to check Mr. Garrison out. I was hoping we'd finally found Contessa's son.

That night, Damon, Shontay, Savoy, and I sat by the pool, laughing and talking.

Earlier that evening, when Damon made it home from showing the condo (which he successfully leased), the two of us slipped away and made up, some of the best lovemaking either of us had ever experienced. I had to admit that Shontay was right: I had made it evidently clear that there were certain things that he could not openly communicate with me. I was woman enough to admit to that, even if I was not yet woman enough to confess my own screw-ups. I was a work in progress and content with being one. Besides, women have some secrets they should take to the grave, and my secret encounters with Kelly would be buried with me.

The four of us had just finished last hand of spades. Damon and I had done nothing less than tapped Shontay's and Savoy's asses.

Utterly defeated, Savoy began filling us in on the upcoming project he was scheduled to begin working on. "An investor by the name of Brooks Incorporated reached out to me months ago and asked me to design their new residential development. The owner actually told me he'd seen the work I did on Ambiance, and he was impressed enough to get in touch with me," he explained.

"Teddy Brooks?" Damon questioned.

"Yeah. You know him?" Savoy asked, looking at Damon.

"Not personally, but we've bumped into each other at some of the land auctions around town," Damon said.

"Well, he purchased the tracts of land just off Highway 53 on Douglas Road," Savoy continued.

"That's a nice area," Damon said, nodding his head.

"It is," Savoy agreed. "When they first offered me the job, I declined due to personal reasons." He cut his eyes over at Shontay.

She looked at him with her eyes wide. "I was going through something," she said. "Can't a girl be confused about what she wants?"

"Mm-hmm." Savoy laughed. "Anyway, once things settled down for me a bit, I hit them up and asked if they were still interested. By the grace of God, they were."

"That's a lot of land," I said, jumping into the conversation. "That project is going to be huge."

"It is," Savoy agreed. "The concept behind the neighborhood is that it will be like a city within the city. The homes are going to be within the $200,000 and $350,000 price range. They'll have a classic look but all the latest amenities."

"I told Savoy he's building the new Mayberry," Shontay teased.

"Basically, that's their concept, little white picket fences and all." Savoy laughed.

"That's going to be interesting," I said. "Dame and I will have take a tour."

We continued to discuss the plans for the new subdivision until the home phone interrupted us.

"Hello," I answered.

"Hi, Octavia. It's me, Amel."

"Hey, Amel," I said pleasantly. "What's up, girl?"

"Sorry to call you at home, but I tried your cell, like, five times," she said.

There was something in her tone that told me there was a problem. "It's okay," I reassured her. "I'm outside, and my cell is on the charger."

"Oh, okay," she said quickly. "Octavia, I just wanted to let you know that the wedding is off." She said it so quickly and nonchalantly that I thought I'd heard her incorrectly.

"What did you say?"

"The wedding is off."

My expression must have given Damon the impression that it was bad news. "What's wrong, babe?" he asked, staring at me.

I shook my head t let him know I was fine, and then I stood and walked away from the table. I walked along the stone walkway leading to my Japanese garden. "Amel, what happened?"

"Tarik and I agree that it's better if we…if we take a break," she sniffled.

"A break?" I questioned. "For how long?" I wanted answers, but at the same time I didn't want to be too pushy.

"He says…um, indefinitely," she said.

"Amel, honey, I'm so sorry," I said soothingly. "Is there anything I can do?"

"No. Just forgive me for wasting your time and money," she said, clearing her throat.

"Wasting my time? Girl, I had fun planning with you," I said honestly. "It wasn't a waste at all."

"It might take me a little time, but I'll pay you for the food and every—"

"No you won't!" I interjected. "I'll take care of it. Amel, are you sure this is what you want?" I asked, concerned.

"Yes. We agreed, and he is currently on a plane, on his way to New York."

"New York?" I said.

"Yes. It's hard, but it's for the best," Amel said quickly.

She was handling the conversation ten times better than I would have. I still remembered the mess I was when Damon and I had called off our engagement temporarily while we were dating. That was the first time I'd ever cried over a man.

"Why don't you take a couple days off?" I suggested. "With pay."

"Thanks, Octavia," she said, "but I'm fine. Really I am. It would be better if I keep busy anyway."

I decided not to pressure her. Amel had been doing well since she'd given up her drug habit, and the last thing I wanted to do was push her toward a relapse. Besides, it probably was better for her to be surrounded by people than sitting home alone. "Okay, sweetie. Call me if you need anything," I said, "even if it's just to talk."

"Thanks," she said pleasantly. "I will."

I rejoined the party of three who were waiting for me on the patio and filled them in on my conversation with Amel.

"That's so sad," Shontay said, shaking her head. "Wasn't the wedding supposed to be in three weeks or something?"

"Two and a half, to be exact," I corrected. "We were planning our trip to Paris for right after."

"Maybe they'll change their minds," Damon suggested. "We did."

"Yeah, but you didn't move to New York," I reminded him.

"Of course not." He smiled. "My home is wherever you are."

"And I'm glad for that, baby," I said sweetly.

"Sometimes distance makes things better," Shontay added. "It helps you realize what you really want."

"Well, when you know what you want, distance is the bullshit that will drive a man to cold showers and chafed palms," Savoy said bluntly.

"Okay," I said, my eyes wide. "So, uh…thanks for sharing, Savoy."

"Anytime." He smiled, looking across the table at Shontay.

She shook her head and rolled her eyes.

"You crazy!" Damon chuckled. "But that's real."

"Both of you are just nasty," Shontay said. She looked from Savoy to Damon, then back to Savoy. "Nasty," she said, erupting in laughter.

I laughed along with her.

"Maybe, but you love us." Savoy smiled.

"That we do," Shontay agreed.

I watched the two of them staring at each other with those big, cheesy smiles on their faces. "You know, the two of you could just get married and save me the trouble of canceling the fabulous reception I've already planned," I teased.

"Hmm. How fabulous?" Shontay asked.

"Chocolate fountain, five-tier wedding cake, three-tier groom's cake, Rosa for the bride and groom, seafood platter, wing platter, veggies, cheeses, and my infamous house specialty punch," I said. "Oh, and of course a live band."

"That's too fabulous!" she said. "Kill the fountain, give me three tiers for the wedding cake, a sheet cake for the groom, wings, cheese, veggies, your punch, and a deejay…oh, and keep my Rosa."

"What am I supposed to do with all that damn lobster?" I joked.

"Okay. I guess the lobster can stay." Shontay smiled. "Do you agree Savoy?"

Savoy shook his head and laughed. "Sounds like a plan, love."

"So you *will* marry me?" Shontay asked.

I looked at her and noticed that her expression was more serious than I had ever seen before. I could feel my lower jaw slowly dropping open as I looked at Damon. He looked just as confused as me, but neither one of us looked as dazed and lost as Savoy. His thick eyebrows looked like they wanted to take flight and go up and away. He lowered his eyes then frowned.

"Um, are we still joking?" he asked, obviously confused. "Or did this conversation just take a major turn?"

"A major, huge turn," I said, still slightly in shock. "The HBIC of all turns—"

"Baby," Damon said, cutting me off.

"My bad," I mumbled, staring at Shontay. "Carry on."

"I'm serious," she said. "I love you, Savoy Breedwell, and I want to know if you will marry me? Will you be my husband?"

"Octavia, maybe we should give these two some time alone," Damon suggested, standing.

Huh? What the hell for? I thought. "I will, just as soon as Savoy answers," I said, cutting my eyes in the potential groom's direction.

"Octavia," Damon said with more authority.

"All right, all right," I said, standing.

"No," Savoy said abruptly. "Stay."

He didn't have to tell me or my nosy behind twice. I was back down in my chair in less than five seconds.

Damon shook his head and walked around the table and stood behind my chair before placing his palms on my shoulders.

I touched my shoulders, massaging his hands with mine.

"Are you sure this is what you want?" Savoy asked. "Because once we say 'I do,' it's over. We'll be Mr. and Mrs. Breedwell till death. No breaks, no separations. Just us…and love."

"I know," Shontay answered, her voice shaking slightly, "and there is nothing in the world that I want more."

"If that is truly the case," Savoy said, "then yes. Yes, I'll marry you." Savoy stood and walked around the table to her chair. The expression on his face was a dead giveaway of what was coming. He turned in her chair so she was facing him. He extended his hands out to her and pulled her up to her feet, right into his arms.

Chapter 22

Damon

I was tempted to address Kelly and the stunt he'd pulled at Ambiance 2 weeks ago, but I decided to do something I'd never done before: let a Higher Power fight my battle. Besides, I knew there's no sweeter victory than the one obtained after a son of a bitch thinks he's ruined your happiness, only to find out his miserable plans have failed.

Detective Jennings contacted me to let me know he hadn't had any luck finding the missing links in Lawrence's murder. Part of me wanted to keep digging and look further, but another voice kept telling me to let it go. I decided to obey that voice and move on with my life.

My new tenant had mentioned that she was a member of New Joy, a fairly new church in the city. Octavia and I had passed by it on several occasions, and each and every time we did, the parking lot was full. When I mentioned paying the church a visit, she was onboard. After the blowup that had taken place between her former stepfather and one of the women on the mother's board at her church home, Faith Christian, Octavia had been open to visiting other congregations, and she was still open to moving her membership. Shontay and Savoy agreed to accompany us for Sunday morning service; much like me and my family, they had a lot to be thankful for.

"It's beautiful," Octavia said as we entered the sanctuary.

I had to nod my head in agreement. The inside of the church had an old-school look with stained glass panes and antique chandeliers dropping from the cathedral ceilings. Behind the choir loft (which looked like it could hold at least 2,000 people), there was a large mural on the wall depicting the crucifixion and the resurrection. To the left and right of the choir loft were huge flat-screen monitors that streamed live feeds from the pulpit.

"Welcome to New Birth." We were greeted by a pretty, slim sister with dark skin and high cheekbones, dressed in a traditional white usher's uniform and gloves. She handed each of us a program and envelopes for collection. "Feel free to sit anywhere you like."

"Thank you," we all said one by one.

"And who is this pretty princess?" she asked, bending down to look at Jasmine.

"Say hello, Jasmine," Octavia coaxed gently, holding our daughter's hand.

Jasmine remained quiet and shy.

"Oh, I can see we have a shy little one," the woman said, standing up straight. "It's okay. She'll have a blast in children's church. Would you like me to take her, or would you prefer to walk her down yourselves?"

"Wait...take her where?" Octavia questioned.

The woman looked surprised that we didn't have a clue as to what she was referring to. "Uh, children's church is held in a separate room, outside the sanctuary," she explained, folding her hands in front of her. "The bishop feels it's more productive for everyone if we don't have the distractions of little ones in the main sanctuary, and the children have more fun down there anyway."

"Oh, so it's like a nursery?" Shontay said, stepping closer.

"Right, our nursery," the usher replied.

"Thank you so much, but we prefer our daughter to stay with us," Octavia replied politely.

"I'm sorry, but it isn't really an option," the woman sated. She continued to smile as she looked from me to Octavia. "All our members are aware of our church policy, and we usually assume they bring invited visitors up to speed. I assure you little Jasmine will be just fine." She extended her hand to Jasmine.

I looked at my wife and could see something in her eyes that the woman was completely unaware of: The two of them were about to have a misunderstanding.

"Yes, she will," Octavia said, stepping toward the woman, "because she'll remain with her family. If that is not suitable, the five of us will choose another place to worship this morning."

I placed my hand on my wife's forearm, trying to keep her calm.

The smile on the woman's face quickly faded. "Well, thank you for—"

"Good morning!"

I turned around and saw my tenant, smiling across the pews and heading in our direction. "Good morning, Ms. Rains," I said, extending my hand to her. "How are you?"

"I am blessed and highly favored!" she chanted, smiling brightly. She was a pretty older woman with smooth brown skin and a petite figure. According to her lease, she was in her late fifties, but she could have passed for far younger. She was dressed in all her Sunday finery, a long orange, floral print dress and wide-brimmed orange hat. "You made it! Praise the Lord!"

"We did," I said, "but unfortunately, it looks like we won't be able to stay."

"You're leaven even before the service starts? Why? What's wrong?" Ms. Rains questioned.

"Sister Rains, are these *your* guests?" the usher asked.

"Yes. This is Mr. Whitmore and…" Ms. Rains paused, I assumed waiting for my introductions.

"This is my wife Octavia and our daughter Jasmine," I said, stepping back.

"Aren't they both beautiful angels?" Ms. Rains smiled, looking from Jasmine to Octavia. "Sister, I love that dress."

I smiled proudly as I looked at my wife. She did look stunning in her pink satin and lace dress that hit just below her knees. The dress had short lace sleeves that stopped just above her toned bicep. Her hair hung freely over her shoulders. She looked classy but stunning as always. Jasmine was also wearing a pink dress adorned with lace. Her full head of curly hair was pushed back with a small pink satin headband. She looked like an adorable miniature version of her mother.

"Thank you." Octavia smiled sweetly. "It's nice to meet you, Ms. Rains."

"Oh no. There'll be none of that." Ms. Rains shook her head. "Call me Sister."

"Uh, okay, Sister," Octavia said. "This is my best friend Shontay."

"Nice to meet you. Sister," Shontay spoke, shaking Ms. Rains's hand.

"I guess good-looking people just flock together." Ms. Rains laughed.

I had to agree with her. Although, I was biased toward Octavia, my sister in-law was holding her own in her cream-colored short skirt and jacket.

"Thank you." Shontay smiled. "Sister, this is my fiancé. Savoy."

"Nice to meet you, ma'am," Savoy said, shaking Ms. Rains's hand.

"Well, now that that's out of the way," the usher jumped in, "please explain to these folks, Sister Rains, that their daughter must go to children's church."

"Please excuse Sister Noels," Ms. Rains said, looking at the woman. "We do have policies, but we also don't want to lose a soul who shows up for a visit. Therefore, we are happy to make an exception"

"But—"

"Please find a seat," Ms. Rains said, cutting the woman off, "and again, thank you for coming to worship with us."

"Thanks." Octavia smiled, and I watched as she cut her eyes in Sister Noel's direction and gave her a cocky smirk.

We left Sister Noel and Ms. Rains whispering, no doubt about the situation that had just taken place, and found a vacant pew toward the front of the church in the middle section.

* * *

Despite the run-in with Sister Noel, the rest of the service was spirit-filled and uplifting, from the song selections performed by the church choir to the sermon delivered by the pastor, Bishop Springs. At the end of the service, he asked if there was anyone who would like him and his associate ministers to pray for them. Savoy and Shontay walked hand in hand to the altar and requested prayer for their upcoming marriage. I'd never been a sentimental man, but something touched me when I heard the bishop praying for them.

After his prayer, he offered them words of encouragement. "Every day is not going to be sunshine," he said, "but just remember that the love the two of you share can fight any battle and slay any adversary, as long as you work at staying together and keep loving and believing."

Octavia slipped her hand in mine. "I believe," she whispered.

"I do too." I smiled.

After the service, Octavia and I were approached by several members. They introduced themselves and invited us back the following week. Savoy and Shontay were surrounded by people wishing them luck and offering advice on how to enjoy a successful marriage. After Octavia and I said goodbye to Ms. Rains and thanked her for inviting us, we reunited with Savoy and Shontay.

"Is it just me, or does church make you hungry?" Savoy asked, rubbing his stomach.

"I thought it was just me." I laughed, shifting Jasmine from one arm to the other. She'd fallen asleep during the service and was still sleeping peacefully.

"Ruth's Chris would be perfect," Octavia hinted.

"Sounds good," Shontay agreed.

"I was thinking about the buffet at Denny's," Savoy said. "I'm in need of multiple trips."

We all laughed.

"Hello," said a voice from behind us.

We turned around, and silence immediately fell upon our group. My first reaction was to look at my wife, who just so happened to already be looking at me.

"Shontay, I thought that was you at the altar." Lena smiled. "Congratulations!"

"Um, thanks," Shontay said slowly.

"Thank you," Savoy also replied. "I'm sorry, but have we met?"

I could tell he was trying to picture where he knew Lena from. The last time he'd seen her was before her dramatic makeover.

"Savoy, this is Alicia," Octavia said sarcastically. "You do remember *Alicia?*"

Savoy looked at me.

Just be quiet, brah, I spoke with my eyes. *Just be quiet.*

Lena stood with one hand on her hips. She was wearing a short, sleeveless red dress that stopped above her knees, and her short hair was spiked all over. "I changed my name," Lena said. "It's now legally Lena, but thank you for that introduction, Octavia."

"No problem." Octavia smirked.

"You look…good," Lena said, still looking at Octavia.

"Thank you, *Lena*. I feel better," my wife said, winking her eye.

"How are you, Damon?" Lena asked, directing her attention to me.

"I'm good, Lena," I said casually. As a man, there are not too many situations that would have made me uncomfortable, but that one was definitely an exception. It was obvious by the look on Savoy's and Shontay's faces that they were uncomfortable, too, especially since Octavia and Lena were standing there like lionesses, prepared to pounce at any moment.

"Where's Janai?" Shontay asked, looking at Octavia.

"Home with her cousins." Lena smiled. "I'll tell her you asked about her."

"Please do." Shontay smiled slightly.

"Well, I need to get going," Lena said. "Take care, everyone…and congratulations again, Shontay." She turned on her heels and sashayed off.

"What was it the bishop said about Satan?" Octavia asked, still watching Lena as she walked away.

"The devil will always try you," I answered.

"That's real talk," Octavia said. "Seriously real talk."

* * *

"What do you think Lena's doing here?" Octavia asked, looking up at me. She lay with her head on my lap as the two of us watched television.

"I don't know, boo," I said honestly. "Probably just visiting. I think she still has family here."

"I just find it odd she invites Shontay to visit her in LA, then she mysteriously ends up at the church we were invited to attend. Doesn't that sound like more than coincidence to you?"

"You think so?"

"I do," she answered. "You think she moved back here?"

I hadn't taken the possibility into consideration. I'd just assumed Lena was in town for a family visit—nothing more and nothing less. "I doubt that," I assured her. "Her business was doing really well in LA, last I heard. Why would she up and leave it behind?"

"One word," she said.

"What's that?"

"Damon," she said, enunciating my name slowly.

It was obvious in that moment that my wife was still convinced that Lena was in love with me. I didn't agree, but I also didn't want to dredge up any bad memories. "Like I said, I'm sure she's just here to visit."

"But if she's not," she said, "you're the only reason that makes sense."

"If that's true, she made one helluva mistake," I said seriously. "I'm 100 percent taken, whether she likes it or not." I ran my hands across the top of her head, brushing her hair back with the tips of my fingers.

"I know that." She smiled. "I just hope she does too."

She better, I thought to myself. I was fond of Lena, sure, but I'd have no problem hurting her if necessary to keep anymore drama from flaring up in my marriage.

Chapter 23

Octavia

Mona, my hairstylist, had advised me of a new boutique called Ianaj that had just opened up a few doors down from her salon. Shontay was looking for a simple but elegant dress to wear for her wedding, so that gave us the perfect excuse to check out the new shop. We were thumbing through a rack of gowns, discussing Shontay's ceremony plans or lack thereof. Shontay and Savoy had planned to get married at City Hall, and their reception would be held at Ambiance, in lieu of Amel no longer needing the facility.

"City Hall?" I questioned, staring at Shontay like she'd lost her mind. "You're rich, and your boo ain't broke, but you want to get married at the courthouse?"

"Of course we want you and Damon and Jazz there," she said proudly.

"Are you sure?"

"Yes, absolutely," she said. "Why wouldn't we want you guys there?"

"Oh, I'm going to be there regardless," I informed her. "I don't care if you get married in a Jacuzzi tub at the Westin, I'll be there. I just want to make sure you're serious about City Hall. You're only supposed to have one wedding, you know."

"This is what I want, and Savoy agrees," she said. "Sweet and simple."

"Believe me, I understand," I said. " It's just that I envisioned you walking down the aisle in a beautiful white—well, maybe not white…hmm… ivory? No, scratch that. The freak you are, you'll need a taupe-colored gown." I laughed.

"Me? Um, what color did *you* get married in?" She laughed. "Wobbling down the damn aisle with your pregnant self."

I laughed harder. "Hey! Jasmine was growing inside of me, and she was pure and innocent so I could clearly get away with white," I said, throwing up my hands.

"A lie don't care who tell it!"

"Well, a person will believe a lie quicker than they will the truth." A voice spoke from behind us.

We turned around and, lo and behold, if it wasn't the Ghost of Hoes Past. Lena stood behind us in her strapless designer dress and five-inch heels, smiling like it was a joyous occasion.

"Lena," Shontay said, obviously unpleasantly surprised. "What are you doing here?"

"I'm fine, Shontay," she said, sounding lightly offended. "And you?"

It was obvious Shontay noticed her tone too. "I'm not trying to be rude," she said. "I'm just…well, I'm a little shocked to see you—"

"Again," I said, taking the liberty of finishing the sentence for Shontay.

Lena looked at me. I could feel there was something she wanted to say, but it was obvious she knew better. "Well, if you must know," she said with a smile, "this is *my* boutique."

"Yours? What happened to your day spa in LA?" Shontay inquired, sounding concerned.

"Still going strong," Lena said.

"Well, that's great," I said sincerely. Regardless of how I felt about the woman, I had to support a sister with an entrepreneurial spirit.

"It is," Shontay agreed. "Are you just here to get the boutique up and running?"

Lena cocked her head to the side. "Well," she said, clasping her hands together, "I guess I forgot to mention at church Sunday that I'm back." She cut her eyes at me. "Permanently."

What the hell? I thought.

"Wow." Shontay seemed speechless for a moment before she said, "I didn't think you'd ever move back here."

"Shontay, I have to give you some credit," Lena schmoozed. "If the two of us hadn't had the conversation in LA, when you told me I'd be fine back here, I probably would have stayed away forever. But I'm here now, and as soon as school lets out, Janai will be here too."

I wanted to blurt out, *"Way to go, Shontay!"* but I chose to remain quiet.

"Well, look, " Lena said, looking around, "it was a pleasure seeing you two *again*." She gave me a fake smile before marching off.

"If she switches any harder, she's going to dislocate a hip," Shontay whispered.

"Well, that is if she doesn't make me break one first," I said through clenched teeth.

"Maybe we should go look elsewhere," Shontay suggested.

"Agreed."

We made our way to the door, then quickly stepped out onto the sidewalk.

"She told me she was in a long-distance relationship," Shontay said as we walked toward her car. "Maybe she moved back because of whatever man she was talking about."

"Could be," I said as we climbed into her Lexus.

"Can I be honest?" Shontay asked, starting the engine of the car.

"Always."

"Even I have a bad feeling about Lena this time."

My bestie had taken the words directly from my mouth. "Me too," I admitted. "I know she has a hidden agenda, and I pray for her sake she's not after my husband. I love Damon and the happiness he brings to me, and I dare a bitch to try and steal my joy."

"I know that's right," Shontay agreed. She pulled away from the curb into traffic. "Uh, there's something I forgot to tell you about Lena."

"Forgot or failed?" I asked, looking out the window.

"You're right. Failed."

"What is it?" I asked casually.

"She *kissed* me," Shontay said lowly.

I snapped my eyes in her direction. "She did *what?*"

"When I was in LA, Lena actually kissed me," she stated.

"Where?"

"Right on the mouth," Shontay said, shaking her head. "It was completely...unexpected."

"Did you kiss her back?" I asked. I had to know what I was dealing with. If my bestie liked to get down with girls, that was her business, but if she got down with Lena, we had a problem; Lena was one I could not accept.

"No!" she yelled.

"Well, how did it happen?" I asked, slightly disgusted but very curious.

Shontay gave me a play-by-play of the night Lena kissed her.

"So you think she may be stalking *you*?" I asked.

"No! Of course not," Shontay said. "I mean, I don't think so. Do you?"

"You never can tell with a nutty wench," I said. "Never can tell."

Chapter 24

Lena

The way Octavia had responded to seeing me made it obvious that she saw me as a threat. *Good! She should!* I'd noticed the way Damon looked at me at the church. Even to a blind person it would have been obvious that he still wanted me. There was only one thing standing in our way: Octavia. When Kelly told me how he'd dropped Damon's secrets on Octavia, I thought for sure they were well on their way to unwedded bliss, but of course Octavia, pathetic as she was, forgave him. All she was good for was holding on to the un-evitable.

I'd hated leaving my daughter behind, but I knew she'd someday understand that what I was doing was for the greater good. She deserved a wonderful father, and Damon was going to be that man. Plus, I knew she would enjoy having a little sister, and Jasmine was the perfect candidate.

I was focused and all about my business. I had managed to find us a home and get my boutique up and running in record time. I accredited my expeditious hustle to the love of my man, and as soon as the two of us had a moment alone, I planned to show him just how much he was appreciated.

I strolled through the doors of Nomad Investments, holding my head high and with a smile of victory on my face. I could sense Damon's presence, and I loved it. "I'm here to see Damon Whitmore," I told the receptionist.

"Do you have an appointment?"

"No," I said sweetly, "but if you tell him Lena Jasper is here, I'm sure he'll make time for me." I walked over to an empty chair in the waiting area and sat down. It was empty, a sign that I'd chosen the perfect time to visit my boo. I smoothed my hands down the front of my skirt and crossed my legs. I had chosen a black fitted pencil skirt and a leopard-print sleeveless blouse for our lunch date. To set the outfit off, I wore red platform heels. I was sexy but classy, just the way Damon liked his women. I looked up and saw the receptionist staring at me. "Are you going to let him know I'm here?" I asked. It was obvious that she wasn't used to an assertive woman. If she had been, she would have been hauling her ass to announce me.

The woman didn't respond. Instead, she picked up the phone and begin dialing. "Um, sorry to interrupt you, sir," she said, but there is a Lena here to see you." After a moment she continued, "Mm-hmm. Yes, of course." She laughed lightly before saying, "No problem." Her smile radiated across her face as she hung up the phone. "Ms. Jasper," she said, calling my name.

"That's me," I said, standing. "Should I let myself in?"

"No." The woman smiled. "Damon asked me to advise you that he's busy. He wants to know if there was anything *I* can help you with." The old hag smiled victoriously.

I could feel my pulse increasing. "You? No. I need to see *Damon*," I told her. "I assure you there is nothing you can do for me."

"I do apologize, but I was asked to advise you that if you need anything, I am the one to assist you."

"If he's busy, I'll just wait," I said humbly.

"No, ma'am," the woman said. "Damon prefers that you *not* wait for him."

"I see," I said. "Thank you." I was humiliated and hurt as I exited the building and headed out into the parking lot. *Damon doesn't even have the decency to speak to me face to face?* I climbed into my car and slammed the door. I knew Damon would never do that to me without an explanation. It was obvious that Octavia had lied to him about something. She'd probably made me seem like a snake when she told him about running across me at the boutique. *That bitch is nothing more than a drama queen! What does he see in her anyway?* I couldn't wait until Damon and I had our chance to be alone. I would undoubtedly show him all he'd been missing and prove Octavia wrong, once and for all.

Chapter 25

Damon

I had brushed Lena off for two reasons. First, I had somewhere to be, and second, the two of us had nothing to talk about.

Octavia told me that Charles had located Stephen Garrison. As it turned out, he actually was in the West Tennessee State Penitentiary. Octavia and I were positive he was Contessa's son and that Jay had been only a nickname of some sort, but we needed to be sure before we started sending money. Charles's contact managed to put me in contact with Stephen's attorney. From there, I monetarily influenced the right personnel to add me to his visitation list, and just like that, I was on my way to Henning, Tennessee.

It was the first time since the trips I'd made trying to track Nadia down that Octavia and I wouldn't be sleeping in the same house. She told me she trusted me, and I trusted her, but that didn't stop me from picking up the phone and calling her as soon as I checked into my hotel. I also wanted to be the first to let her know about Lena's pop-up visit. "I didn't leave my office to see what she wanted," I said. "Louisa handled it."

"Boy, that Lena is sure determined if nothing else." Octavia exhaled softly.

"Determined to do what, babe?"

"Make me beat her black as—" she started.

"You're too beautiful to get your hands dirty," I told her. "Besides, I think she finally gets it this time, since I refused to see her and likely made her feel like a fool."

"She better, Damon," she said. "She better."

"I love you," I said, smiling.

"I love you more," she said.

"Where's Jazz?"

"Right here next to me," she said sweetly. "I put on her flower girl dress tonight to make sure it fits. She looks too cute in it!"

"Since when do they have flower girls at the Justice of the Peace?" I questioned.

"Since I declared that my baby will be a part of her godparents' wedding."

"You are determined to turn this into an event."

"Yes." she laughed. "Yes I am. Shontay and Savoy do not get the honor of ruining this for me."

We both laughed.

"Speaking of weddings," I asked seriously, "how is Amel?"

"She sounded fine when I spoke to her today, but tomorrow I'm going to go by and put some work in at the office," she explained. "That'll give me the opportunity to see for myself and make sure she's okay."

"Sounds good, baby," I said, looking at my Blackberry screen. "Hold on for a second, sweetheart. That's Ms. Rains."

"Sure."

"This is Damon," I said, answering the other line.

"Damon, I am so sorry to call so late, but I need to let you know my refrigerator stopped working," she said frantically.

"What is it doing?" I questioned, sitting up against the headboard.

"Sweetie, it's not doing a thing," she said. "It's all warm inside, completely hot. I was wondering if you could come check it out."

I had checked all the appliances before I released the keys to the condo, but I also knew that some appliances don't stop working until you start using them on a daily basis. "I apologize, Ms. Rains. I'm out of town right now, and I won't be back until tomorrow afternoon, but I can have a friend of mine come by."

"Oh, sweetie, no," she said. "I can wait. There's no need for you to go to all that trouble. I'll just put my food in a cooler until you can get here tomorrow. I don't keep many groceries on hand anyway, since it's just me."

"Are you sure, Ms. Rains?" I asked.

"Yes, absolutely, dear."

"Okay. Well, I'll call you as soon as I get back in tomorrow," I said.

"Praise the Lord and goodnight," she said before hanging up.

"Baby, I'm sorry," I said, clicking back over.

"Everything all right?"

"Yeah. Ms. Rains says the fridge is acting up," I explained. "I offered to have Savoy stop by to check it out for her, but she said it can wait till tomorrow."

"Is she sure?"

"Yeah," I said. "I'll be back on the road first thing in the morning, as soon as my visit with Stephen is over. I'll handle it myself."

"Well, let me know if I can help," Octavia volunteered.

"Thank you, love. I will."

We talked until the only thing I could hear on the other end of the phone was the sound of Octavia breathing.

* * *

Stephen Garrison was a big brother with braids, who strangely resembled Rick Ross. He sat on the other side of the metal table in his prison whites, staring at me and his attorney, Eric McDaniels, a short, scrawny man with wire-rimmed glasses, dressed in a blue suit that looked liked he'd slept in it the night before.

"Stephen, my name is Damon Whitmore," I said, "and your mother used to work for me."

"What you do you mean she used to?"

"I'm sorry, but Contessa passed away," I said empathetically. "We've been trying to find you every since."

"You been looking for the wrong one," he said. "My mama's name ain't Contessa."

"Really? My wife found your inmate number in Contessa's things, so I assumed you are her son," I explained.

"You assumed wrong, mister."

"Stephen, this is the picture Damon provided me," Eric said. He opened his briefcase, removed the photo of Contessa, and slid it across the table toward the inmate.

I instantly saw it in Stephen's eyes, even behind the harsh exterior, that he recognized the woman in the photo.

"Is this your mother?" McDaniels asked.

"Yeah," he said.

"She was my daughter's nanny," I said. "She passed a month ago from a diabetic seizure."

Stephen ran his hand down over his face. "I'm done talking," he said.

"Stephen, you may want to hear Damon out," Eric interjected. "It may turn out to be very beneficial to you."

"How so?" he asked.

"Give us a minute," I said to Eric.

He hesitated slightly before getting up and walking away from the table.

"Contessa requested that her savings help maintain your commissary," I explained, leaning forward. "That's about $2,000. However, I can make sure you get whatever you need on the inside." I could tell he was considering my offer, but he wasn't onboard just yet. "Anything you need. I can even get you another lawyer."

"That's my mother," he finally said. "But her name wasn't Contessa. Her name was Mary-Ellen Garrison."

"Did she ever tell you about me or my family?" I asked.

"She told me about this chick who took her in," he said. "Said she pulled her off the street and gave her a job. Until she started working for that chick, my poor moms was in a real fucked-up place. I hadn't spoken to her or seen her in, like, fifteen years or so, but then, out of nowhere, some chick offers to help her turn her life around, to give her a new beginning. I think that was about nine months ago." He exhaled. "Anyway, my moms couldn't refuse a gig like that. The lady cleaned her up real nice and hooked her up with a job. Even moved her down to Alabama."

Stephen's story about the woman I knew as Contessa was interesting, but it was all new to me. I was confused but determined to get to the bottom of it all. I asked Stephen a few more questions about his mother before wrapping up our meeting. I advised him that I would be in contact and that I would honor my word. We shook hands and started to go our separate ways when I remembered I had one more question. "Oh,, just one more thing."

"Yeah?"

"Do you happen to know a man by the name of Kelly Baker?" I questioned.

"Who?" Stephen asked, staring me in the eyes.

"Kelly Baker."

He shook his head. "Nope. Never heard of him."

G STREET CHRONICLES
A NEW URBAN DYNASTY
WWW.GSTREETCHRONICLES.COM

Chapter 26

Octavia

After lunch, Amel and I sat in my office at TheAmbiance, going over paperwork and catching up with each other. My visit was nothing more than an excuse to sit down and talk with her face to face about her breakup with Tarik. She looked healthy and sounded fine as the two of us chopped it up. There was no evidence that she'd slipped back into her life of drug abuse. She told me she didn't want to go into details about Tarik, but she was fine with their mutual decision, and she said again that she knew it was in both of their best interests to go their separate ways. "Besides," she said with a smile, looking across the desk at me, "we never know what the future holds."

I wanted to tell her the future didn't hold shit for the two of them if she was willing to let the love of her life walk away, but I decided against it. As long as Amel was happy, I was happy for her. I was skeptical about asking her to attend Shontay and Savoy's upcoming reception, but she seemed genuinely thrilled about the invite and was extremely happy for Shontay.

"Are they registered?" she asked.

"Please," I said, turning up my lips. "Registered? Not going to happen. Shontay still hasn't even agreed to let Jasmine be her flower girl."

Amel blinked several times, staring at me with a questioning look.

"Octavia, people don't have flower girls if they get married at the JP. There's not even an aisle to walk down, let alone throw flowers."

"Y'all better stop hating on my baby," I said, waving my finger in the air. "She will be there with her basket and her rose petals, flower girl on deck."

Amel shook her head. "Never a dull moment," she said.

"You know that's right, girl!"

We both laughed.

"Thank you, boss lady."

"For what?" I asked.

"Just for...for being you." Amel smiled.

Knock-knock!

"It's open!" I said.

Tabitha opened the door and smiled. "You have a visitor," she said, "and yes, he is handsome."

I laughed. "You know me well," I said. "Amel, do you have anything else you want to discuss?"

"No, I'm good," Amel said.

"Okay. Great," I said, standing. I walked around my desk and leaned against the edge. "Tabitha, you can send him in." I looked at my watch, surprised that Damon had made it back from Tennessee in record time. I was anxious to see him and to hear about Stephen.

Five seconds later, Kelly strolled through my office door, flowers in hand. He was dressed rather casually in jeans and an emerald-green button-down. "Hello." He smiled and shut the door behind him.

"Kelly," I said, standing up straight.

"Did I catch you at a bad time?" he asked.

"Well, I am a little busy," I lied.

"This won't take long," he said, staring at me. "These are for you." He held up the roses and extended his arm out to me.

"Roses? What's the occasion?" I asked, removing the bouquet from his hand.

"So now I need an occasion?"

"Kelly, I think it's best if we don't see each other anymore," I said, exhaling. "You know, after everything that has happened, I just think—"

"Are you referring to what I told you about Damon?" he asked, standing with his hands in his pockets. "Or are you referring to everything that has happened between us?"

"Both," I said, setting the flowers on my desk.

"You find out the man you married isn't half the man you think he is, and you want to push the man who cared enough to tell you the truth away?" he asked, cocking his head to the side. "Octavia, what is it about him that has you so blind that you can't see the truth? If he lied once, he'll do it again and again and again. But he gets it honest." Kelly spoke with a passion I had never heard him use before.

"I forgave Damon," I said firmly, "because he is my husband and because his sin doesn't outweigh mine. We both have secrets, and we've both been very wrong."

Kelly laughed and shook his head. "How do you know Damon didn't sleep with Nadia?" he questioned.

"Because I trust and believe him, and he said he didn't," I said sincerely.

"Like he trusts and believes you when you say nothing's gone on between us?"

It was obvious Kelly was attempting to make a point—a point that was obviously being wasted on me. "He can trust and believe me," I said strongly, "because it's true."

He moved toward me, closing the short distance between us. "Denial is a terrible thing," he said.

"You should go," I said, stepping to the side.

"Octavia, why are you pretending this doesn't exist?" he asked. He stared at me with an expression of pain. "The chemistry is real."

"I'm not doing this, Kelly," I said. "I have too much to lose."

He nodded his head. "Okay," he said.

I held the office door open for him. I wanted him to go and right then.

"By the way, I'm still looking for my cousin," he said. "Hopefully I'll find him soon."

"I think we may have already found him," I said, happy for the change of subject. I did want him to leave, but I didn't want it to be on such uncomfortable terms.

"Really?" he asked with raised eyebrows. "When?"

"A few days ago," I said. "When I was cleaning out Contessa's room, I found some papers tucked away with his inmate information. We weren't going to tell you until we were sure, but Damon went up to Tennessee to see him."

"Good," he said abruptly. It seemed as if his whole demeanor had changed. "I better get going. Take care." And in a second flat, he was out the door.

Chapter 27

Kelly

I sat in my truck in the Ambiance parking lot with my phone pressed to my ear. "Just answer the damn phone," I grumbled aloud.

"Hello," Lena finally answered.

"What the fuck took you so long?" I snapped.

"Excuse me?" she asked, sounding offended. "I don't like your tone."

"Do you know where Damon is right now?"

"Yes, of course I do," she said sarcastically. "He's out of town."

"Not just out of town," I said. "He's in fucking Tennessee, visiting Contessa's son."

Lena sounded like she dropped the phone on the other end. "Wait... what?!" she blurted loudly. "How did he find him?"

"According to Octavia, Contessa left his inmate information in her room."

"That stupid old cow! That stupid, stupid wench!" she shouted. "Even after she's dead, she's ruining everything."

"Not only that," I said, "but if Damon figures out how it all ties together—how *we're* all tied together—sooner or later he's bound to link us to other things," I said, thinking about my involvement with the deaths of Emerson and Victor.

"Nadia's death was ruled an accident," Lena reminded me.

"Yes," I said, "but once people start snooping in your background, they start reevaluating things and look for other hidden details. They tend to dig up other dirty little secrets."

"You're right," she said. "I think I know what I need to do."

"Meaning what?"

"Don't worry, Kelly," she said. "It's going to be fine." She hung up before I could comment.

I wanted to tell her that the only way things were going to be fine was if someone put a complete stop to Damon's little investigation. It was obvious that telling Lena would be a waste of breath, though, because she was too far gone. Knowing her, she was still trying to figure out a way to make Damon her man. For all I knew, he already knew about our connection. Lena's over-emotional ass had packed her shit and moved back to Huntsville on a whim, and now everything else was falling apart. The situation seemed to be going downhill with every breath I took, and I debated about what my next move would be. I knew I could always pack up Donovan and move back out to the West. It would put distance between me and the crimes that were sure to start unraveling, but it would also dig my grave even deeper with Gator. I had hoped things were finally going to turn around for me, but now it seemed things were shifting again. Now I was faced with yet another dilemma. I had to come up with a solution...and quickly.

"You had me concerned," Gator said when he answered on the second ring.

"Sorry I've been out of contact," I said. "I've been working."

"Any luck?"

"Yeah," I said. "Actually, I've found out a lot."

"I'm listening."

"It turns out the missing link in the equation is a woman," I said.

"Continue."

I spun another tale of lies to Gator, in an effort to protect my own ass and possibly throw a wrench in Damon's investigation. I wasn't proud of myself for it, but I really didn't have an option. *"Sometimes money even trumps love."* Ilene's words echoed in my head. *Scratch that,* I thought. *Sometimes survival trumps everything.* After wrapping up my phone call with Gator, I called to let Donovan's afternoon babysitter know I was headed home.

Chapter 28

Damon

Whoever Kelly was, he'd played his hand and played it well. I didn't know who he was or what was on his agenda, but I knew he had made one of the biggest mistakes of his life by coming into the lives of me and my family. I opened the center console and pulled out my .45, then climbed out the driver side door. The parking lot of the complex was nearly empty, with the exception of Kelly's truck and a silver Mercedes-Benz, which was parked a couple spots down and appeared to be empty. Of course, with the anger I was feeling at that moment, it wouldn't have mattered if there was a gathering of spectators outside. I wanted Kelly to tell me who he was, and if he failed to comply, I was going to see to it that he choked on his own tongue.

I banged once, then twice, and finally a third time on the door until he finally answered, looking annoyed but not surprised. I could practically feel my adrenaline flowing through my veins as my heartbeat resounded in my eardrums.

"Listen, man, this ain't a good time, so you best just—"

I drove my fist into his jaw before he could complete his sentence. Kelly stumbled backward, I hit him with another right before he had time to recover, knocking him to the floor. I planted the heel of my shoe in the center of his chest.

"Fuck!" he panted, grasping his chest.

"Is it a good time now?" I asked, standing over him. "Who are you?" I gripped the handle of my .45 and aimed it right at the center of his forehead.

Kelly remained silent.

"Tell me who you are!" I demanded.

"Don't do it, Damon."

I whipped my head in the direction of the voice of Kelly's savior. I couldn't deny the voice, but it didn't stop me from doing a double-take. There stood my own mother, in the hallway of Kelly's apartment, dressed in a long, flowing, coral dress and gold open-toe sandals. She looked beautiful as always, but there was something different about the crease of her mouth and the arch of her brow. I remembered the Mercedes I had seen outside; it was my father's. I lowered my weapon and took two steps back. "What... what the hell are you doing here, Mama?" I asked. "What's going on?"

"I guess you're not the only one with secrets," Kelly said, choking out a laugh. He looked at me and grinned while slowly pulling himself up to his feet.

The thought of Kelly touching my mother made my stomach churn. I raised my arm, aiming the gun straight at his chest. "What is he talking about?" I snapped, looking into my mother's eyes.

"Damon, it's not what you think, darling," she answered gently.

"I'm sure it's ten times worst," Kelly taunted, "brah."

I rushed in his direction and grabbed him by his shirt, then backed him up against a wall, pressing my steel into his neck. I was prepared to blow his throat and his voice box out if he didn't start using them to answer my questions. "Are you fucking with my mother, you sick fuck?" I asked through clenched teeth. "Tell me what you're up to, you piece of shit!"

"Damon!" my mother called from behind me. "Enough!"

Kelly's gray eyes were wide with what I could only describe as laughter. He gave me a crooked smile. "Come on now," he said slowly. "Is this any way to treat your big brother?"

I wondered if I had stepped in the middle of a bad trip without even managing to get high. "What is he talking about?" I asked.

My mother inhaled deeply, then exhaled. "Kelly is not my lover,

Damon," she said lowly. "He's my…son."

I thought my ears were playing tricks on me, so I asked her to repeat herself.

"I said he's my son, Damon," she repeated firmly. "Kelly is your brother."

I looked back at my mother just long enough to see the expression on her face. For the first time in my life, she looked humiliated and ashamed. I released my grip on Kelly and backed away, lowering my weapon as I moved. I looked at Kelly, who only smiled as he looked at me. I was lost in my confusion, bombarded with the desire for the truth.

"Sit down," Mama instructed. "The three of us need to talk."

* * *

"I was twenty-one when I met Kelly's father," Mama began, as the three of us sat around Kelly's dining room table. "Back then, I was waiting tables to pay my way through college, and I met an older, charming man whom I lovingly nicknamed TD. He came into the diner every evening and order one cup of coffee, black, and a cinnamon roll." She smiled as if she was reliving the sweetest of all memories. "He always tipped me three times the amount of his bill, and sometimes he wouldn't even order anything at all but still left a tip on the table for me. This went on for approximately a month, and finally, one night he asked me out on a date. Of course I accepted."

I could tell Mama was enjoying her flashback, but I wanted her to fast forward to the part where the bastard sitting on the other side of her became my blood.

"About a three months after we started dating, I found out I was pregnant," she continued. " When I told TD, he informed me that he was a married man, with a wife and family in another city. I was clueless," she said, touching her hand to her neck. "The man was living a double life, and I had no idea."

"Sound familiar?" Kelly smiled mischievously.

I looked at him angrily, knowing I still wasn't above killing him.

"I was heartbroken and terrified. I didn't want to raise a child alone, but at the same time, I knew I couldn't kill my baby."

"So you put him up for adoption?" I concluded.

She nodded her head and dabbed at her eyes. "Yes," she said.

Best decision you ever made, I thought to myself. "How did the two of you reunite?" I questioned. "Kelly you led me to believe your meeting Octavia was a mere coincidence. Why don't you tell us what really happened?"

"Look, what I told you was the truth," he said, throwing his hands up. "I didn't find out we were brothers until after Nadia passed and I was going through some of her things. She had information on my birth mother, along with other details about the family. Hell, that gold-digger played all of us, wanting to get her hands on the Whitmore money, one way or the other. I think that was the only reason she took up with me, because she knew I was Ilene's son. Anyway, when I saw Ilene at that family gathering, I couldn't resist telling her who I was. After that, we exchanged numbers, and I visited her in Atlanta."

"Where?" I quizzed.

"Kelly came to our home," Mama told me.

"When?" I asked.

"A couple weeks ago," Mama answered. "Why?"

"Nothing, "I said. I knew it had to be around the time I had Lawrence following Kelly, back when Lawrence had advised me that he'd lost him. That explained why Kelly was paranoid to the point that he noticed Lawrence following him. "How do we know this is not all a lie?" I asked.

"We had a paternity test," Kelly said, "and it came up 99.9 percent positive." He was gloating, working my last damn nerves.

"Who performed this test?" After my run-in with Nadia and Gia, I knew anything could be faked, including medical test results.

"I called Dr. Jack," Mama told me.

I knew Jack was a trusted family friend; if he said the test was positive, it unfortunately had to be so. "So you didn't find out about the blood connection until after Nadia's death?" I asked, redirecting my attention to Kelly.

"That's right," he said, clearly annoyed with the interrogation.

"And what about Contessa?" I questioned. "How does she fall into the equation?"

"Contessa?" Mama asked. "What do you mean, Damon?"

"I went to see Contessa's son in prison," I informed them. "He's never heard of you, Kelly. If he's your cousin like you say, that doesn't make sense."

"Listen, I didn't want to say anything because I knew you guys were fond of my aunt, but I'd never even heard of Auntie until a year or so ago, when she contacted me and told me she was my mom's—uh, I mean my adoptive mom's—sister. I was just so happy to have someone left that I could call family that I accepted what she told me. We forged a bond and went from there. I never even met her son Jay. For all I know, her name wasn't even Contessa and she was in on Nadia's little scheme."

I remembered what Contessa's son had said about Contessa being on the streets until some wealthy chick came along. *Is it possible that Nadia was the woman?* "But why?" I asked. "Why pull Contessa into it?" I wasn't buying into Kelly's explanation.

"My aunt was the one who told me your family was hiring," he said. "When I didn't get the job, I turned right around and referred her."

"That could have been the plan from the very beginning," Mama said, "so it wouldn't be so obvious." She looked like she actually believed him. "Nadia was sneaky, and sneaky whores have scandalous agendas."

"Do you really believe that?" I asked, looking at my mother.

"I know Nadia discovered years ago, back when you were still in college, that I had a child before I met your father," she explained. "I kept a lockbox in my closet with mementos of Kelly, and Nadia discovered it during one of the summers when she was staying with us. Although she agreed to keep my secret, I know she would have done anything to weasel her way into our family and get next to you. Maybe she had the information because she planned to use it against us someday."

I nodded my head. "Is that why you didn't like Nadia?" I asked my mother. "Because of what she knew, what she could hold against you?" I was positively sure that Nadia had threatened or attempted to use the information against my mother, and that would explain her hatred for the woman.

"One of many reasons," she said, looking from me to Kelly.

"So what are your intentions now?" I asked Kelly, looking him directly in the eyes.

"I just want to get to know my family," he said. "Before you showed up, our mother and I were discussing our intentions to get to know one another."

"Do you want to know the family…or our finances?" I asked sarcastically.

"I don't want money," he barked.

"Sure you don't."

"DJ," Mama said lowly, "I offered Kelly money, and he turned me down."

"Maybe you didn't offer him enough," I said, continuing to stare Kelly down.

"I asked him to name the amount," she said, "and he still declined. That's why I am here today—to apologize and to try to make things right."

"Does Dad know?" I asked, ignoring my mother's statement.

"He does not," Mama said quickly, "and, DJ, darling, I ask that you please keep this between us until further notice."

I didn't like that she was keeping secrets from my father or even that she had kept the secret from me, but at the same time, I was in no position to judge. Besides, even if I was, I would never judge or allow anyone else to pass judgment on my mother. "We can do that," I said. I had heard enough of the drama for one day. "I have to get going. I've got to go check on a tenant. Mama, where are you staying?"

"She can stay here," Kelly suggested eagerly, "with me and her grandson."

"No, I'm going to get back on the road," she said. "I told Damon I would be home tonight, and I keep my promises."

"I think it'd be better if you stay with me and Octavia," I suggested. "You can leave first thing in the morning." I didn't like the idea of my mother traveling alone. I worried about her…and with good reason.

"Thank you, DJ," she said, "but if I leave now, I'll be home before 7. Besides, your mommy is a big girl. Believe it or not, I can handle my own. Don't let the class fool you. I am a force to be reckoned with, and nobody better mess with me."

I looked at Kelly. "I know," I said. "I've always known that, but I guess I believe it now more than ever."

* * *

I called Octavia and told her I had some news for her.

She told me she had a little news for me too. "Something's wrong," she said. "I can hear it in your voice."

"Yes, but it's not us," I reassured her. "We'll talk later. I'll see you when I leave from Ms. Rains's place."

"Okay, love," she said cheerfully. "I love you."

"I love you more."

I stood on the front step of the condo and rang the doorbell. After five seconds, I rang the doorbell again, then knocked. I wasn't in the mood for the waiting game. I was carrying too much baggage at the moment, and the only thing I wanted to do was go home to my wife and daughter and relax. I slipped my Blackberry out of the holster and dialed my tenant's number.

"Hallelujah! Praise the Lord!" she answered.

For a moment, I thought there was something slightly off about her voice, but I assumed it was just me and all the thoughts running through my head. "Ms. Rains, it's me, Damon."

"Oh, baby, I completely forgot about our appointment," she whined. "I am so sorry! Sugar, just go ahead and let yourself in."

As the landlord, I reserved the right to do so per our lease, but I preferred not to. "I can just come back," I said, turning to leave.

"No, just go on in," she insisted. "Honey, I ain't got nothing you ain't already seen probably times three. I'm at the church right now, helping with a ladies' seminar. I don't know how long I'll be, but I'm going to need a refrigerator tonight, sweetie. I'm bringing home a few trays of cheese and meat."

"Okay," I told her.

"Bye," she said sweetly.

I used my master key to unlock the door and stepped inside, leaving the door slightly open behind me. Inside the condo, I couldn't help but notice how nicely Ms. Rains had decorated the living room with leather and wood furnishings and beautiful pieces of black art on the walls. The walls, which had once been off white, were now burnt orange in the living room and two-toned with chocolate and cappuccino in the kitchen. Granted, she was only leasing the unit, but I approved of her painting and the color selection. It gave the area a warm feel.

I removed my suit jacket and laid it on the back of one of the mahogany dining room chairs. I opened the refrigerator door. Just as Ms. Rains had stated, it was completely off and warm inside. I walked to the hallway and found the breaker box so I could double-check the switch to make sure it was on; it wasn't. I hadn't even thought to inquire with Ms. Rains over the phone to see if she had checked it. After flipping the switch, I headed back to the kitchen to check the fridge again. Sure enough, it was up and running.

"That was simple, huh?"

I jumped slightly from the surprise of seeing Lena standing on the carpeted floor behind me. I hadn't even heard her come in. She was wearing a pair of open-toe high heels and a sheer black nightie that stopped well above her knees and showed every inch of her skin. She smiled at me like everything was normal, like she wasn't standing before me practically naked, like she wasn't an unwanted guest.

"What are you doing here?" I asked.

"You're here, baby," she said, stepping toward me, "and wherever you are is where I want to be."

I looked around the room and realized it was all strangely familiar. The condo was decorated and painted almost exactly like Lena's townhome in LA.

"Where is Ms. Rains?" I asked.

"At the ladies' luncheon, *sugar*," Lena stated, mocking the woman's voice.

It became clear to me that it was Lena I'd been on the phone with. I had called Ms. Rains's number, but Lena had answered the phone. "What did you do to her?" I demanded, taking a step forward.

"Nothing, Damon," she said, shaking her head. "Why would you automatically assume the worst of me? Geez! I would never hurt my own mother."

Mother? At that moment, I put it all together. It's amazing how foggy pieces of a puzzle can become clear in an instant. "Octavia was right," I said, shaking my head. She had taken my friendship for something other than platonic. "Reaching out to Shontay. The church. Opening the boutique. Falsely occupying my condo. All that shit was because you have feelings for me?"

Her eyes lowered to almost invisible slits at the mention of my wife's name. "Please don't mention her during *our* time!"

"What?" I questioned. "You tricked me, Lena. I would have never come here if I had known it had anything to do with you."

"Of course not," she said, "because Octavia has turned you against me! Don't you remember how we used to hold hands and laugh? How we kissed and made love? Damon, it's supposed to be us…forever!"

"Lena, we were kids!" I yelled. "We don't have a relationship. In fact, there is no we!" I was sick and tired of the nonsense. Normally, I would have tried to be more gentle and considerate of a woman's feelings, but enough was enough.

"You're just saying that, Damon," she insisted. "I see the way you look at me, the love in your eyes. You want me." She stepped across the carpet until we were standing toe to toe. "Damon, everyone knows your first is your best," she said, searching my eyes with hers. "We were reunited for a reason. You did everything you could for me for a reason. You told me you loved me, and I know you still do. Look how long we've been part of each other's lives, even when we didn't know it! Our future has already been prepared. We just have to live it."

I looked in her eyes and saw that I was fighting a losing battle. Lena was delusional and quite possibly psychotic. The only thing left for me to do was try and make an exit without someone getting hurt. "Lena, you are a wonderful woman, but you are mistaken. I did love you as a friend, but nothing more. I did what I did for you because I wanted to help you as a friend and because I wanted Shontay to be happy. I did it because of my love for Octavia." I said gently. "I love my wife. I went through hell for the love of my wife, and I'll make my bed in hell before I'll lose her. There is, nor will there ever be, anyone else." I could see the tears swelling in her eyes, and I decided it was time for me to exit. "I need you out of this condo within ten days or I will put you out." I walked over to the kitchen table and grabbed my jacket. I didn't bother putting it on. Instead, I moved quickly out the door and down the steps.

As I walked toward my car, I noticed a van parked across the street. I had an unsettling feeling that I was being watched. Once I was in the safety of my Range, I started the engine and looked in my rearview mirror. I saw Lena in the doorway, watching me, and I pulled off as quickly as possible.

* * *

As soon as I placed my key in the door to turn the lock, the front door of my home opened. Octavia stood in the doorway in a white, low-cut maxi-dress and a smile. Her hair was pulled high on her head in a long ponytail, and her lips shimmered lightly from her pink lip gloss.

"Where are you going, beautiful?" I asked, kissing her on the lips lightly.

"Nowhere right now," she said, "but a little later I plan to take a trip to ecstasy, and guess who I'm bringing with me."

"Sounds like a plan," I said, stepping inside our home. I placed my arm around her waist and led her to the kitchen with me.

"Something is still wrong," she concluded, placing her hand on my chest. "Did something happen on the trip? What did you find out?"

I had temporarily forgotten all about Stephen. "I don't even know where to begin," I said, dropping my arm from her waist. I pulled out a chair and sat down.

"How about we start with a drink?" she suggested.

"Hennessey on the rocks," I requested.

"Coming right up."

* * *

Fifteen minutes later, Octavia sat across from me at our kitchen table with her eyes and her mouth wide. I had just finished bringing her up to speed on Stephen, as well as Kelly and my mother. "Say something," I egged.

"That explains why Donovan and Jasmine look so much alike," she said slowly. "They're cousins."

I nodded my head in agreement. "You said all along that something wasn't right with Kelly. I guess we now know why."

"Yes," I said, "but I still don't know whether or not to believe him. For all we know, he could have plotted the whole thing or enlisted someone else. I mean, we thought Contessa was actually named Contessa, but—"

"Instead she's Mary-Ellen," Octavia recited. "I didn't have a clue when I brought her into our home. I still don't know who she really was."

The last thing I wanted was for Octavia to feel guilty. Even I had fallen for the deception. "We both made mistakes throughout this whole journey," I told her.

She smiled. "Now I see why you sounded like you did on the phone," she said. "This is a lot to digest in one day."

"Yeah," I agreed, "but I have something else I want to tell you."

Chapter 29

Lena

"Do I have a son-in-law yet?" Mama asked, walking through the front door of my condo. I had given her a key for emergencies, but she chose to use the place whenever she pleased, which was mainly when she came over to ask me for cash, and that seemed to happen often.

I sat on my living room sofa with my bathrobe wrapped around me. I was staring into space, focusing on nothing in particular. "Not yet," I said, sulking.

"What happened?" she asked, walking over to the kitchen table.

"He rejected me…again," I said, following her with my eyes.

"You wore the negligee and the heels?" she asked. She opened the kitchen cabinet where I stocked my wine and pulled out a bottle of Moscato.

"Yes," I said, sighing lightly. "He still turned me down." I watched her as she retrieved a wine glass from the cabinet and filled it to the rim.

"Seriously?" She exhaled. "I don't know who's more pathetic, you or that sister of yours."

"What?" I asked, slightly shocked.

"Don't what me," she said. She took a long sip from her glass and then topped it off again. "I take that back. Clearly, the more pathetic wench is you. I mean, at least your sister has a man. You can't even get one naked.

Then again, you are facing some fierce competition." She laughed. "That wifey of his is a hot little number. You'd probably be better off getting with her than with him."

"Please, Mama. I don't want to hear about Octavia," I snapped.

"Don't you get loud with me!" she ordered.

I watched as she turned her head up and guzzled what remained in the glass.

"You're here getting all pissy with me, when you should have been handling your business with Mr. Whitmore. I mean, I practically dropped that fine, rich-ass man in your lap, and you still couldn't secure him."

"He loves her," I reasoned.

"What does love have to do with his dick?" she questioned. "Not a damn thing. You take what you can get from him and let the rest work itself out."

"It's not over yet," I said.

"Please," she blurted, erupting in laughter. "You might as well pack up and head back West. You lost. Game over, you stupid girl." She set her glass on the counter, then walked over to the couch and stood in front of me. "Alicia, you must learn to accept defeat graciously," she said. She snatched the cell phone off the coffee table in front of me. "By the way, please remember to pay my phone bill. This is the only number my friends can use to contact me."

"Leave your key," I instructed.

"Excuse me?" she asked, staring down at me.

"Damon ordered me to vacate within ten days," I said.

"Great," she said, shaking her head. She slid the key off her key ring and tossed it on the sofa next to me.

"Can I stay with you until I find a new place for Janai and me?" I asked. It wasn't that I needed my mother; I just didn't want to be alone, and I figured crappy company would be better than none at all.

"Of course not," she said. "I can't have the bishop coming through and finding you all in my space. Just because you ruined your game doesn't mean I'm gonna let you ruin mine like you ruined my figure so many years ago. I'll call you if I need you," she said before exiting out the door.

I could feel tears swelling in my eyes. I snatched my own cell off the end table and dialed Kelly's number. The phone rang three times before his voicemail came on. I called him again, but this time his voicemail came on immediately. *He turned his phone off,* I thought to myself. I scrolled through my contacts and located Joni's number.

"Hello," she greeted me.

"Hey, Joni."

"Hey, Lena. How's it going?"

"Great," I lied. "Can I speak to Janai?"

"Sure. Just a sec."

I waited until I heard my daughter's voice on the other end of the phone. "Hey, baby. How are you?" I asked happily.

"Fine."

"How is school?"

"Good."

I was starting to get frustrated with her cold, one-word answers, but I decided to overlook them. "Are you ready to come home?" I asked.

"No. I want to stay here with Joni."

"Huh? Baby, what do you mean?"

"I like it here," she said, "and Joni's really nice, and…"

I tuned her out as she ranted and raved about Joni. "Well, what about me?"

"You'll be okay, Mommy," she said.

In that moment I felt like I had nothing else to lose. "You're right, sweetie," I said, forcing a smile. "I will."

* * *

I hated reaching out to my old contacts. It was a step backward, an unsettling reminder of where I'd come from. I don't care what people say: It is not always good to remember from whenst you came. For me, it was like taking a dump and going back and reflecting on the shit floating in the toilet. I had made that mistake with my mother, and all that had gotten me was disappointment and less cash than I had in the first place. Nevertheless, I needed a major favor, and for that, I would have to reach way down low to the bottom of the barrel for backup.

"What can I do for you?" Freddie answered.

Freddie was a brother Donna and I used to mess with back in the day. We only hit him up when we wanted to get high or needed something. Not only was he a weed man, but he could get almost anything anybody wanted. He was one of the hottest boosters in the projects. He wasn't an attractive man, but he got plenty of play in the 'hood because he only snatched high quality.

"Hey, baby," I said sweetly. "How you doing, Daddy?"

"Who dis?"

"Boo, it's me, Len...er, I mean Alicia."

"Alicia who?"

"Lee-Lee," I said, sighing lowly.

"I ain't got it, and even if I did, you can't get it," he said quickly.

"I don't need it," I said. I had forgotten that our last visit had ended on bad terms. Freddie had fronted me a $20-sack for which I had agreed to give him a little head. When he slipped in the bathroom to take a piss, I snatched the bag and hauled tail out the door. If Freddie had been any other man in the projects, I would have had a well-whooped ass, but back then Freddie was a lame. As long as we could get out of his sight, we could get away. "To tell you the truth," I continued. "I've got some work for you."

"Work? What kinda work?" he asked.

"I need your help with something," I said. "I'll make it worth your while."

"Your credit has expired with me," he said roughly.

"Don't worry," I said. "I can pay you in advance."

Chapter 30

*I*t had taken everything in my power not to ride over to the condo and beat the black off of Lena. Actually, it took Damon hiding all the keys and Shontay refusing to drive me. I know grown mothers should not express themselves with violence, but to hell with that. She had gone above and beyond the call of duty with her hoe-ism! Damon had given her ten days to move out of the condo, and she had obeyed. We hadn't heard from her nor seen her, so I was counting my blessings.

Granted, Damon and Kelly were half-brothers, but they still had no contact or interaction whatsoever.

I looked at Shontay and smiled. She was dressed in a champagne, off-the-shoulder fitted gown that flowed down to her ankles, almost covering her open-toe gold heels. She wore a single yellow daisy in her curly hair, just above her right ear. She looked beautiful, and she had a natural glow about her.

Savoy was dressed in a classic black tuxedo and champagne-colored silk tie. His dreads were neatly secured in a back ponytail.

The two of them held hands as they recited their vows.

"I, Shontay, take you, Savoy, to be my husband…"

I listened as I looked over at Damon. In his black tux and bowtie, he looked just as handsome—if not more—as he had the day the two of us recited our vows on the lawn of our home. He turned his head, winked his eye at me, and smiled. Our daughter stood in front of us, wearing the fluffy pink dress I'd purchased for her and holding a small champagne satin-covered basket. *I told y'all my baby was gonna throw her petals!* I thought. I felt happy and beautiful as I stood amongst some of the ones I loved in my spaghetti-strap pink dress and crystal-covered, see-through heels. Despite the weeks leading up to that day, my life was good and nearly perfect—so perfect that if it had been chosen as the last day of my life, I would die complete.

"I now pronounce you husband and wife," the Justice of the Peace said. "You may kiss your bride."

Damon and I watched as Savoy laid a kiss on Shontay, so passionate I almost blushed.

"Congratulations! "I smiled. hugging my bestie.

"Thank you," she beamed proudly. "I'm married now!"

We both erupted in laughter.

"Congrats, brah," Damon said, as he and Savoy exchanged a brotherly hug.

After the four of us exchanged hugs and kisses, we posed for the photographer Savoy had hired before, and then we left City Hall to head to Ambiance.

* * *

By the time we got to the reception, a small crowd had gathered in honor of Savoy and Shontay, including my parents and Damon's. Savoy's mother and sisters, though, were MIA. I thought their failure to appear was tasteless and tacky. Regardless of their feelings about Shontay and what she did or didn't do, Savoy loved her, and I had learned that life is far too short to be without the ones you love.

"You should have seen Jazz throwing rose petals on top of my shoes!" Shontay laughed, speaking to my parents.

"I told you my baby was going to have her moment." I laughed.

"I'm so happy! Both of my girls are finally happy," Mama said, taking us by the hands.

She and Ilene wore mother-of-the-bride dresses. Mama's was pink and off the shoulders and came just above her knees, while Ilene's was pink and strapless and also stopped above the knees. Both my father and Damon's wore black suits and ties.

"Finally, you're each complete," Mama continued.

The three of us embraced and struck a pose for the photographer.

"Excuse me, ladies," Savoy interrupted. "If you all don't mind, I would love to dance with my bride."

"By bride he means me!" Shontay cheesed.

"I got a man, so I don't mind at all," Mama said. "Catch you later, pretty girl."

"Bye, gorgeous." I laughed and watched as Mama made her way across the floor to where my father was standing with Damon Sr. and Ilene.

Scar, my deejay began spinning Keith Sweat's "Make it Last Forever."

Damon walked up to me. "Care to dance?" he asked, taking me by the hand.

"I would, but my boyfriend wouldn't like that," I teased.

"Good." He smiled, pulling me in his arms. "Today has been a good day," he said as he held my waist tightly.

"A perfect day," I said, wrapping my arms around his neck, "and tonight will be a perfect night."

"Now you know we have to get up early in the morning," he reminded me. "Straight to the airport!"

"Paris...finally!" I said excitedly.

The two of us finally had our flights confirmed and were set to depart, along with my parents, at 8 a.m.

"Do you think your parents will be the same?" I asked. "After a week with their granddaughter?"

"I don't think Jasmine will be the same." Damon laughed. "We'll have to de-divatize her when we get back."

"I know," I agreed. "A week of shopping with your mother? Priceless."

"Not for Pops," Damon said. "You know he's picking up the tab."

"Like father, like son," I said. I yawned lightly.

"Tired, baby?"

"A little," I admitted. "I think with all the excitement, I've been running on E."

"Why don't you call it an early night?" he suggested. "I can lock up here."

"I don't want to leave you with all the responsibility," I said. "I'll be okay."

"We're partners," he said. "We've got each other's backs, remember?"

"Yes, you're right." I smiled. "We are…and we do." I rested my head on his shoulder as the two of us swayed slowly to Keith's crooning. "That's why I'm going to stay here to help you."

"You're stubborn as hell," he said, shaking his head, "but I love you."

I lifted my head and stared into his eyes. It felt like the first time I'd ever seen him. There was a depth in his stare that could only be described as true love—the kind of love forever is built upon. "I love you more," I replied.

* * *

Shontay's and Savoy's well-wishers had all departed, with the exception of my employees, who were now in cleanup mode, my parents, and my in-laws. The happy couple insisted on staying to see everyone off. It was just like the two of them to break an age-old tradition.

"Baby girl, your mom and I are going to head home so we can get some rest," Daddy said, kissing my cheek. "We'll see you in the morning."

"Okay, Daddy." I smiled brightly. "I love you."

"Love you, baby," Mama said, hugging me.

"Love you too," I replied. I watched as the two of them walked out, saying goodbye to everyone who was left in the building.

"We are departing, too, darling," Ilene said. "The Embassy is calling."

"Are you sure the two of you don't want to stay with us?" I asked. "We have plenty of room."

My mother-in-law had requested for Jasmine to go ahead and stay the night with her. In my mind, she and my father-in-law would have been a lot more comfortable at our house with a toddler.

"Now, dear, you know your mother-in-law," Damon Sr. said, shaking his head. "She'll do anything to get in my pockets."

"You know me so well." Ilene smiled proudly. "Besides, Jazz is two. She's long overdue for her first stay in a luxury suite. We'll see you in the morning, darling." She gave me a nice, warm hug. "I love you," she said quickly.

I looked into her pretty gray eyes and smiled. "I love you too." It was the first time in the history of my relationship with Damon that she'd ever said the words to me. I hugged my father-in-law, kissed my daughter, and stood there, savoring the moment I had just shared with Ilene.

"Hey, bestie." Shontay smiled, walking up to me.

"Hello, beautiful."

"Are you sure you don't want Savoy and I to stay until everything is locked down?" she asked. "Really, we don't mind a bit."

"Positive," I said. "Go get started on your wedding night."

She smiled mischievously. "Girl, you don't have to tell me twice."

"You are a freak," I teased.

"Super freak," she said, correcting me.

We both laughed.

"Savoy and I will take the presents back with us. That'll be one less thing for you and Damon to deal with."

Shontay and Savoy had received an abundance of gifts, despite the fact they requested none be given. It just goes to prove that when you're good people, others don't mind doing for you, even if you can already afford it.

"I don't think they'll all fit in his car," I said. "Why don't you two take the Range, and Damon can take Savoy's car?"

"You think Damon will mind?"

"Of course not, but I'll ask him just in case," I said. "Just my little way of letting him think he's in control."

"You mean he's not?"

"Choose a side," I joked, "and stay on it."

"I did! I chose the truth."

"So, have the two of you decided where you're going to live?" I asked as we walked toward the exit doors.

"Uh, no," Shontay said. "We plan to make that decision in the next few days."

"So while most couples would be honeymooning it up, you'll be house-hunting? How romantic." I laughed.

"I know. We're so backward." She laughed. "But we work well together. We'll probably seek temporary housing here while Savoy works on the new job. Who knows? Maybe we'll buy a home in the new Mayberry."

"Either way, there's always room at the Whitmores'," I offered sincerely.

"I know." She grinned. "That's why I'm in no rush!"

Outside, night had come. I admired the light the full moon cast down upon us. In the sky was a cluster of stars, including the constellations. I briefly admired the Big Dipper before turning my attention to Damon.

"Savoy and I are going to swap rides so they can take the gifts home," Damon told me.

I looked at Shontay and smiled. "Great minds think alike," I quipped.

"And marry," Shontay added.

Savoy held the passenger side door open for Shontay before jogging around to the driver side. "See you back at the house," Savoy said, throwing his hand up.

"See you later." I smiled, wrapping my arm around Damon's waist.

"Be careful," Damon stated.

"You too," Savoy recited.

Chapter 31

Damon

Octavia and I waited as her last employee clocked out and headed for the front door. After double-checking all the doors, she set the alarm, and the two of us exited.

"What do you say we go for a ride?" I suggested while we walked hand in hand toward the parking lot.

"Sounds like a plan." She smiled. "We can let the top down and let the wind whip through our hair." She paused, looking up at my head. "Whip through *my* hair." She laughed.

"You got jokes," I said, "but I got you."

The sound of her Blackberry ringing interrupted us.

"Hello" she answered cheerfully.

"This is Octavia. What? When? We're on our way!"

"What is it, baby?" I questioned, concerned by the look on her face and the sound of desperation in her voice.

"That was a nurse at Crestwood. Shontay and Savoy have been shot!"

* * *

Octavia and I sat in the waiting room of the ER, waiting to speak with the doctor. Although we had only been there for three minutes, it felt like we'd been there an hour.

"I'm sure they're fine," I said to Octavia. I took her hand in mine and squeezed it gently.

She nodded her head but remained quiet.

A tall, balding brother in green scrubs pushed through the doors, into the waiting room. "Mr. and Mrs. Whitmore!" he called, looking around the room.

"Yes," we answered, standing.

"I'm Dr. Riddick," he said as he walked up to us.

"Are our friends okay?" Octavia questioned.

"Ms. Holloway—"

"Breedwell," Octavia corrected him. "They got married today."

"Mrs. Breedwell sustained a gunshot wound to her chest," he began.

Octavia gasped loudly.

I wrapped my arm around her waist, holding her tightly.

"The bullet missed her heart by mere inches, but she's lost a lot of blood. We've managed to get her stabilized, but right now it's touch and go."

"What about Savoy?" I asked.

"I'm sorry," he said. "Mr. Breedwell didn't make it. His injuries were too substantial, and he died moments after arrival. We did everything we could, but there was too much damage."

"No!" Octavia whispered. "Oh no…"

I was in a complete daze as I stared at the man, waiting for him to tell me he was mistaken and that he didn't really mean to say that Savoy, my partner, my brother was gone. I waited, but in my heart I knew that my waiting was in vain.

"Baby, I'm sorry." Octavia sobbed, wrapping her arms around my waist.

I rubbed my hand up and down the middle of her back. I fought against the tears that were attempting to rush from my eyes. *I need to be strong,* I told myself, *for my wife and for Shontay.* "Can I…see him?" I asked.

"This way," Dr. Riddick said, nodding his head. He led us through the automatic doors to a small room. "I'll give you a moment," he said, walking away.

"I'll be right here," Octavia said. She must have read my mind, because my next request was going to be that she wait for me outside.

I stepped in the room, allowing the door to close behind me. Savoy lay on his back on the small metal table, a thin white sheet covering his body. I stared at him, thinking about how happy he'd been just moments earlier, wondering who had done it and why. I felt an unbearable weight bearing down inside of me, making my knees shake. I felt weak and helpless, and the tears I'd been fighting won. I dropped to my knees next to the table and cried until I could barely breath. I felt a warm hand on my shoulder and then another on the top of my head. I looked up into my wife's eyes.

"It's okay," she whispered. "It's okay."

I wrapped my arms around her waist, allowing my tears to saturate her dress. After I gained my composure, I contacted Savoy's mother. Breaking the news of her only son's death was one of the hardest calls I'd ever had to make, and I silently hoped it was one I would never receive. I knew death is certain for everyone, but I couldn't imagine having to outlive my child.

Before we left the ER, an officer with the HPD advised me that a motorist found Savoy lying facedown in the street by the driver door with his cell phone in his hand. Shontay lay by the curb on the passenger side. Both of them were unconscious and bleeding. Savoy had been shot at point-blank range, while Shontay had been shot from a short distance away. The officer said it looked like a possible robbery or attempted carjacking.

I ruled out robbery as a possibility when he told me they discovered that Savoy still had his wallet, all his cash and credit cards, and that Shontay still had her purse and all of its contents. I ruled out carjacking when he told me they didn't take the damn car. It didn't make any sense whatsoever. I understood that he was grasping at straws, attempting to come up with some viable explanation, but I wasn't buying the story. However, I chose to keep my thoughts to myself. One of the biggest mistakes one can make is to have too much knowledge in the presence of any authority you don't employ yourself.

"It's possible Savoy fought back," the officer continued, "and the assailant panicked."

I nodded my head in agreement.

"We do know there was at least two shooters," he continued.

"How can you be sure if there were no witnesses?" I questioned.

"The shell casings found at the scene," he said, "were from two different weapons."

I had never been in the business of robbery, but even I knew one thing to be true: A robber doesn't waste his time and risk his freedom to come up empty-handed, and they never spend too much time at one crime scene. It was just common sense. My heart was telling me there was another motive behind the crimes. My first thought was to take the law into my own hands and do my own investigation, but then thoughts of Lawrence came to mind. I had done so many things my way, and the last time had cost a good friend and a loyal man his life. I couldn't risk harm coming to anyone else I knew or loved. I decided to wait and let the police do their job.

* * *

Octavia insisted on staying at the hospital with Shontay. It took myself and the hospital staff to convince her that it would be better if she went home and returned in the morning. Even then, the only way I could convince her to leave was by promising we would stay the next day.

Later that night, I lay in bed, staring up at the ceiling. I still hadn't come to terms with what had taken place that day. It seemed unreal that Savoy was gone and Shontay was fighting for her life.

"Are you asleep?" Octavia asked, lying with her back turned to me.

"No," I said.

She rolled over to face me. "Can't sleep either?" she asked, running her fingers across my bare chest.

I turned on my side so the two of us were eye to eye. I grabbed her hand and pressed it against my lips, giving it a brief kiss. "Too many thoughts running through my mind," I said truthfully.

"Mine too."

"I was just thinking about the night Savoy and I met." I laughed lightly.

"Oh, the infamous Taliyah." she smiled. "You know, to this day, Shontay and I believe there's more to that little story."

"More? Like what?" I asked innocently.

"Like the two of you accepting her offer," she said.

The night Savoy and I met, we ended up in the apartment of a female we'd both been dating. When we confronted Taliyah about seeing both of us, she invited us in for a threesome. Thinking back, some men would have ended that situation in bloodshed or at least beef, but it wasn't like that for Savoy and me. It was like we'd known each other our whole lives, and we were destined to be friends. Thinking back, I realized it was already written that Savoy would be my brother and friend for life.

"I'm waiting," Octavia said, staring at me with her honey-brown eyes.

I suddenly saw my wife in a new light. Before that day, I'd always known she held her own personal strength, but I also knew she could be weak in front of me. What I hadn't realized until earlier was that it was okay during certain situations for me to be weak.

"We told you." I chuckled and rolled onto my back. then pulled her into my arms. "Nothing happened."

"Mm-hmm."

"Thank you," I said seriously.

"For what, babe?"

"For being there…and for being you," I said, my way of thanking her for allowing me to cry on her shoulder.

"No," she said. "Thank *you*."

"For?"

"For allowing me to do so."

"They'll find out who did this," I told her.

"I hope so," she said. "I really hope so."

The two of us lay in silence until she fell asleep, and my own sleep soon followed.

* * *

I sat straight up in bed and grabbed the ringing cordless off my nightstand. I assumed it had also awakened Octavia, because she bolted up next to me.

"Hello."

"Mr. Whitmore, this is Stephanie, Shontay's nurse."

I couldn't deny that I was nervous about what was to follow. "What is it, Stephanie?" I asked.

"We're just calling to let you know Shontay is awake."

"Thank you," I said, relieved. "We'll see you soon."

Chapter 32

Lena

I propped my feet up in front of me on the bed and stared at the .25 I held in my hand. I had purchased the gun from Freddie, and it had served its purpose. I looked at the piece, wondering how I had gotten to that point—the point of complete isolation and desperation. I had left my passion, my daughter, and my home to move across the country in pursuit of the man I loved, but all that had gotten me was a stay in a lonely suite at the Extended Stay and my mother's phone bill. *How did I get here? By trusting my heart and feelings to self-centered assholes, that's how. I give and give and give, and all they do is take, take, take. Not anymore! Enough is enough!*

I laid the gun on the nightstand next to the bed and turned on the television. I was channel-surfing, in search of something that might entertain me and occupy my thoughts, when I saw Shontay's and Savoy's faces on the screen, followed by pictures of a black Range Rover. I recognized the car immediately as Damon's. The photos were replaced with live feed of a short brunette, standing in front of the camera, holding a microphone.

"The couple was on their way back to the home of some friends after leaving a celebration in their honor at this local restaurant."

The camera cut to a view of Ambiance.

"Mr. Breedwell died within minutes of arriving at the ER. Mrs. Breedwell is in stable but critical condition. Authorities are asking anyone with information to come forward and contact the Huntsville Police Department at 256-555-5595."

I stared at the TV in a complete state of shock. *Savoy's dead and Shontay is fighting for her life? How did that happen?! That was Damon's car. I know it was, but why weren't he and Octavia in it?* "Shit!" I said, shaking my head. "Shontay."

I rocked back and forth on the bed thinking, replaying the scene of that evening. I had sat in the passenger side of the Dodge Charger, parked by the curb. I had been waiting for over an hour, but I knew it would all be worth it when everything was done. I'd looked up in the rearview mirror, checking my reflection. I'd even thought to cover my head with a dark baseball cap that matched the dark sweats and sneakers I wore. From my position, I could see Ambiance in the distance. Freddie had sat behind the steering wheel, looking impatient. I had dropped him some cash and broken him off some head to get him to accompany me. I was disgusted about the latter of the two, of course, but it was all for a greater good. We'd sat in the parking lot two buildings over from Ambiance, waiting, watching vehicles entering and leaving from the restaurant parking lot.

"There they go!" I said excitedly.

Freddie started the car but hesitated before pulling out.

"What are you waiting for?" I asked impatiently.

"Are you sure that's them?"

It was obvious that Freddie was still a lame, and he'd suddenly become a bitch. "Yeah, I'm sure," I snapped. "I know that car anywhere!"

Freddie shook his head but finally pulled out of the parking lot. He was taking his own sweet time as he drove down the street.

"You're going to lose them!" I snapped. "Speed up!" I was sitting on the edge of my seat. I had the gun in one hand and my other hand planted firmly on the dashboard to brace myself. Thanks to Freddie's non-driving ass, I knew we were sure to miss the chance to catch who I was sure was Damon and Octavia, slipping.

"The light is going to catch them," he said loudly. "Be easy. Shit." We rode behind the car, following it turn for turn. "Is that car following us?" Freddie asked, looking in his rearview.

I turned my head briefly but saw nothing. *This asshole is paranoid,* I thought. I redirected my attention to the road and the car in front of me. Damon's car came to a stop as the traffic light turned red. I felt the sweet taste of victory as we pulled up behind them. "Tap the truck," I said.

"What?"

"Bump them!" I ordered, cutting my eyes over at Freddie.

"Hell no!"

"Do it," I said, aiming the gun at him. "Do it now!" I was through playing with him. He had the option of doing what I said or doing nothing ever again.

Freddie eased off the break and hit the Range lightly from the back. The impact was light, but it was enough to push the Range slightly forward under the light.

I climbed out of the car with the gun at my side. The passenger side door of Damon's car opened, and she stepped out wearing what looked to be an evening gown.

"Yo, someone's coming," Freddie said.

"Are you guys all right?" I heard the driver ask.

I cut my eyes to the left and saw him moving closer.

"Are you okay?" she asked, looking at me as she moved in closer. She stayed what some would consider a safe distance away, but it wasn't safe enough.

I lifted my arm and smiled. I could see the surprise and the shock on her face as I pulled the trigger. She fell like an angel falling to Earth.

"Noooo!!!!!" I heard him scream, rushing to her side.

"Let's go!" Freddie ordered.

I hopped back in the car, barely getting the door closed before Freddie mashed out and away from the scene.

"Shontay?" I repeated to myself over and over again. *It was dark on the street, but it couldn't have been Shontay! It was Octavia! It had to be! There had to be some mistake,* I told myself.

I dug through my purse until I located my cell phone. I scrolled through my contacts until I located Shontay's name and pressed send.

The line rang several times before going to voicemail.

"Shit!" I cursed, slamming my phone on the bed.

A few seconds later, my phone rang. I hastily picked it up and looked at the caller ID. It was the number, calling me back. "Hello" I answered slowly.

"Who is this?" she asked.

There was something annoying and familiar about the voice. It was Octavia.

"I…I'm sorry," I said. "I must have the wrong number." I pressed the end button, hanging up in her ear.

What have I done? I asked myself. I quickly scrambled, grabbing my purse and my keys. I opened my hotel door and ran straight into a tall brother who looked like he ate the damn weights rather than lifted them. "Sorry," I said, attempting to step around him.

"Let's talk," he said, blocking my path.

I looked in his hard, dark face and knew my ass was in trouble. "No thanks," I said, planting my heel in his crotch.

The man didn't budge. Instead, he smiled.

What the hell? I thought. I saw a flash of gray before I felt a heavy blow to my head, and everything around me faded to black.

Chapter 33

"How long have I been out?" Shontay asked, looking over at me. Her voice was almost inaudible in the room, thanks to the wheezing and beeping of the monitors and machines surrounding her.

"Just twenty-four hours," I answered, standing by her bed.

"Thank God." She breathed lightly. "I just knew you were going to tell me it had been years."

"No." I smiled.

"Good," she said slowly. "Although I could probably wake up fifteen years from now, and you still wouldn't have a single wrinkle."

"Good genes," I joked.

"Too stubborn to grow old." She laughed, then winced.

"Did that hurt?" I asked.

"A little," she said. "Getting shot hurts like hell."

"You remember what happened?" I asked.

"Yes," she said. "I remember Savoy and I were talking when someone bumped the car from the back…"

I listened as Shontay told me the story.

"They pulled the trigger and shot me, then just drove off," she said. She stopped and looked at me with her eyes wide. "Wait…where is Savoy?"

I looked at her in silence.

The look of panic and fear on her face slowly broke my heart.

"Shontay…"

"Oh no!" she cried. "Noooo! Noooo! Savoy? Noooooo!" A river of tears flowed down her cheeks as she covered her mouth with one hand while squeezing mine with the other. "Noooo! Why?!" she asked as she began to sob uncontrollably. "Why?! This isn't how it was supposed to be Octavia!" She coughed lightly. "Not like this!" She cried hysterically while coughing uncontrollably.

"I know," I said. I leaned over the bed, stroking her head softly with my fingertips in an attempt to calm her down. "I know."

Shontay's coughing became worse.

I pressed the button for the nurses' station.

The machine that monitored Shontay's heart began to beep erratically, and her eyes rolled back in her head as she released the grip she had on my hand. Her body began to shake violently.

"Shontay!" I cried. "Shontay!"

Everything passed in a blur as the door flung open and a team of nurses and doctors rushed in. Their voices played in my ears, mingling together. I moved backward, one step at a time, until I was standing outside the door.

Shontay shook and shook again until she finally shook no more. I saw the line on the monitor as it dropped from its plateau to the even valley. I heard the doctor's words, as he tried frantically to revive her. Shontay's body jumped from the electric shock they applied to her chest, but that dreaded flatline refused to climb again. My stomach turned into a painful knot, sending me to the floor. I felt a piece of my heart being torn from my body. I tasted my own tears as I opened my mouth and screamed in sorrow and horror at losing my best friend.

Chapter 34

Octavia

We buried Shontay and Savoy just as they would have wanted it, side by side. That day, it rained from sunup to sundown, but it wasn't one of those gloomy, depressing rains. It was more of a calming, soothing kind of rain, the kind that lullabies you to sleep. I told Damon it was Shontay's mother Josephine celebrating their reunion and Ely, Savoy's father, celebrating theirs. I knew that wasn't the reason, but in a small way, it gave me peace.

Damon said the day of the funeral was the first time he'd seen Savoy's mother and sisters in years. He made a vow to stay in contact and advised the ladies to get in touch with him if they needed anything. I was polite to each of them, but I did not try to hide the fact that I had some ill feelings. I felt it strange that they would show up for a funeral but not a celebration of love. Damon reminded me that Shontay would not want me to hold a grudge. I reminded him that while she would not have wanted me to, she knew me well enough to know I still would.

The authorities had yet to find the people responsible for the murder of my best friend and her new groom, and I was getting more and more impatient with the wait. Knowing that their killer or killers were walking around only added insult to my emotional injury, and not a day went by when I didn't think of them.

Despite our original plans to refrain from daycare, Damon made the suggestion that I go back to work at my restaurants, and we put Jazz in a daycare facility. My first thought was to protest, but I knew that sitting at home all day would not be a good way to deal with my friends' deaths, even if I did have my daughter there with me. So, we found what was considered to be a prestigious daycare not far from Ambiance, and I was back to my day-to-day grind. Damon begged me not to overdo it, so I agreed to work only half-days for the first couple of weeks.

It was already after 1 p.m., so I decided to wrap up my work at the restaurant. I still had to pick Jasmine up, and I wanted to pick up something good to make for dinner before I headed home. "See you tomorrow." I smiled at Tabitha as I strolled toward the door.

"Octavia."

I turned around and saw Gator sitting at the bar. He had an empty shot glass in his hand. "Hello," I said. I was in a hurry and was in no mood for his down-low flirting.

"Leaving?" he asked, standing and adjusting his suit jacket.

"I am," I said, looking at the watch on my wrist. "I have got to go get my daughter."

"Well, let me walk you out," he volunteered. He reached in his pocket, pulled out a $100 bill, and laid it on the bar.

"No need," I said quickly.

"I was just leaving myself," he said, standing.

"Very well," I said, walking off. I didn't have to turn around to know that Gator was not far behind me. "Have a good evening," I told Amel as I walked by.

"You too," she said hesitantly, looking from me to Gator.

I could only imagine how the scene looked, but at that moment, I didn't have time to explain. Outside I saw a dark blue passenger van parked across the street from the restaurant.

"Have a good evening, Octavia," he said as he crossed the street, walking toward the van.

"You too," I said, throwing up my hand.

* * *

I was making record time as Jasmine and I came out of Target. I'd decided to cook Damon a nice T-bone steak and a baked potato. I figured we could light some candles and enjoy love. "Ready to see Daddy?" I asked Jasmine as I strapped her in her car seat.

She smiled brightly.

"Me too." I laughed, shutting the back door.

I was backing up when a tall brother appeared out of nowhere behind my car.

"Damn it!" I yelled, slamming on my brakes. "Sorry, Jazz," I said, feeling bad for cussing in front of her. I'd always believed a mother with a potty mouth would raise a child with a potty mouth, and I normally only swore when Jasmine was out of earshot, figuring what she didn't hear wouldn't hurt her.

The man looked equally terrified. He stood with one hand on my trunk, clutching his chest.

"Please let him be all right," I prayed silently. "Are you okay?" I asked as I exited my vehicle. I walked back to the trunk of the car where he was still standing, still clutching his chest.

"Yes," he said, standing upright. "I'm just fine."

I instantly knew something was wrong. I saw the van Gator had entered earlier speeding toward us. I tried to make a run for it, but it was too late. The man grabbed me by my hair. I screamed as pain shot through my neck. He pulled me back against his hard body, lifting me in the air as the van came to a screeching halt besides us. The door of the van opened, and he tossed me in. I screamed, kicking wildly as thoughts of my daughter being left alone filled my head. A second later, I felt a blow as someone sucker-punched me, and everything around me went black.

Chapter 35

Damon

"They're working the leads they have at this very moment," Charles advised me in regard to the search and investigation to locate Octavia. "I've called my connects, and they're also checking out the information the witnesses provided."

I listened in silence as images of Octavia flashed through my head. I couldn't imagine the fear she must have felt at the time, not only for herself but for Jasmine. They were devastating and unsettling thoughts. Someone had taken my wife and left my daughter alone and vulnerable in the back seat of a car. I was thankful to the good Samaritans in the parking lot of the Target shopping center who'd witnessed the kidnapping and come to Jazz's rescue. They'd even returned Octavia's handbag and its contents without touching a dime. They were living proof that there were still some good people in the world, but the men responsible for her kidnapping were proof that there were still individuals who didn't value their own lives. I was a firm believer that whatever a man does not value, he should lose.

I sat for forty-five minutes and listened to the police jargon and investigation bullshit. It was forty-five minutes of my time that was clearly wasted. I had trusted HPD to solve the case of Shontay and Savoy, and they'd gotten absolutely nowhere. I would not make the same mistake with my wife. It was obvious that someone was personally attacking my family. What I couldn't understand is why they hadn't contacted me yet. "I can't wait for them to find her," I said.

"I don't expect you to," Charles said. "That's why were going to find her ourselves."

I nodded my head in agreement.

"Charlene called your mother, and your parents are on their way," he continued.

I hadn't planned on telling my parents what was going on. The only reason I'd told Charlene was because I knew she would eventually get suspicious when she didn't receive her nightly phone call from Octavia. "How is Charlene doing?"

"Worried," he said.

"Understandable. How are you?" I asked.

He looked at me and bit his lip. "Worried and pissed."

"Me too," I told him. "Me too."

I gave Charles a list of Octavia's employees, as well as mine. I also disclosed the information I'd learned about Contessa and her son Stephen, as well as everything I knew about Lena. In our eyes, everyone was a suspect, and no one was exempt. When the police interviewed Octavia's employees who were on duty, none of them seemed to recall any strange visitors or anything out of the ordinary.

When Amel came to me, I found out that she'd purposely lied to the HPD. "When Octavia left, she was talking to a man," she said quietly.

"What man?"

"His name is Leon," she said, "but everyone in the streets knows him as Gator."

"How do you know this man?" I asked, looking her in her eyes.

"I knew him through Beau," she said, lowering his eyes. "He's a dealer."

I frowned. *Why was Octavia receiving visits from a drug dealer?* "What else do you know about this man, this Gator?" I questioned.

"He's big time," she said, "and he's bad news," she said, and then she offered me the best description she could.

I now regretted not insisting that Ryan put surveillance cameras throughout the entire dining room. I understood that it was an invasion of privacy, but a hidden camera doesn't hurt anything unless someone is up to no good. I decided to call Charles to bring him up to speed on the new information. "Amel said a dealer by the name of Gator was in here talking to Octavia yesterday."

"Gator?" Charles repeated.

"Yes. You know him?"

"I know *of* him," he said. "Back before you and Octavia got married, she asked me to investigate Beau. I discovered that Beau was connected to a major supplier out of Queens, a man by the name of Montay. This Montay had a couple people in the area whom he did business with, including—"

"Gator," I concluded. "Do you think this is payback for what went down with Beau?" I was responsible for Beau's death, and if anything happened to Octavia because of me, I wouldn't be able to live with myself.

"I doubt it," Charles said. "If anything, Gator probably saw Beau's death as an opportunity to come up and take over."

"Why would he be visiting Octavia at the restaurant?" I questioned.

"That's a good question," Charles said. "The man is a major player in the streets. Anything he's involved with is guaranteed to get sticky. He's a professional, and he has a whole slew of flunkies to handle his dirty deeds."

In an instant, I remembered telling Octavia about Lawrence's death, telling her that hiring a professional to kill a professional would take money. "Charles, can you check and see if you can find a connection between a boy named Emerson Bailey and Gator?" I asked.

Jennings had advised me that he'd found nothing, but I wanted to try again. Granted, Jennings was on my payroll, and if Gator was as big as I was beginning to think he was from everything I was being told, the possibility existed that he could have more than one officer on the force on his team. No one was exempt.

"Emerson?" Charles repeated. "Where have I heard that name before?"

"He was found dead a couple months ago," I told him, "along with an associate of mine."

"I'll check on it," Charles said. "I checked out Contessa, Mary-Ellen. Her son's story checks out. She was clean. I have someone working on the employees."

"What about Lena?" I questioned.

"I haven't been able to locater her yet," he said. "Her mother says she hasn't heard from her in days. I also went by her boutique. It's closed. The other shop owners said they haven't seen anyone in or out for days."

I wondered if Lena had finally decided to just leave town. Maybe she'd decided enough was enough.

"I'm going to check out the Emerson connection," he said. "I'll let you know as soon as I hear something."

"Sounds good," I said. "Later."

Thirty minutes later, Charles called back. "Damon, I've got something on Emerson."

"What's up?" I asked, impressed with Charles's speedy turnaround.

"Emerson Bailey is the son of Terrance and Venetta Bailey. Venetta Bailey is the sister of Leon Douglass, also known as Gator."

"Emerson was Gator's nephew?"

"Yes," Charles answered.

Gator was linked with Emerson, and Lawrence was linked to me. Gator was acting out of revenge. *But where does Kelly fit in?*

"Can you think of anyone else who may have been involved?" Charles asked.

"Just one," I said, "but I'll handle it."

* * *

Before paying Kelly a visit, I went home and retrieved the case I kept hidden behind one of the panels in my bedroom closet. I always kept two things of value in the case: my .45 and a half-million dollars. I slipped my .45 under my seat, then climbed out my Benz with the case in hand. I hadn't had any contact with Kelly since my mother made her grand announcement. In my mind, there was nothing to be said, nor was there anything that needed to be discussed. I felt I had no obligation whatsoever to the man. However, now that I was on a desperate search, I needed to make sure I crossed all my t's and dotted all my i's.

"I swear you have the most imperfect timing," he said when he opened the door. "What ever happened to calling before you come?"

"I need to speak with you," I said, ignoring his question.

"Now is not a good time, Damon," he said, looking at his watch. "I just laid Donovan down for his nap."

"It's never a good time," I reminded him. "But my wife is missing." I saw what looked like a glimmer of hope flashing in his eyes.

"She left you?" he asked.

I could almost smell the happiness in his voice. "Never," I said, shaking my head. "She was abducted."

The way Kelly felt for Octavia would have been crystal clear even to a blind man. He took a deep breath and exhaled. "Come in," he said, stepping away from the door.

"Octavia was snatched yesterday," I said, as the two of us sat at Kelly's dining room table. "From the parking lot of the Target over on University Drive."

"Were there any witness?" he asked. "Have you heard anything from her abductor?" Kelly shot question after question at me.

"There were witnesses who said the person who took her threw her in a blue van." I waited to see if his expression changed, but it didn't. I knew then that Kelly was not involved. I don't know how I knew, but I did. "Her captors have not contacted me."

"Shit, man," he said, shaking his head. "That's not good."

Kelly was right. The fact that the abductors hadn't contacted me was not a good sign, but I refused to think of Octavia as anything but alive. "Before she was taken, she had a visitor at Ambiance," I continued. "I need to know your connection to that man."

"Who?"

"Leon Douglass," I answered. "Gator."

Kelly looked away, and I could see in his face that he was going to lie.

"Kelly, I think this man has Octavia," I said, "and I think *you* know what he's capable of."

"Why would you assume he's linked to me?" he asked.

"Because Gator's nephew Emerson was killed by an associate of mine," I confessed. "You may know him as Victor Henson. He was the private investigator I hired...to follow you. I know something went wrong between the two men, and I know you were involved, but none of that matters. All I want is to get my wife back." I lifted the case up on the table and opened it before him. "This will be yours, and the rest will be history."

Kelly stared from me to the money. I had turned on the light in his head by putting it all on the table. Now it was up to him to prove he was smart enough to eat.

Chapter 36

Lena

I'd never been one to dwell on how or when I'll die. Why would I? I was too busy living, trying to claim what was mine. I won't lie, though. My current situation has me rethinking a lot of things.

Days ago, when I awakened, I found myself tied to a chair in the middle of an abandoned warehouse. Inside the warehouse were several chains hanging from the ceiling, and four dust-covered fluorescent lights, along with an equally dusty mattress. For the first two days, I sat thinking about ways to escape, until I finally concluded there wasn't one. The metal doors opened from the outside, and the windows were so high that it would literally take a lift to reach them. When I first came to, my head was still throbbing from the blow I'd received, but now the spot was numb. I knew without even touching it that there had to be a knot, undoubtedly a large, disgusting one. It was unbearably hot and humid in the warehouse, and there was sweat dripping from my body like rain falling from an umbrella. I hadn't heard nor seen anyone since I'd been dumped in this hellhole, and I was beginning to wonder if they had forgotten about me. My lips were chafed and cracked to the point that when I licked them, I only tasted blood and raw meat. I swallowed, attempting to cool the burning sensation in my dry throat, to no avail; in fact, it seemed my saliva only made things worse.

My dress and panties felt like they were singed to my skin, saturated by my own sweat and urine. I was so miserable with all the pain in other parts of my body that I had no time to focus on the hunger pangs that coursed through my stomach in waves. All I could do was wait for my captor to return so he could do whatever it was he had planned.

But then it hit me: *Maybe this IS the plan. Maybe he WANTS me to suffer and rot slowly away.* Either way, I was already tired of waiting to find out. I was ready for whatever he had prepared.

The sound of a car pulling up made me squeamish. A minute later, I heard several locks being opened and saw light as the door was opened. The breeze that flowed in from outside was brief but refreshing. I watched as the asshole who'd knocked me out at the hotel entered, carrying a woman on his shoulders. He dropped her on the mattress and then stood over her, watching her briefly.

She wore a cream pencil skirt and pink, short-sleeved blouse. Her long hair covered her face, and her hands and feet were bond by plastic ties.

"I brought you a little company." He smiled, turning to look at me. "You two play nice. I'll be back soon."

"Can I please have something to drink?" I asked, watching him as he walked toward the doors. "Please?" I was thirsty as hell, and I had no clue how long it would take for him to come back again.

He looked like he was contemplating my request. I thought he was until I saw him unzipping his pants as he walked toward me. He stopped directly in front of me with his hands wrapped around what had to be the world's smallest dick. "Suck this and you'll have something to drink in just a minute."

I rolled my eyes and turned my head.

"Hmm?" he said, attempting to rub his tiny black pecker across my lips. "Open up, bitch," he ordered. "Open up!"

"Leave her alone."

We both looked over at the woman as she slowly sat upright.

"What's wrong?" the man asked. "You want some too?" He walked over and grabbed her by the hair, pulling her head back.

Octavia, I thought, staring at her face.

"Don't touch me!" she screamed.

"Here you go," he said. He held her by the hair with one hand, holding himself with the other. "Take it. Come on...take it!"

"Darth!" the voice at the door echoed loudly.

I turned and saw a tall, dark-skinned, handsome brother wearing a designer suit.

"Let her go."

"I was just playing with her, Z." Darth laughed and released his grip on Octavia, then backed away. He didn't turn around to face the man until after his pants were zipped up. I assumed he was ashamed for another man to see the travesty he was walking around with between his legs.

"Let's go," Z ordered. "We got other shit to handle besides messin' around with these hoes."

Darth followed behind Z as he exited, leaving Octavia and I alone. I stared at her; she appeared to be allowing her eyes to adjust to the light. Her right eye was swollen and an off shade of purple and blue. She finally looked like she had gained her bearings. She looked at me and frowned.

"Are you serious?!" she snapped.

Chapter 37

Octavia

The smell of urine and funk floating in the air made me want to throw up, and seeing Lena didn't make it any better. She sat there, bound to a chair looking, like shit run over. I stared at the large gash on her head and wondered what Darth's weapon of choice was when he went upside her head. When I had awakened from Darth's punch, I'd found myself tied to a metal beam inside someone's basement. The room was empty, with the exception of a sheet-covered mattress and a toilet. There were four rectangular windows at the top of the wall; each had to be either boarded or covered, because the only hint of sun were the rays that peeked through the random cracks.

During my time at the home, the man known as Z stood guard over me. Z was a tall, chocolate brother with a clean-shaven bald head, full mustache, beard, and glasses. The first time he'd offered me something to eat, I'd declined for fear that he was trying to poison my ass. However, once my stomach started to feel like it was beating down my back, I accepted. Granted I knew that Z could kill me at any second in cold blood, but I all-out refused to take every breath in fear. After several hours, Darth had returned and made the announcement that they were relocating me, and now, here I was, stuck in a nasty –funk-filled hellhole with an even nastier person for company.

"What?!" I asked.

Lena sat staring at me for a moment before she answered. "Of all people for me to spend my last days with," she said, shaking her head. Her voice was scratchy and rugged.

"I'm not exactly thrilled about the accommodations," I snapped sarcastically, "and don't worry. You're dying by yourself." I was claiming it, for my own sake and for the sakes of Jasmine and Damon.

"I heard about Shontay," she said.

My mind had kicked into survival mode, to the point where I'd forgotten my sorrow, but the mere mention of my bestie's name jolted me back to the morning she took her last breath. "She and Savoy are...in a better place," I said confidently. I shook my urge to cry. "At least they're together forever, like she wanted."

"In a better place? Together forever? What do you mean? I thought Savoy was...gone. That's what it said on the news, and—"

"They're both gone," I said, clearing my throat and cutting her off. I looked at her and frowned.

Her eyes widened slightly, and she shook her head. "No, only *he* died," she said.

"How long have you been here anyway?" I asked.

"Since the morning after the shooting."

It was obvious that Lena hadn't heard the newest news, so she didn't know Shontay had died from her injuries.

"Shontay passed too," I said gently. Regardless of my problems with Lena, Shontay was her friend too. "We buried them together."

Lena made a strange, shrill sound and began to cry. "I'm so, so sorry, Shontay." She looked at me again, still shaking her head. "It was supposed to be you! It was supposed to be you!"

Me? What? I stared at her, wondering what in the hell she was talking about.

Chapter 38

Damon

I stood in the family room of my home, surrounded by my family.

"Damon, I don't like this one bit," my mother said, shaking her head. "Something doesn't feel right."

"It's going to be fine, Mama," I reassured her.

Her concern was justified though.

Kelly had contacted Gator, advising him that I was ready to talk.

"Seems you are a very lucky man, Mr. Whitmore," Gator said from the other end of the phone.

"Where is my wife?"

"She is in a safe place," he said.

"What do you want?"

"Your life," he said.

"It's yours," I said sincerely. "Just let Octavia go with hers."

The two of us agreed to meet at his storage warehouse, and he promised to bring Octavia to the spot alive and in one piece. Though I wasn't sure how much I could trust a promise from a man like Gator, I had no choice but to comply.

* * *

An hour later, Kelly and I stood in a field behind a large brick home. On our way to the warehouse, I received a phone call from Charles advising me that Octavia was still at the original holding spot.

"He didn't move her," Charles said.

"What?"

"She's not at the warehouse. She's on a farm in Triana," he explained.

"Are you sure?"

"Positive," he said. "The information came from an insider. He said you have one hour to get in and out before someone returns."

I listened to him carefully as he gave me directions, then pressed end on my phone. "Charles said he received a tip Octavia's still at the original holding location, a farm in Triana. We have an hour to get in and out."

"Triana?" Kelly's eyes widened. "I know exactly where it is," he said. "Let's go get your girl."

I was dressed for action in jeans and a thick sweatshirt. I told Kelly I wanted to wear something warm in the event that Octavia might need it when we found her. Under my jeans, I was wearing the leg holster Charles had provided, secured tightly with his .25mm tucked inside. More than anything, I wanted to bring my wife home safe and sound, but I wasn't about to get caught slipping.

"You ready?" Kelly asked, looking over at me.

"Yup. Let's go," I said, clutching my .45 in my hand.

As the two of us ran through the knee-high grass, thoughts of my family ran through my mind: the day I'd met Octavia, our first kiss, the first time we made love—all of those beautiful moments I'd spent with her. I also pictured Savoy and Shontay smiling down on me.

When Kelly and I reached the house, the back door was unlocked. I slowly pushed it open and eased inside, with Kelly right behind me. The house was dead quiet—too quiet, as far as I was concerned.

I looked around, checking the area around me before walking toward the stairs that led down to the basement. I eased down the steps one by one, clutching my piece in front of me. I could feel the sweat on my brow, hear my heartbeat increasing. I slowly turned the knob to open the door. I looked around frantically. *Fuck!* I thought as I held my .45 by my side, realizing the room was empty. *What in the hell has Gator done?* "She's gone,"

I said through clenched teeth. I looked at Kelly and saw it in his eyes as he aimed his gun at me: I was too late to react.

In the next second, my bastard half-brother pulled the trigger and hit me three times in the chest.

Chapter 39

Kelly

When Gator asked me to help find the missing link in the case with Emerson, I did what anyone with common sense would do: I made up a lie. I told him about a love affair gone wrong, and I threw Lena under the damn bus. I explained to Gator that Lena was playing house with a married man, but she had a thing for the young bucks. I advised him that I had discovered she was breaking Emerson off, and her other lover, supposedly Victor, who was found dead with Emerson, found out about it. Damon would have never been included in my plot for revenge, but he was seen leaving Lena's condo, and his name came up in a discussion about the case with Emerson.

Detective Jennings was a man who liked to play as many sides of the game as possible. When Damon asked him to check into the case, he had no clue that Gator already had approached Jennings about it. See, Jennings loved money, regardless of the source. He also liked to treat his nose and veins; Jennings was a junkie. Working for Damon was a win-win situation, but working for Gator was a double. Damon had money to offer, but Gator had money and drugs. When Gator was informed that Damon had an interest in the case and saw him coming out of Lena's spot, it was a wrap.

I handed Lena over to Gator as the missing link, and I thought that would be the end, but then he requested that I off Damon too. I should have known that canceling my debt was going to involve more than just providing him names. Nothing in life is ever that easy. I was also sure his request was a test of my loyalty, and my only option was to honor that request and pass that test.

The night of the reception at Ambiance, I sat in the passenger seat of the van Gator used for his dirty work, with Darth behind the wheel. We had noticed the white Impala tailing the Range Rover, so we fell back. I heard the first gunshot and thought sure someone had beaten me to the job, until we moved in closer. I didn't notice Shontay lying beside the car, so I assumed I'd just mistaken a car backfiring for a gunshot.

Part of me was torn with what I was about to do, but it came down to being either Damon or me; with those odds, I had to choose me. I climbed out of the van and rushed up to the scene. As I moved closer, I knew the man standing by the car door wasn't Damon, but I pulled the trigger anyway with the ill hope that Gator would be satisfied and it would be over—once he got Lena, of course. I let off five rounds before running back and jumping in the van.

Needless to say, when the news broke that it was not Damon, Gator ended up taking things into his own hands by grabbing Octavia. I couldn't deny being pissed off about that little turn of events, because I cared about Octavia more than anyone, but I also knew there was a way I could redeem myself from one end by helping Damon get Octavia back. When the call came through that the plans had changed, I decided it was a perfect opportunity for me to make good on my agreement to off Damon. It would make me look good with Gator, and when I got Octavia back, it would be in my arms where she'd seek comfort, and it would be my dick she'd ride—not to mention that Damon's fool ass had dropped me a half-million for my "assistance." I would finally be able to have a new start with a real woman and my own money.

I left Damon's body at the bottom of the stairs and hurried out of the house. As I rushed, I dialed Gator's number.

"My patience is wearing thin," Gator said as soon as he answered his phone. "Talk to me."

"I'm on my way," I said. "We had a change of plans that required me to go ahead and, uh…handle that problem. He's gone."

"It's done?" he asked lightly. "Really?"

"Yes."

"Very good. I'll see you when you get here," he said. "Thanks for a job well done."

I cut through the grass until I reached the road where Damon and I had parked. I climbed in my truck and started the ignition. I felt the cold steel pressed against my neck before I heard his voice.

"Going somewhere?" he asked.

I glanced up in the rearview mirror. "You gotta be shittin' me," I said as he looked back at me.

Chapter 40

Octavia

"I thought she was you," Lena ranted. "I would have never hurt Shontay. She was good."

As much as I hated the girl, I had to agree with her. Shontay was good, and I loved her too.

Lena explained to me all the sick, twisted details of her plot to take my life the night of the reception, only to find out Damon and I weren't in the car. She told me about her "perfect plan" to win my Damon over, a plan for which she enlisted help. As she spoke, I actually felt pity for her. She was lost without a damn cause, and—worse—she was absolutely clueless to it.

The door opened, and Gator entered the room, accompanied by a tall, slim brother who didn't look like he was playing with a full deck. For this reason, I wondered if he and Lena were related. He looked at me, then began to stare at Lena. Darth entered next, pulling the door closed behind him. He looked at me, then squeezed his pathetic crotch. I turned my eyes in disgust.

"It seems we've had a slight change of plans, ladies," Gator said. "I was hoping Damon would be able to join us."

My heart fluttered at the mention of my husband's name.

"Damon? Where is he?" Lena asked eagerly. She smiled, looking like a madwoman.

"Unfortunately, due to unforeseen circumstances, young Mr. Whitmore didn't make it," Gator continued grimly, without the slightest bit of emotion.

"Where is he?" Lena asked, turning her head frantically from side to side.

"Dead," Gator said, looking at me.

I remained silent, telling myself it was nothing but a lie to get to me. I forced my tears that were attempting to surface to stay still.

Lena, on the other hand, unstable as she was, flipped out. "No!" she screamed, bucking in the chair. "I fucking hate you…you bitch!" She screamed and cried while looking across the room at me. "You did this! You! If Damon's dead, kill me!" she ranted, looking at Gator. "Kill me so I can be with him! Kill me now so—"

Her frantic plea was cut short by the bullet that burst through the side of her head. I watched as fragments of her skull and brains fell on her shoulders like tainted rain. The sight pushed the contents of my stomach up. Tears streamed down my cheeks as I hurled on the ground next to me.

The man who'd entered with Gator stood with his gun still aimed in the air. There was a look of satisfaction plastered on his face.

I looked at Gator, as he stood there, still emotionless. "Ask and it shall be given," he said, adjusting his tie.

The lights inside the warehouse suddenly went out, and three pops, followed by a loud boom, sounded outside. The doors flew open, spilling light in, followed by the terrifying exchange of gunfire.

Chapter 41

Damon

"Son? Son, are you all right?"

I lay on my back with my eyes closed. The impact from the bullets had knocked the wind out of me, but I was alive. I opened my eyes and saw my father kneeling beside me. I rolled over on my side, then quickly pulled my sweatshirt up over my head. There was a stinging in my chest that was annoying as hell, but it was ten times better than the alternative: death. I quickly pulled open the Velcro straps on the bulletproof vest and slipped it over my head. I took a deep breath, then exhaled through my lips. After catching my breath, I replied, "Yeah, Dad, I'm good."

He extended his hand to help me up.

"Octavia's not...she ain't here," I gasped.

"I know," he said. "Charles is on his way to the warehouse as we speak."

I carried the sweatshirt and the vest Charles had loaned me as the two of us cut through the grass toward Kelly's truck. I was thankful that I'd taken the vest when Charles had offered it. "How'd you get here?" I asked, looking over at my father.

"A friend."

When we reached Kelly's truck, my father told me to drive.

"Where's Kelly?" I questioned as I climbed in behind the wheel.

"Uh, in a safe place," he responded.

* * *

We reached the warehouse just as the smoke began to clear, literally. Charles was on the scene already, along with a team of officers and HEMSI. When he saw me, he smiled a smile that could only mean one thing. I looked past him and saw my beautiful wife sitting on the back of the ambulance.

She looked shaken, and she had a black eye, but she was alive. "Damon!" She cried as soon as she spotted me.

I ran to her like a man running for his life. Now that I think of it, I was; Octavia was my life, and I couldn't get to her fast enough.

Charles later explained that before we arrived, there'd been an exchange of gunfire outside, and Gator's drive, AJ, was taken out. When Darth came out to see what all the commotion was about, he saw the officers and opened fire while attempting to retreat back inside the warehouse, but he was struck down, along with Terrance Bailey. Gator was smart enough to duck and take cover. When the gunfire ended, he came out and surrendered peacefully.

Lena's body was carried out, and I admit I felt no sympathy after Octavia explained that Lena had confessed not only being responsible for Shontay's death, but that she—along with Kelly and Nadia—had all planned and been involved in the intricate plot to destroy my marriage. In the end, not only did her plan fail, but in some ways, it brought Octavia and I closer together.

Chapter 42

*D*amon's on his way," Charles said, looking at me. "Both of them."

"Everything okay?" I asked.

"They're both fine."

"I'm going to head out," I said. "I have another meeting, and I don't wanna be late. Plus, I don't wanna blow my cover."

"I appreciate everything," Charles said, extending his hand to me.

"It was my honor," I said, giving him a firm handshake.

Charles reached in his back pocket and removed an envelope and handed it to me. "For your trouble," he said.

I put my hand in the air. "No need," I said, "I've already been paid in full."

"Um, okay," Charles said, nodding his head. "Be safe, Lawrence."

"And you do the same."

Once I was snuggly sitting in the cab of my F250, I removed the plastic glasses from my face and pulled back the fake mustache and beard. As I drove down the gravel road, away from the scene, Kelly's Armado came speeding past me. I knew Damon should be in the truck if all had gone well, but I just wanted to be sure. I came to a stop and checked the rearview mirror; I saw Damon Sr. and Damon Jr. hop out. "Crazy-in-love motherfucker!" I laughed to myself as I continued to my destination.

If I had known that helping my boy on his journey to happily ever after would have caused my black ass so many problems, I probably would have declined the first assignment. For starters, I almost got shot once by Octavia, and then I actually *did* get shot by Emerson. *Emerson.* The poor kid. That night that changed everything. Emerson came out like a soldier on a blazing trail, but only two of his rounds actually touched me: one to my chest and a graze on my neck. When I heard the first shot go off, I immediately started retaliating. Glass was flying everywhere like gnats swarming in the wilderness. I knew Terrance and Gator were looking for someone to blame for Emerson's death, but the guilt lay within the two of them. They were the ones who'd sent the boy—their own nephew/godson and son—out to do the job of a man. Against someone with less experience and training, Emerson may have survived, but I was the shit, and that li'l boy didn't stand a chance. His own kin had sent him out to the damn wolves.

After that, I pretended to be dead until the coast was clear. Then, I snatched the cell phone Emerson had handed me to call Kelly and headed to a safe house I had established in the event of an emergency. I called a colleague of mine, and he patched my wound up. He also had access to cadavers so that was how the world learned of Victor Henson's death.

After I healed, I got back on the job. I staked out the home Emerson had shared with his parents, and when I felt the time was right, I introduced myself to Terrance who later put me on to Gator. If I had been a little earlier, I could have saved D.'s boy Savoy and possibly his wife Shontay, but I was a little too late. When the orders came down to snatch D.'s wifey, I, posing as "Z", insisted on doing the grabbing. I was determined to return the beauty to him unharmed. Leaving Jasmine behind was a last-minute decision, but it was for the best. I'm convinced that if Gator had snatched both Damon's wife and daughter, he certainly would have killed one of them.

I was the one who tipped Charles off about Gator and Emerson's connection. I was the one who contacted him about a change in the meeting between Damon and Gator. The goal was to keep Damon out of harm's way until I, along with Charles and his colleagues, could properly handle things at the warehouse. I knew Damon well enough to know he wanted a piece of the action, and he would have enjoyed nothing more than killing Octavia's captor personally. Normally, I wouldn't fuck with cops, retired or otherwise, but Charles was a special breed, a good dude—not dirty enough for my taste, but still a good guy. Things didn't go quite as planned, but for the most part, they turned out well for everyone involved—well, almost everyone.

When I pulled up in front of Damon's condo, I parked behind the silver Benz. The doors to the car were unlocked, just as we agreed, giving me easy access to the trunk. I popped the trunk and walked around to the back of the car. "Remember me?" I asked, staring down at Kelly. I could see the fear in his eyes as he stared back at me. I smiled, letting him know his fear was justified.

Epilogue

Ilene

I sat behind the wheel of my car with the radio turned up slightly to help muffle the grumbles and moans coming from my trunk. After my husband had held Kelly at gunpoint, then bound and gagged him, together we lifted him into my trunk. I drove him to the condo, parked the car, and removed the keys, leaving the doors unlocked.

I sat there thinking about how time had passed so quickly and about all the events that had led up to that moment. I was capable of loving Kelly, but I loved my DJ more. Having the capability to do something and actually choosing to do so are two entirely different things. Even though I'd given birth to the boy, my relationship with Kelly was never meant to be. He would forever envy DJ and lust after Octavia, and he would undoubtedly do anything within his power to cause DJ harm. So, when my husband suggested that we deliver him into the hands of Lawrence once Octavia was safe, I did what any woman dedicated to her husband and their child would do: I agreed. When I reached out to Kelly after he declined my money, I did so with the intention of finding out what it would take to make him go away. I was slowly building to the question when DJ caught me in Kelly's apartment. I immediately played it off but getting Kelly out of my life was always my plan. There was a slight possibility that things between Kelly and

I might have turned out differently, but that was a chance I was not willing to take.

I strolled away from the condo with my phone in hand. A few minutes later, I rode in the back of a cab back to DJ's home. I had delivered Kelly to Lawrence, and it was up to him what happened next.

One Year Later

When DJ and Octavia announced their plans to renew their vows, I felt it only fitting that the two of them do so at our home in Stone Mountain. After all, I'd been promising to have a family get-together, and there was no time like the present.

I watched the two of them spinning around on the rented dance floor that my loving husband had installed on our lawn for the wonderful occasion. Octavia was wearing a long, cream, strapless, fitted-bodice gown with a chapel-length train, and of course her shoes were open-toe, five-inch heels that had been custom created for her by my favorite designer. The bodice of her gown was adorned with pearls and sequins. Her hair was swept up on top of her head in a cascade of curls, and around her neck she wore the stunning teardrop pearl and diamond necklace I'd given her. On her wrist she wore a diamond bracelet, a gift from her husband.

Damon looked just as handsome as he had when the two of them had exchanged vows the for the very first time. He complemented his queen exquisitely in his cream tuxedo. The tie he wore was a shimmering gold that reflected majestically against his skin.

I nodded my head as Charles escorted Charlene out onto the dance floor. The two of them looked so happy. Charles wore a simple black tux, and Charlene wore a stunning purple gown. After a week in Paris, where my husband and I had joined them, they looked refreshed and so alive. The City of Love could have that effect!

I admired my grandchildren as they laughed and played amongst themselves. Soon, Octavia and DJ would be adding another beautiful addition to our cozy little family. She was only six weeks along, but she was already glowing. "Jasmine, Donovan, please be careful, darlings," I called out to my grandchildren as they ran across the lawn.

At first I was completely and utterly against disclosing Kelly's paternity to my husband, but I couldn't justify bringing Donovan into our home without some feasible reason. When I broke the news to him, he didn't even blink. The fact was, he already knew. I came to find out that Nadia had, in fact, disclosed my little secret while she was involved with my husband. I had faith that Donovan had potential to grow up to be a strong, successful man. How could he not being in the presence of influences and role models like DJ and Octavia?

"You got everything you wanted, didn't you?"

I turned on my heels to greet the giver of the dreaded voice that came from behind me.

My mother-in-law was there, in her wheelchair. She was dressed in a gold, sequined gown with a flowing skirt that stopped just below her scrawny knees. I had chosen the gown, along with the lovely salt-and-pepper duo curl wig for her to wear for the occasion. She looked pretty on the outside, but there was no accounting for the ugly inside her. Nonetheless, I was thrilled to see that she was adjusting more and more to her new form of transportation.

See, a month after Octavia's rescue and the untimely death of Kelly, Odessa paid us a surprise visit. Unfortunately, her trip was foiled when she took an unsightly tumble down the flight of stairs in my home. She was unconscious for nearly a week, and I thought she might pass, but just like an old, determined dog, she pulled through. In the fall, though, the stubborn one had fractured her hip in three places and severely damaged her vertebrate, leaving her partially paralyzed. She'd been confined to a wheelchair every since, stuck in my home. To be honest, if she hadn't been paralyzed, I would have kicked her out without a second thought. Truth be told, I still wasn't above considering that.

Odessa had burned so many bridges with me. When she thought she was on her deathbed, she disclosed that she was the one who'd encouraged Nadia to carry Donovan to term, and she'd even supported her in her nasty plot to wreck Damon and Octavia's marriage. Nadia was Odessa's favorite of all of DJ's girlfriends, and Octavia was mine.

When I casually left the copy of *Black Woman's Monthly* lying on my kitchen counter, I knew Octavia would catch his eye because she'd caught mine. I knew she'd make the perfect daughter-in-law, and once Damon saw her, he knew she'd make the perfect wife. The first step to a successful marriage is knowing what you want; the second is knowing how to get it. My husband often told me that he knew I'd be his wife, right from the first moment he saw me. What he didn't know was that I'd already seen *him* a week before at the bank where he worked, and I'd already declared the same thing to myself. I knew how he liked his coffee, who cut his hair, and two of his pet peeves before we ever said hello. A good whore does her research, but a bad chick does too.

I looked at Odessa and smiled. "You're right, Odessa. I think I did get everything I wanted," I bragged, "and it is such a wonderful feeling."

Octavia

I swayed my hips from side to side while resting my head on my husband's shoulder. After our family party, the two of us had a flight to catch to France, a just-the-two-of-us trip that was long overdue. The past year had been hard as hell, but Damon and I had done what we always did: We'd survived.

I missed Shontay and Savoy something crazy, but I knew the two of them were with me in spirit. Gator sat in jail, awaiting his trial for his involvement in mine and Lena's kidnapping and a slew of other criminal activities. I was ready to get the trial over and put it behind me.

Four months after Contessa's death, we were informed that traces of Drano, along with other household products, had been found in the poor woman's bloodstream. The examiner concluded that she'd died from meth complications, but I was pretty sure she died because she was tired of Lena and Kelly's game. Contessa had warned me about Kelly, but I'd just brushed her off. I didn't have any proof, but I refused to believe that Contessa died only for one reason: because she was trying to warn us. When I think about her warning and how she came to my rescue when Damon questioned me about the earring he found and even how the camera that would have showed me entering the guesthouse with Kelly, mysteriously stopped working around that time, I can only conclude she was trying to save Damon and me. Yes, she was wrong for her deception and her participation in Lena's plan, but I knew she was a good person underneath all of that.

The night of my release, Kelly's burned body was found in Damon's rental property. The property was engulfed in flames, due to what authorities called "a natural gas explosion." Their guess was that Kelly had taken Damon Sr.'s car and drove to the condo to hide from the authorities. When I asked why he took Damon's car, Daddy suggested that Kelly probably wanted to throw investigators off track. Kelly's death was ruled an accident and was never mentioned again.

I looked across the lawn at my mother, Ilene, my father, and Damon Sr. I looked at Odessa, sitting in her wheelchair with Isabella pushing her toward the house. As I did, I reflected on how Damon and I met and everything that had taken place over the last few years. I concluded that there were no accidents when it came to our family, nor were there any limits when it came to our love.

Mz. Robinson

Mz. Robinson, born in Huntsville, Alabama is a licensed Realtor and the author of the tantilizing Love, Lies, and Lust Series. Mz. Robinson is an avid reader and advocate for literacy. Although, she began writing as a child, it was not until much later in life that she began to pen short stories. After falling in love with the characters she created, she turned one of her short stories into her debut novel: What We Won't Do For Love. After completing her first manuscript, Mz. Robinson took a break from writing to pursue other career opportunities. Five years later deciding to pursue her passion, she secured a home with G Street Chronicles. Today Mz. Robinson has six published novels. When she's not writing Mz. Robinson enjoys reading and shopping. She is currently working on her next title and other projects.

The Love, Lies & Lust Series

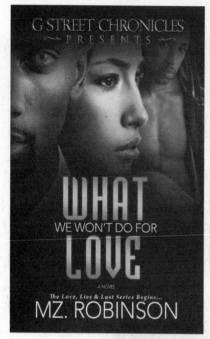

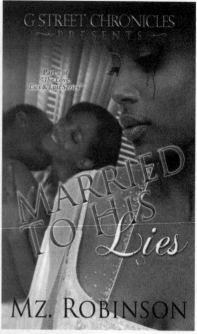

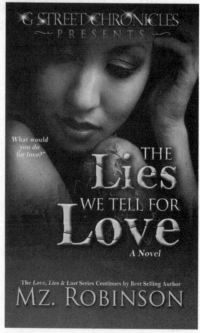

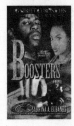

We'd like to thank you for supporting G Street Chronicles and invite you to join our social networks. Please be sure to post a review when you're finished reading.

Facebook
G Street Chronicles
&
G Street Chronicles "A New Urban Dynasty" Readers' Group

Twitter
@gstrtchroni

My Space
G Street Chronicles

Email us and we'll add you to our mailing list
fans@gstreetchronicles.com

George Sherman Hudson, CEO
Shawna A. Grundy, VP